THE SURVIVORS BOOK SIX
OLD ENEMY

BY

NATHAN HYSTAD

Cover art: Tom Edwards Design

Edited by: Scarlett R Algee

Proofed and Formatted by: BZ Hercules

ISBN-13: 9781731351975

Also By Nathan Hystad

The Survivors Series

The Event

New Threat

New World

The Ancients

The Theos

Old Enemy

Red Creek

ONE

Rain pelted down to the streets, and as we watched through the window, the roadways grew deep puddles. We were perched on the second floor of a squat building, overtop of a mechanic shop, and we were all growing tired of the endless downpour.

"Is it ever going to stop?" Mary asked. We'd made bunks of the offices, each personalized with things we'd found around the city. We were now sitting in what we called our living space, where floor-to-ceiling windows allowed us to see outside even when conditions weren't ideal.

"I don't think so," Slate offered. "For a world with a lava ocean, where does the precipitation even come from?"

Suma was perched on a chair, and she wiggled her short legs back and forth, her feet not quite able to touch the ground. "There has to be a large source of water other than the small sources we've found out there." She said the words in a mixture of English and Shimmali. Our translators were turned off, but we'd spent the last three months trying to learn each other's languages, since we didn't have much else to do.

"Should we try to find it?" I asked. "We haven't been able to get a vessel to function. Maybe we should just leave the city."

Mary was beside me on the couch. Some things were universal no matter what race we came across. She leaned back, sighed, and rubbed her ever-expanding belly. "Is it a good time to go exploring? I think we need to hunker down, hope the rain stops, and keep working on the ships."

"I agree," Slate said. "There's still a lot of the city we haven't explored. Who knows what we'll find?"

"Hopefully an engine with a technology familiar to me. Whoever these people were, they did things their own way." Suma slipped off her chair and went to the window to stare at the ceaseless rain.

We knew enough about the race that had abandoned their world, but we didn't know where they'd run to. After spending three months here, I was beginning to understand why they left. When it wasn't gusting wind or firing electrical storms at the city, it was raining for weeks at a time.

I set a hand on Mary's leg and gave it a light squeeze. "You're right. We'll keep working on the ships. How are you feeling?" I asked her quietly, not wanting to mention the bags that had begun to grow under her eyes. I knew she hadn't been sleeping well, and often woke to her screaming out in her sleep. She wouldn't admit it, but I thought she was having nightmares fueled by her time under the Iskios' control.

"I'm fine. As worried as I am about the baby, I want

her to come out already." Mary closed her eyes, and no one spoke for a few minutes. The sound of the rain hitting the glass was the only noise in the room.

Slate stood, rushing to the window. "What was that?"

Mary's eyes darted open, and I got up to stand beside my large friend. "What did you see?" I asked.

He pointed to the east. "I saw something flash over there."

"More lightning, probably," I said.

He shook his head. "No. This was different."

We watched for a few moments, and I saw it too this time. "There!" I called, pointing a little more south. It was a circle of light, the kind made from a ship's searchlight. "Someone's here."

Suma finished the thought. "And they're looking for us."

Mary was beside me, her eyes wide. "Maybe it's our people," she said hopefully.

"Maybe not. We can't take the chance right now." Slate gripped a pulse rifle in his hand. I had no idea where it had been stashed, but it had to be somewhere close. I was glad someone was always ready and alert. I'd grown a little complacent in my time on this planet.

Part of me had actually enjoyed being stranded, because I was with Mary, and Slate and Suma were some of the best company I could have asked for. We were living like Robinson Crusoe on an alien world, with no one to bother us. Nobody to save from extinction, no threats to our lives other than dealing with our own basic day-to-day survival. Food. Shelter. Water. The lights we saw were a compromise to that new life, one way or another. If it was our people, I was glad to go home to New Spero, but I knew my life would never again be like the last three months.

"We have to get a closer look," I said. "Suma, is there any way they can detect us?"

Suma looked thoughtful, concern etched over her forehead, and her snout twitched as she considered my question. "I don't think so. If they have technology similar to that on Shimmal and New Spero, then they can't pick up the small frequencies we may be emitting with, say, our pulse rifles or comm devices."

"Suma, can you stay here with Mary? Slate and I will run point on this." I started toward the door, where I could get my EVA on. It would keep me warm and dry in the downpour.

Mary got up and advanced toward me. "Where do you think you're going?" I asked her.

"With you. I don't want to sit around helplessly." Mary started to put her jumpsuit on and nearly screamed when it didn't zip up over her baby bump.

I touched her hand, and she pulled it back. "I've done nothing but wait around for three months now, and I'm getting tired of it," she said. "I know you're having fun here on desolate-city-world, but I'm about to have a baby, and I want to go home. If this is our people coming to get us, I want to be there."

"Mary, I'm all for that, but they could be hostile," Slate said, stepping into a fight he wasn't invited to. I was still glad he did.

Mary looked from Slate to me and sighed, stepping out of the undersized jumpsuit. "Fine. Be careful, okay?"

"We will." I grabbed my earpiece and passed Mary hers. "This way, it's like you're with me."

In the last few months, Mary and I had remained close. At first I hadn't let her out of my sight, worried she'd disappear again. I wouldn't let that happen. Eventually, I started to try to give her space, and now it was her turn to make sure we didn't get too far apart.

Mary accepted the earpiece and placed it in, giving me a half-hearted smile as she did so.

"Suma, can you still see them searching out there?" Slate asked, clasping his EVA helmet on. The air was breathable here, but we always used oxygen when performing laborious tasks.

Suma stared out the window across the room and pointed to the east. "It looks like they're doing a short pattern. Down a few blocks, then over one and down again. They don't want to miss an inch."

I nodded, scratching at my unruly beard before clasping my own helmet on. Slate passed me a pulse rifle, and I clipped it to my back. "We're just going to survey the situation, report back, and analyze." I looked to Mary, who seemed concerned, her hand resting on her belly.

"Come on, boss. Let's go."

A few minutes later, we were down the stairs and onto the street. Cold rain barraged us and everything in its path as we jogged along the buildings on the side of the street.

"Let's head east, but past the line they're following.

That way, we can see them from a block away before they have a chance of spotting us," I said, hoping my logic was sound. We turned north and ran two blocks, before heading east once again. This part of the city was full of shorter buildings, the odd high-rise scattered among them. Over here, the tall ones were residences. I'd spent countless days searching through the ancient civilization's homes, trying to get a sense of who they were and what they'd fled.

The videos we'd found suggested it was the neverending storms and the lava that had caused them to run from the world we now knew to be named Sterona, but after being here all this time ourselves, we found they likely could have stayed. Unless there was something we were missing.

It was still daytime, but the dense black cloud cover made it darker than normal. Lightning flashed, and thunder followed behind as we kept moving down the vacant streets.

"Up there." Slate pointed a few city blocks over, where a bright search light shone down while an alien lander roamed the skies above the buildings.

"Do you recognize it?" I asked, trying to recall if I'd ever seen one like it. I used the zoom on my visor, and a green grid appeared as I followed the lander. I tapped my arm console and snapped a few images of it. It was boxy and larger than I'd originally thought. Our landers were small transport vessels, but this looked like it could house two dozen people.

"A dropship?" Slate asked, mirroring my own

thoughts. "It could be full of some race's military. We don't have the ammunition to take on an invasion, boss."

"You're right. Let's stick around and see if we can learn anything else." I leaned back, covered by a derelict restaurant's awning. Maybe they'd just leave if they didn't find anything. Or maybe it was our friends, borrowing a ship. There was no way to be sure, and I didn't want to make a gamble that could cost us our lives. With a baby on the way, I couldn't make those kinds of rash decisions anymore.

We stood there, rain pelting down to the street before us for at least an hour, watching the dropship wind its way over the city on a systematic path, almost as if a computer program was controlling it.

"Slate, have you noticed that the ship's on a pattern?" I asked, feeling like I was onto something.

"Yes, it is. I haven't seen any variance in it. There's no one at the manual controls on this ship," he answered, confirming my suspicion. "But that doesn't necessarily mean anything."

"How so?"

"It could be a program. Hell, it could be Dubs flying a borrowed ship," Slate said, referencing W, the robot we'd found on Larsk Two.

"I wish we knew. It's time to leave this world and get Mary back home, where there are doctors – and our homes." Suddenly, I was homesick. I'd been playing at surviving this world for three months, but it finally hit me. Home. Without the portal working, it seemed so far away.

"Me too." Slate looked to the sky. He was fiercely missing the new woman in his life, Denise.

"Let's head back. We have enough images. We can see what Suma and Mary think." It was nice to have a team around me to help make decisions.

We went back the way we'd come, the dropship now past the dwelling where we were holed up. As we made our way inside, water dripped off our suits, and we took them off downstairs in the garage, hanging them up to dry. Slate grabbed his pulse rifle, found mine leaning on the wall, and passed it to me.

"We can't be too careful," he said, and I took it, feeling the metal handle dig into my palm.

As much as I wanted to be done with guns, portals and spaceships, I knew I wasn't. I never would be. We moved upstairs, and I told myself to lift one foot at a time. One foot at a time.

TWO

"I've never seen anything like that, but it's not in my tablet database," Suma said, scrolling through the images on her handheld device. Her English was nearly perfect, and I was amazed that our vocal cords could even remotely duplicate one another's speech. Our Shimmali sounded like a herd of cats attacking a bird sanctuary, but she picked up most of it.

"How about the shape? Can you reference that? With the size?" Mary asked, and Suma's snout straightened as she tried that.

"Nothing exactly the same, but it does look like there's something similar from a faraway system. We only had the drawings, though, so I could be wrong." Suma showed us some line art, and it was similar in style.

"Where's it from?" I asked, feeling like we were about to learn if they were friends or foes.

"It's blocked!" she exclaimed. "How's that possible? I've never seen it before. The text says 'encrypted'."

"That doesn't bode well for us. Okay, what do we do?" Mary asked.

I shifted in my seat, grabbing a cup of water and drinking it in one big gulp. "We have a couple of choices.

Stay put, don't show ourselves, and wait here until someone we know shows up."

"Which might be never," Mary chimed in.

"Correct. Or we flag them down and hope they aren't here to kill us," I finished.

Mary leaned as far forward as she could and rested her face on her palms. She was clearly upset, and my arm curled around her, bringing her to rest her head on my shoulder. I kissed the top of her head and whispered to her, "We'll get home."

"When? When can I get home?" She shouted the question.

Slate stood, a grim look on his face. "I'll flag them down. Suma, we have the flares we found last month, right?"

"Yes, but…" Suma started to say.

Slate cut her off. "I'll go to the other side of the city, fire off some flares, and get their attention. If they're hostile, then you three will still be safe. If it's Magnus or Leslie, or anyone else we know, we'll come for you."

I wanted to laugh at him, but I could tell he was absolutely serious. "Slate, you can't do that."

He shrugged. "I'm tired of being here too, boss. For the first time in my life, I feel like I have a home. Someone to get back to."

"Then getting yourself killed isn't the answer," Mary said. "We wait it out and see what happens. If it *is* Leslie or Magnus and Natalia, they won't leave without finding out evidence of us."

She was right. "We wait and watch," I said.

Slate sat back down, and nodded. "What I wouldn't give for a hamburger right now," he said, grabbing a piece of fruit and biting into it.

"And a beer," I added. We were all feeling the effects of the local-vegetation diet. Other than the fruit we'd first found, we'd managed some sort of bean and a variety of nuts, giving us a slightly more balanced diet. My own pants were always trying to fall to the ground. It was a good thing we mainly wore the jumpsuits.

We sat into the night, talking about home for the first time in months. Not only mentioning it like it was a destination, but discussing all the things we couldn't wait to get back to. The conversation led back to Earth and the things we missed from there too. For Slate, it was action movies. Mary missed going to her hometown's fall carnival when she was a kid, and I missed so many things that I couldn't keep track.

Suma watched silently, laughing and smiling as we reminisced.

By the time we couldn't see the ship's lights in the distance out the far window, we decided to get some sleep. Tomorrow would be another day. Tomorrow might determine our futures.

Dim light shone through the window of our room, and I rolled onto my back, covering my eyes with my arm. Mary made a noise beside me, and I draped myself over her, feeling the warmth radiate off her body in waves.

"Morning," she said sleepily.

"Morning." I sat up in bed, swinging my feet to the ground. "I'm going to check on Slate."

"Okay. I'll be out soon," Mary said.

I hopped into my jumpsuit and plodded out into the shared common space. I'd had nightmares that Slate had left us to expose himself to the ship hovering over our city. I was grateful to see the big man still with us.

"Slate. How was your watch?" I asked him. Suma had taken first watch, I took the second, and Slate rounded us out with the last.

"Uneventful." He was still staring out the window, and I could tell something was weighing on him.

"You almost did it, didn't you?" I asked, not having to say what *it* was.

He nodded. "But you were right. I have someone to get back to now. Otherwise, I wouldn't have thought twice about it."

"Did you ever think how your dying would affect us, Slate?" I asked him, and he finally turned to me.

"Sure. But if it meant I was the one to roll the dice and get you home safely, then I would," he said.

"We'll do this together. Let's suit up and see what else we can learn today," I said as Suma emerged from her bedroom. "Suma, we need you to activate the drones this morning. Have them ready to attack if necessary."

She knew exactly what I meant. The three of us had been attacked by the automated drones the first time we'd hooked power back up to the section of the city holding the portal. It had been a close call, but now, with Suma's programming skill set, they were under her control. "Will do."

"I'm coming today," Mary said from the doorway. "I want to see what we're looking at. In person."

I shrugged, knowing I could only talk her out of things for so long. She'd had another bad night, crying out for me and holding her belly. I thought the baby was nearly ready to be born.

After another fruit-filled breakfast and some fresh water, we were all suited up in our EVAs, walking down the street toward the last region where we'd spotted the vessel hovering below the clouds. It was still raining as we went, but the clouds were less dense, more gray than black today, and I felt better for it.

Slate held his pulse pistol, ready to attack, even though we'd seen no sign of any beings on the ground yet. They could have dropped in the night and might even be stalking us now.

A few drones hovered out of view behind us, guided by Suma's control. The rest were tucked away, ready to attack if needed.

"I see them ahead, boss," Slate said, his voice ringing in my earpiece.

"Affirmative. I have visual too," I said, seeing the boxy dropship flying slowly in the same pattern, only over a different section of the city. It took us an hour to get underneath it, hiding behind a commercial high-rise. The rain slowed to a drizzle, and I took it as a good omen.

"Does anyone have a line of sight on it?" Mary asked

as we all peered into the sky toward where we'd last seen the ship.

"Negative," Slate said. He rushed across the street, making himself visible from the air, and I cringed, hoping no one could spot him. For all we knew, they had their own micro-drones hovering around the city too.

"Wait, what's that?" I said, seeing a form down the block.

"Is that…" Slate started to ask as I used my face-mask's zoom feature on the figure.

I saw it clearly just as Slate stepped from the edge of the sidewalk and into the street. "Slate, no!" I called, but it was too late. The robo-pirate had seen him.

A red beam shot down the street, hitting the ground just in front of Slate as he dove away from us. "What the hell is that?" he asked, getting to his feet as another volley of shots streaked toward him. He was running now, away from us.

"Those appear to be the same model as the pirate robots we told you about!" I called and ushered Suma and Mary around the high-rise, far from the firing guns.

"I take it they're not friendly?" Slate's voice asked through my ear. He was panting while he ran. "I'll lead them away."

"Them?" I asked.

"They're coming from every street now. You need to hide. There's at least ten of the bastards," Slate said, and we could hear the blasts from their guns tearing apart the streets and nearby buildings.

"Suma, get the drones," I ordered and saw they were

already advancing behind the robo-pirates, walking and rolling down the street after Slate.

The ancient drones chased after the robots, targeting them and firing away. We watched on Suma's arm console as they blasted apart two of the pirates before they realized where the fire was coming from. Once they knew, they turned their attention to the attack from the skies, leaving only three to follow Slate.

"Stay here," I said, running in the same direction as Slate had gone, but a block over. I looked back, and the two women weren't where I left them. "Mary, what are you doing?"

"I'm pregnant, but I can still fire a gun. We'll cut them off on the other end," Mary said through my earpiece.

"Fine, but take care of each other," I said, running faster as I heard more pulse fire from the adjacent block. "Slate, where are you?" I hadn't heard his voice in a while and was beginning to worry.

"I'm here," he whispered. "Damn it, they have me surrounded."

"I'm coming." I slowed, rounding the corner to see a group of five robots heading down the next block. "Suma, what's our status on the drones?"

"They're coming. ETA two minutes," Suma said.

I wasn't sure we had two minutes. "I'm going in."

My heart was racing, and an alert appeared on my visor, warning me of the spike in my heart rate. I dismissed it with a tap on the console and took a deep breath. Slate needed me.

I fired toward the robots. "Over here, you freaks," I said, remembering Rivo's captors, especially the one with skin hanging over his twisted metal face.

As they turned, I fired at will, striking the lead robot in the chest. It didn't drop, so I made a head shot, sending sparks flying as it blew apart. I ran across the alley, rolling as the barrage of fire came back toward me. Slate was shooting at them from the other end, so we had to be careful not to get caught in each other's crossfire.

"How many are down?" I asked, peering around the corner of a wall.

"Three down, four to go," Slate said. I saw beams cutting through the air and ran from my cover, heading for the alley they had Slate blocked into.

I fired at one's back, striking it perfectly. It fell, but I kept shooting. Two of them emerged from the shadows of the side road behind me and fired. I ducked and rolled, their blasts narrowly missing me as the ground tore open.

"The drones are coming," Suma said through the channel, and I hoped they were quick enough. I ran toward Slate, who was hiding at the far end of the blocked alleyway. Ancient trash bins lined the streets here, full of metallic waste; anything organic had decayed a thousand years prior.

"We stand together, boss." Slate stuck a fist out, and I bumped it, breathing heavily.

"Let's hope the drones do our work for us." I leaned against the wall. Everything went quiet as the pirates' fire ceased. All I could hear was my own breath, and I strained to listen down the alley.

I heard substantial footsteps, and the whirring of the robo-pirates' rollers. "They're coming," I whispered, pointing in their direction.

Slate nodded, gripping his rifle and moving into position. He pointed right and then to himself, then left and to me. I understood what he meant. I'd duck and shoot the left ones, while he took high and right.

His fingers shot into the air. One. Two. Three.

We moved into the open and fired away just as the drones appeared above our attackers. The pirates didn't stand a chance. They were torn apart before they had a chance to target either of us.

"Yes!" Slate yelled, pumping his fist in the air. "Take that, robot demons! You think you can come to our world and win? I don't think so!"

We were cheering and hugging in the alley when Mary's voice cut over the line. "Guys, I hate to break this up, but you might want to come over here."

Her tone was no nonsense, with a hint of fear laced into it.

I checked my arm console and saw their blips faintly glowing a couple blocks away. "Come on," I said to Slate, and we ran for them.

I scanned over the broken pieces of the robots as we hurried around them. I noticed the symbol stamped onto them: a triangle in a circle, two wavy lines in the center. It was the same image I'd seen on the pirate ship where I'd found Rivo. It was from one of Lom of Pleva's companies.

If Slate recalled me mentioning it, he didn't seem to

notice, and we kept moving, heading for our friends' position. We saw them soon enough, backs pressed against a wall.

"What is it?" I asked, close enough for them to spot us now. I didn't need to wait for the answer. Around the corner was the dropship. Its doors were wide open, empty. Another ship was lowering, then another. The first landed a block away, and the doors hissed open. Even from where we stood, watching from a concealed spot, I could hear the whirring of the robots come to life.

The second ship from the sky landed, and the same thing happened. A few dozen of the robots descended as the doors lurched open.

"We're screwed," Slate said.

"We have to get out of here," I whispered, taking one last peek while the others began to move. One of the robots turned to look toward me, and I ran.

THREE

"Where do the drones put them?" I asked. We had a dozen drones trying to stay hidden, feeding us locations of the invading robot pirate army. We were lucky to have escaped unscathed.

"Every sector of the city. We're technically surrounded now, but I think we can distract them enough, giving us time to carve a path toward the outside of the metropolis," Mary said, eyeing the cameras on the tablet.

I walked around the room, trying to see if we'd left anything useful behind. I hated to leave the security of our sanctuary, but with the invaders, we weren't safe anywhere anymore.

"Let's do it. Suma, how's the rover?" I asked the young Shimmali girl.

She smiled. "Right as rain," she said, reminding me it had started pouring again. My good omen from earlier had been proven wrong, and now it was mocking me with even more precipitation.

"You're getting good at these terrible human puns, Suma," I said, and she smiled wider. "How can you be so happy? We're being hunted by robots."

"It's better than sitting around wondering if someone's going to rescue you. If this Lom guy knows where we are, then so does Magnus."

I wondered at that. How could it have taken our people so long to get here? And just how had this mysterious Lom of Pleva tracked us down first? It didn't add up, but we couldn't sit around contemplating it. We had to leave the city.

Slate came back into the room. "Rover's loaded with everything I could fit. It's going to be a tight fit. It usually seats two, but we can make it work. I figured Mary can drive. Dean, you and Suma will cozy up in the back seat, and I'll hang on for dear life. Think of me as a turret on top of the vehicle."

I couldn't help but laugh at him. "Is there no way for us all to fit inside?"

"Not with our suits on, and the supplies. Don't worry about it. I've had worse jobs." Slate helped Mary up off the couch, and there we stood, each looking around the room we'd called home for the last few months.

"Everything must come to an end at some point," Mary said. "Who's up for a vacation in the country?"

We all raised our hands.

Ten minutes later, we were stacked inside the rover as the large tires started to rotate, pulling us from the cover of the garage.

"Now, Suma," I said, and she used the tablet to direct the drones toward the explosive we'd thrown together. Once they targeted the cylinder and fired, we heard then felt the rumbling from our seats, and the plume of smoke rose high into the sky. That would keep their attention for a while.

We waited, watching the feeds from the other nearby drones, until our pathway was cleared.

"Gun it, Mary!" I called and was pushed back into my seat, Suma pressing tightly against me from her perch on my lap.

I peered around Suma's head, watching through the windshield as we raced down the streets. Buildings zoomed past us as we sprinted through the cityscape.

"Suma?" Mary asked from the driver's seat in front of us.

"Drones aren't showing any robot movement this way," Suma announced confidently.

"Slate, all good?" I asked into my mic.

"Glad I'm strapped on here; otherwise, you'd have lost me five blocks ago. All good." Slate sounded like he was having fun.

Everything was going to plan. We neared the edge of the city some time later, still not having seen signs of any robo-pirates.

We'd been to this area a few times, and I knew that in a couple more city blocks, we'd be exiting into the countryside where, to our surprise, there was green grass, vegetation, and water. There were homes here, likely a suburb of the ancient race. It was almost like estate living, with old metal fences separating the structures. Some were built out of stone, which was rare in this land.

I had the urge to investigate these homes, feeling like there might be more to them than the small apartments in the city center. But we had bigger fish to fry.

"All clear," Suma said.

"Suma, pull a few drones to follow us. Let's leave some high over the city, and a couple along this border, to see if anyone crosses," I said, and Suma set to tapping on the tablet.

"Mary, you know where we're going?" I asked.

She didn't reply.

"Mary? Everything good?" I asked again, worry carved in my voice now.

"Dean, I think I'm having a contraction."

———————

*T*wo hours later, we pulled over under a thick copse of trees. The dense underbrush would keep us hidden from prying eyes, or drones and ships searching from above. The trip had been frantic, Mary refusing to stop the vehicle to trade positions.

My door hissed open and I ran to the front, opening Mary's door by the manual handle. She smiled sweetly at me and took my offered hand. "I'm sorry, Dean, but there was no chance we could fit any other way. Suma wasn't going to want to squish up to a woman in labor, and you and I couldn't fit in one seat."

She was right, and I fought the urge to argue. We were going to have a baby. We'd been as prepared for this as we could and had gathered what little supplies we were able to muster. None of it seemed like enough at that moment.

Slate was beside us, untethering himself from the rover. "I'll get the tents set up. Suma, can you give me a hand?"

Suma nodded, leaving us alone.

"We can do this," I said quietly to Mary, our heads close together.

"What choice do we have?" she asked before grimacing through a contraction. She let out a groan, squeezing my hand in the process.

"Stay here, and we'll get everything set up," I said, unsure what that even meant. We'd been through so much, but the idea of delivering my own baby on this deserted planet was the most frightening thing yet.

I left her there and assisted Slate and Suma as they erected our shelters. We'd found and salvaged some supplies from the city. These tents were a large cabin style, with a peaked roof and ample room inside, giving a bedroom separate from living space. The fabric was thick, insulated, and the poles dense and heavy. They would make near-permanent homes for as long as we needed.

I tried to shake off my exhaustion and anger. We should be at our real home. The only way to free Mary was to kill the portal, so we'd had no choice, but I still felt like I'd failed her.

"Boss, has her water broken?" Slate asked.

"No, not yet," I said.

"Then this might be a false alarm. I've seen it before. It's called Braxton-Hicks, I think. What?" he asked, after getting some strange stares directed at him. "My aunt was a nurse."

"You think it's only some unwelcome discomfort?" I asked.

He shrugged. "I'm just saying there's a chance. She should have another month, right?"

"Three weeks, we think, but who knows for sure?" I tested the doorway, which had a seal similar to Velcro, but much stronger. The two materials touched and acted as a closure. Clare would love to see it.

"Dean!" Suma called.

"What is it? Mary?" I asked, running for the rover.

Suma shook her head, her snout twitching inside her EVA helmet. "Look," she said and pointed at the tablet.

We saw two of the dropships crossing under the drones we'd set to watch the city boundaries. They were heading straight for us.

"This isn't good."

"Do we keep going?" Suma asked.

Slate already had his gun in hand.

I looked around our bare camp, and to Mary, who was clutching a blanket and watching us with wide eyes.

"Suma, call all the attack drones. Get them here fast, then take Mary farther in the rover. We'll make our stand here." I tried not to make eye contact with Mary but couldn't help it. I expected her to fight me on this, but she just nodded as tears streamed down her face.

---

*W*e'll stay in contact," I said, kissing her forehead.

"Magnus, Leslie, and I took down a ship full of them a few months ago, and then we did the same with the squadron on the ground just yesterday. We'll survive this attack, like all the rest before it."

"I know, Dean. I know. Be careful," Mary said.

I squeezed her hand. "I'll be with you soon." I shut the rear door and walked to the front of the rover. "Suma, take care of her. Whatever happens, you take care of her." I said the words more harshly than I intended, but Suma took it with grace.

"I will," she said in Shimmali, and I understood the words.

Slate and I stood there watching the rover drive off. When it was out of sight, we dragged the tent into an opening in the trees, so it could be seen from above.

Slate patted me on the shoulder and headed for the treeline. "Come on, let's get into position."

"How many do you think they're sending?" I asked.

"Probably all of them. I'd say two or three dozen at least," Slate answered.

That was a lot. Far more than I wanted to stand and fight here in the trees. I wished we had more time to prepare. We could have made some traps. The wheeled robots weren't ideal in rough terrain.

Soon I could make out the hum of the ships' engines as they neared our position. Once again, it had all come to this: isolated on an empty world, with robots attacking. Leonard would have a fun time drawing this comic issue if he ever learned our fate.

The ships landed right where we expected, in the

opening near the tent. We were at higher ground here and watched the dropships touch down on the ground, the doors clinking open. Dozens of the robots piled out, weapons ready and pointed toward the tent. Simultaneously, each of their guns began to fire at the structure, tearing it to pieces in seconds.

Then the drones attacked. We had twenty or so left, and they surrounded the robots from the air, firing beams down like rain. The robots rolled and ran toward the ships, shooting up at the drones as they went.

Slate took this as the time to attack. He ran forward, rifle raised, and I followed him, pulling my trigger and sending beams at the unsuspecting targets. We hit a few, but they were getting the better of our drones now. Only a few robots were on the ground, immobilized, and I saw no more than a handful of drones still firing from the sky.

Slate ran for the treeline to the right, and I went left, shooting wildly as we crossed the opening. I pressed my back against a tall, wide, smooth tree trunk. Then there was silence. The drones had all been destroyed, along with my hope of making it out of here alive. With a quick glance, I saw twenty or so of the robots gathering. At least a dozen were still on the ground, sparks shooting from a few of them.

"Any ideas?" I asked through my helmet mic.

"None that don't involve me going berserker mode on these bags of bolts," came Slate's reply.

"Go the long way around, cutting back into the forest. We'll meet a mile north of here," I said.

"Okay, I'm on..." Slate's voice cut out, and I slid

around the tree, palm on it now as I looked toward his position.

"Slate?" I asked and got a mangled message in reply. There was an issue with our mics and earpieces.

Before I could react, a shock coursed through me. I fell to the ground to see a robot leaning over me, blue energy crackling at the end of a metallic rod.

FOUR

I opened my eyes and surveyed my situation with a strange detachment. My body ached, and my toes and fingertips were numb. I was standing and felt chafing at my ankles and wrists. I was inside one of the buildings in the city. I recognized the vanished alien construction. The robots had captured and shackled me in this dim room. There was a small window across the space, water seeping through it onto the floor.

I tugged on my arms, but the restraints were too strong to break. I could only hope Mary and Suma had gotten away. And Slate. If he'd seen me taken, there was no way he would have gone quietly. He probably ran at them, guns blazing.

"Mary? Suma? Slate?" I tried each name in my mic but received no response.

It was at least an hour later that I heard the whirring of a robot coming toward the room. I braced myself. I'd seen how cruel they were. I remembered Rivo on death's doorstep, her tattered clothing hanging from her emaciated blue body.

The robot that entered the space was disfigured, like the rest of them. This one had two legs instead of wheels, and it methodically stepped over to me. Its body was a thick metal armor, its head small in proportion, and two glowing red eyes looked straight at me, with darkness behind them.

"Where is Dean Parker?" it asked in monotone English.

I was taken aback. We hadn't known whether they were looking for us particularly, but evidently, they were. They were searching for me.

"Never heard of him." I said the words in Shimmali tweets and squawks. This appeared to confuse the robot, who stood silently, calculating before speaking again.

"Where is Dean Parker?" it asked again, still in my language.

"Look, I'm just visiting. I work hard and get three lousy weeks of vacation a year, and you interrupt it without even saying 'I'm sorry'." I felt the zap before I saw the rod in the robot's grip. Blue energy raced across my skin, and my knees fell weak. My arms jarred as the shackles held my weight.

"Where is Dean Parker?" it asked with the same tone.

I struggled to regain my footing but eventually did. Was there any point in lying to these guys? They already had me. Maybe there was a way to leverage my name, a way to keep myself alive another day. I needed to distract them from searching for Mary. Had she delivered our baby out there in the wilderness, alone with Suma?

I stood as tall as I could, cleared my throat, and said firmly, "I'm Dean Parker."

The robot lowered the energy rod, turned around,

and plodded out of the room, the floor shaking slightly with each step. The door shut, and I was once again alone.

When I came to after passing out, someone was standing in the room with me. Its back was turned to me, and it seemed to know I had woken. Maybe it was the light jingle of the chains binding me as I shifted. "*The* Dean Parker." It spoke rough English, but clear enough to understand. The being was tall, and I struggled to make out its features in the dim corner of the room.

"I suppose so. Who am I speaking with?" I asked. The robots were one thing, but seeing a sentient being in here with me elevated my distress.

"I'll ask the questions." A couple of steps, and the being stopped short of the light carrying in through the window. "Do you ever feel badly about the things you've done?"

I took a second to consider the question. "Every damn day."

It paused, as if not expecting that reply. "Interesting."

"Not really. I've had to do some messed-up things since Earth was attacked, and I'm not proud of many of them. But I've done what I had to for my race to survive," I said, my voice getting heated. Who was it to judge me?

"Do you ever think the ones you've fought were only doing what they thought best for their own race to survive?" it asked calmly.

"Sure. I do think it's always a matter of perspective. Instinctively, we protect our own, and ourselves, before considering the repercussions for others," I said, wondering why I was stuck in a philosophical debate with this shadowed alien.

"Your logic is sound. I didn't expect this, Dean Parker," it said.

"Neither did I. Now can we shake hands and call a truce?" I asked, fishing for its response.

"I don't think so, Dean Parker. I hereby charge you with the murder of…" The mysterious figure didn't have a chance to finish its sentence. The far wall of the room ripped from the building with a boom. The being stumbled but kept to the edge of the space.

A ship appeared in the newly-formed opening, and two armored bodies jumped from the top of it, landing on the floor with a thud. They ran for me, blasting my chains loose. They dragged me toward the ship, which had turned around, its rear ramp opened, guiding us to enter.

As we retreated, the whole scenario leaving me in a blur, I glanced to the side of the room, where the figure still stood. I was still, eyes wide, unbelieving.

I recognized its features and nearly fell to my knees. Across its face was a long, horizontal scar. I was half-carried, half-dragged to the ship, and tossed inside. The ramp closed, and I lay on the hard metal floor thinking about what I'd just seen.

It was a Kraski.

"We have to go to them! They're still out there!" I shouted as the ramp closed and the people in armored suits surrounded me. The largest of them knelt down to me and lifted their visor.

Magnus smiled widely and barked a laugh. "Man, am I glad to see you."

It was my friends. With everything going on, I truly had no idea who was extracting me from my capture.

I sat up and took his offered hand. "You're glad to see me? *I'm* glad to see you!" I hugged the big man, my arms unable to wrap around the thick armored suit.

The other two lifted their visors, and emotions rolled through me. The hybrids, Leslie and Terrance, stepped in, each taking their turn to greet me.

I followed them inside the ship. "Mary's still out there."

Terrace shook his head, and I took that for the worst-case scenario. I didn't know how long I was tied up alone. I'd passed out, and it might have been a day. He must have seen the look on my face, because he quickly explained, "We got her, Dean. She's okay."

My knees gave way, but Magnus was there to catch me. "Where is she?" I asked.

"Safe. We're heading there now." Leslie started to work on the shackles. We were inside the belly of the ship, and she led me down a basic corridor, then down some steps.

"Is she… is the baby…?" I asked.

Leslie smiled. "Nick's with her now. He thinks everything's going to be fine."

"And Slate?" I asked, hopeful.

Magnus stepped down the last rung and into the engineering room with us. "We haven't found him yet, Dean."

Damn it. "We have to go…" I started, but Leslie put a hand up.

"First things first. We're heading to Mary at the camp now. Come over here, and we'll cut those off."

Minutes later, Leslie had finished using a cutting tool to remove the metal bands on my ankles and wrists. I removed the safety glasses and slouched to a lone chair by the desk.

"We need to hydrate you, Dean." Magnus led the way, and before I knew it, we were in a kitchen, Leslie passing me a water bottle. Unfamiliar beings were walking the halls, and one spoke quickly in a language unknown to me. She was strong-looking, skin as dark as midnight, with what could only be described as built-in armor scaled over her body. When she caught me staring at her, she smiled, showing sharp teeth before going back to her task.

"Whose ship are we on?" I asked, taking a long drink of the water.

"We'll get to that." Magnus leaned against the wall. "How did you four survive here so long?"

"We found water and a food source. Not much more to it. We were trying to get a ship functional, but everything here was just too old and worn down," I said before grabbing another water bottle.

"We're close to the base," Leslie said, tapping her earpiece.

I took the lead now, heading back to the cargo bay, where the ramp would lead us to the surface. I felt a slight lurch as the vessel landed, and Terrance was beside me, hitting the ramp release. We walked through a containment field, and onto the lush grass outside.

I generally knew the area. There was a mountain in the distance. We were about forty miles from the lava ocean here, the mountain range directly between our location and the lava.

There was a flurry of activity around me, and I tried to get my bearings. Three large vessels sat on the ground. Each would hold a crew of at least thirty, their markings unfamiliar once again. Sleek and rounded, they reminded me of a peanut: narrow in the center and bulbous on each end. They were black with yellow symbols on the sides, each with a series of letters I couldn't read. At first, I hadn't even noticed I was only in a jumpsuit, the EVA taken off by the robots upon my capture.

I hoped Garo Alnod didn't want his flying suit back; otherwise, he was going to be sorely disappointed.

"Where's Mary?" I asked, and Leslie led me to the second ship in the field.

I ran behind her, and various aliens parted. Many looked like the woman I'd seen in the kitchen. They moved with the smooth grace I usually associated with a skilled predator.

Leslie took me down a series of corridors, and we climbed upward until we reached a doorway. "In here," she said, and I hesitantly moved to it, the door sliding open to reveal a medical center.

"Mary." I rushed to the bedside, where Mary lay sobbing and breathing heavily.

"Good, almost there," a familiar voice said from behind a surgical mask. He turned, noticing the new person in the room. "Dean Parker, as I live or die. Someone get him suited up." He winked at me, and I instantly calmed down. Nick knew what he was doing, and if he felt comfortable with how things were going, then I could too.

"Dean! I tried to help you," Mary said between breaths. "They wouldn't let me come." Tears fell from her damp eyes, and I couldn't help but love her more for it.

"I'm fine," I said. "How are you?" I asked, but a woman in scrubs stopped me.

"Decontamination, next door," she said as she pointed with determination.

I nodded. "I'll be right back."

It was happening. Mary was safe, and she was giving birth to our baby. My exhausted body felt rejuvenated, and it was nothing compared to what Mary was going through. In a few minutes, I was back in the room, clean and wearing green scrubs.

I ran to Mary's side, and she was screaming, pushing as per Dr. Nick's orders. "You got this, Mary. I'm so proud of you."

"Ahhhhh!" Mary squeezed my hand, and I happily took the pain.

"Almost there," Nick said from the bottom end of

the bed. "One more push."

Mary cried out, and then a moment of silence until our baby took over. Thin wails carried through the room, and Mary pushed the blankets aside, trying to get a look at our child.

"It's a girl!" Nick called, and I instantly felt my eyes well up.

With quick and efficient movements, Nick snipped the umbilical cord, and the nurse wiped our baby girl clean before placing her in a small, warm blanket.

Mary was crying, and she stuck her arms out, grasping for the child she'd carried while possessed by the Iskios, then while stranded on this lifeless world.

I helped Mary sit up, and Nick passed the small bundle to Mary's waiting arms. "Dean, she's so beautiful."

She was the perfect specimen, and I took a moment, watching her wiggle her little hands. I cried as I watched Mary interact with our baby. Tears streamed down her face too, and we caught each other's gaze, locking in for a second before we heard a knock on the door.

The nurse answered it, and Leslie stuck her head in, smiling as she saw Mary with her baby. "It's Slate. We've found where he is, but we're going to need to extract him, and quickly."

I looked at Mary, leaning in to kiss her before she said, "Go. Bring him home to us. He needs to meet his goddaughter."

FIVE

"We tracked into his frequency and found out where he was hiding. The connection was lost shortly after, but we understood enough to know he was underground, not far from where you were taken." Magnus picked up the lead on the rescue mission, and I was relieved.

We'd elected to use the lander instead of the large ship. Leslie was piloting it, Terrance beside her. One of the aliens, whom I now knew as Rulo, was with us. Her built-in armor impressed me, and when she'd caught me staring, she'd nodded and stuck her arm out. I tapped it and felt the solid impact. She was hairless, had no visible nose, and her eyes reminded me of a snake's. Otherwise, her silhouette was human, albeit a large one.

"Dean, do you know of a spot like that?" Terrance asked from the front bench.

I tried to think. "There are some visible rocks by the lake there. They had a mineral embedded in them, something that sparkled in the rare times we were there when it wasn't raining. I bet they go underground. Slate must have found a crack and hidden down there."

I pointed through the viewscreen, and Leslie took the directions with ease.

"What happened to the robots you came across? The dropships?" I asked.

"All destroyed," Magnus said quickly.

"And out there?" I pointed up toward space. "Those dropships must have come with a fleet."

My friend nodded. "They attacked as we came in range. We flanked them and ended the threat."

I thought to the Kraski's words, asking if I'd ever felt regret. Magnus looked tired in that moment.

"I understand," was all I said. Below, the shapes of five robot pirates huddled around a section of rocks, a half mile from the lake.

"Blast them?" Leslie asked.

"No. Slate could be right under the surface. I don't want our rescue mission turning into a funeral." Magnus grabbed his pulse rifle and passed me one. "We're going to the mats on this one."

The lander lowered, and Magnus opened the door before it landed, jumping the last six feet. We were in the new armor suits, and I was trying to get used to it. For their bulk, they were lightweight. Magnus explained that the suit accentuated our movements, making them easier on our bodies to use. So far, I liked what I saw.

The helmet's visor was slim, shaded, and details showed up on the heads-up display to the right side. When I looked at Magnus, his suit's serial number scrolled across, with his name underneath. My name wasn't programmed into my suit, so I'd only be identified as XA-1927. I liked the ring of it.

Leslie stayed in the lander, ready to cover us with

gunfire if necessary. Rulo hopped out, not wearing armor like ours. She held a massive weapon, something like a minigun you'd expect to see mounted to an all-terrain vehicle in battle.

Magnus signaled to follow him and spread out, which we did: Terrance to the far right, me between him and Magnus, and Rulo on the far left, her minigun resting on her shoulder as she smoothly covered the distance.

"Hey! We meet again, you rust-bucket bastards!" Magnus called, using his suit's external speakers.

The robo-pirates turned red on my HUD, their IDs appearing as unknown enemy models. Either way, there were five of them and four of us, but I felt the odds were with us. When we were sure Slate wasn't hiding behind them, we were clear to attack.

"Fire at will," Magnus ordered, and we did. Terrance kept moving, getting closer to their right side; Rulo braced herself and opened fire on the robots. Out flew a series of small pulse beams, blowing strong and yellow. The first barrage hit the lead robot, who'd turned toward us, firing his weapons in our direction. A single beam flew at us as the robot exploded into a million pieces.

The others were shooting now, and I dropped to my knees, firing my pulse rifle recklessly, knowing that if I fired enough beams, they'd be cut down. It was over soon, all five robots destroyed.

Everything was quiet for a moment. The light hum of the lander was all I could hear as we walked toward the rocks.

"Slate!" I called from inside my armor suit. "Slate, it's

clear!"

No response.

Rulo said something, and my suit translated it. "There's an opening here."

I ran now, feeling the hydraulic boost from the suit as my legs pumped forward. I was the first to her and saw what she was pointing at. The rocks were large and smooth, a dozen or so twenty-foot-wide gray-black slabs. In the center was a hole, leading into the ground.

With my rifle raised, I stepped over to it and activated my left arm's light beam. I couldn't make out much inside, but it looked like a cavern, at least fifteen feet down.

"Slate!" I called again and waited, but there was no response. "We're sure this is the spot?"

Magnus nodded. "It has to be. Slate was near the water, under the rocks, and this is where the robots had congregated, searching for him. All signs point to this hole."

"Then we go in," I said.

"Then we go in," Magnus repeated. Terrance ran from the lander and had a rope tethered to the vessel. He dropped it into the hole and started to climb down it without hesitation, making it look easy in his armor.

Rulo cut in front of me, flashed me a toothy smile, and jumped down, not even bothering to use the rope.

Magnus looked at me, and I could see his eyes roll even through the tinted visor. "Show-off."

I went next and found the climb down easy in the suit. A guy could get used to this.

Magnus appeared beside me, and Leslie was standing

above, rifle in hand. "I'll stay here and make sure no one bothers you," she said.

"We should be right back," Terrance said, and we took a look around.

The cavern was, as I thought, less than twenty feet deep, but it was wide. From here, it appeared to have four corridors leading away from it, one in each direction. It felt like too many choices.

"Which way do we go?" I asked.

"There are four of us," Magnus suggested.

"I've seen that movie too many times. Friends go spelunking in the caves, and when they get separated, they each get picked off by the monster living underground," I said.

Terrance stated the obvious. "This isn't a movie, Dean."

"I know. This is worse. We live in a universe with ancient god races, wormholes, and bugs addicted to drug pollen. There could be something much worse than a monster down these halls." I smiled under my helmet, but I didn't think any of them saw it.

"Dean's right. We stay in groups of two," Magnus said, once again taking charge.

"I'll go with Rulo. Terrance and Dean, why don't you try that one first?" Magnus showed me how to scroll on my HUD to see the locations of the other armor suits. "This way, we can see where each of us is at all times."

"I'm liking the suits, Magnus. Where'd we get them?" I asked.

"Our friend Rivo had them shipped to Haven. She

thought we might need them." I could hear the smile behind his words.

"Rivo? You've talked with her?" I asked, surprised.

"She was worried about you. They helped in a lot of ways," Magnus said. I couldn't wait to catch their whole story. So far, I'd only heard pieces.

"We'll talk about it later. For now, I need to find our friend and get back to my baby." I'd been trying not to think about that little pink human bundled in Mary's arms. The moment she was born, I had to leave her. I vowed to change that. I would be there for her, growing up. I wouldn't be the father who missed everything because he was out chasing disgruntled aliens.

Magnus and Rulo headed to the opposite end to us and disappeared into the corridors.

"After you," I said, clapping Terrance on the back.

The hybrid led the way, heading into the entrance to the rocky hallway. It was dark, and we turned on our visors' infrared function. Everything glowed a soft green in the narrow passageway.

"Where is he? Why wouldn't he stay in the cavern?" I asked.

"I would have run too if five robots were shooting down at me," Terrance said.

"They hadn't fired, though. The ground wasn't blown to pieces," I said.

"True. Then I'm not sure. We'll find him. These tunnels can't go on forever," Terrance said, and I didn't argue with him. The lake was close, so unless the robots had burrowed beneath it, they'd have to recalculate around the body of water.

I looked to my HUD, seeing two blinking green dots showing us where Rulo and Magnus were. Rulo didn't have a suit on, so I guessed they'd added a beacon to her minigun or somewhere on her body. Their icons were moving smoothly in the opposite direction as us.

"Magnus, you there?" I asked, testing our connection.

"We're here. Nothing but rock. How about you?" he asked.

"Same. How far before we double back and try the other corridors?" I asked.

"Let's do another fifteen minutes in, then turn around. Slate wouldn't have gone that deep. It doesn't make sense." Magnus ended the call, and I thought about what he said.

Slate would have stayed close, unless something forced him to leave. This realization sent shivers up my spine.

The tunnels were narrow, but at least eight feet tall, staying consistent in size as we moved through them. I stepped on something and nearly slipped on it.

Terrance stopped and stuck a hand out, keeping me from falling. "What is it?" he asked, and I stepped back. In the infrared light, I could see it for what it was in an instant.

"Animal scat. And a large one at that." I was grateful I didn't have to smell it with the armor suit on. It was larger than the cow pies from the neighbor's fields growing up.

Terrance spoke into his mic. "Magnus, we have a

problem. Feces. From a big animal."

We received no reply. I checked their position and saw they were standing still down in their tunnel. "Magnus, come in."

For a second, their connection linked, and we heard yelling and pulse fire before it cut out and we lost them.

Without asking Terrance what we should do, I turned and ran back the way we'd come. The suit made running easy, and I booted it as fast as it would allow me to. The walls raced by as I made it into the cavern. With large leaping steps, I wound my way into the corridor they'd entered, heart pumping with every kick of my feet. I scanned to their position on the HUD, seeing I was closing in on them. I was panting by the time I approached, and I kept my back to the wall, trying to see what was happening.

"Magnus, I'm right behind you." No answer. The gunfire had ceased. Terrance was behind me now, his rifle raised, ready to attack.

I waved a finger forward and crouched low, gun up and steady. What I saw almost made me stop in my tracks. Magnus was on the ground, and he was being dragged down the hall by his feet. Rulo lay in a crumpled heap close by.

Terrance ran to her and carried her back. She was alive, her chest rising and falling slowly.

"Rulo, what happened? What are those?" I asked, and she blinked her eyelids open wide.

"Death. Go hunt..." Her words translated, and I wasn't sure I grasped what she was suggesting. Were they hunting us, or should I hunt them? She passed out, blood seeping from her cheek where a gash had opened the thick skin.

"We'll be back for you, Rulo," I said and moved, trying to get a visual on the creature dragging Magnus down the hall.

We tried to stay silent. It pained me to not go help Magnus at that moment, but as long as they were dragging him, they weren't attacking, and that was the only solace I had in the situation.

The sound of his suit being carried over the rocky ground ceased, and I could finally see the outline of the creature. It was tall, seven feet if an inch; broad shoulders led to long arms that dragged on the ground when it stood there. I zoomed to its face, which had a wide nose, four nostrils sniffing at the air like a bloodhound. A single beady black eye sat under its nose, its mouth near the top of its head. The creature was something out of a nightmare. Its thin torso made for a narrow target, and it finished off with thick powerful legs and stubby feet.

Terrance's hand trembled, telling me he'd seen the monster too. It stopped sniffing and grabbed Magnus' legs again, continuing on down the hall.

We followed for a few minutes, and eventually, it wound into another cavern. More feces littered the halls here, and we waited a few moments after it entered the cave.

The creature appeared to use smell as a hunting technique, and I hoped our suits hid our musk well. We flanked the entrance to the cave, and I peeked inside, my infrared vision allowing me to make out the heat of the creature and Magnus. Only there were at least a dozen heat sources inside, ten of them much larger than those two.

"Slate and Magnus are both in there," I whispered into my mic. Terrance nodded slowly.

We could hear the animals start to make noises: a sort of pack howl. We didn't have time to wait. I had an idea.

SIX

Terrance understood what I was suggesting, and we prepped our suits and our minds.

I looked to him across the doorway and counted down with my gloved fingers. Three. I tapped the controls for all of my armor suit's lighting. Two. *Confirm?* One. *Yes.* Tap. We shone like a star in the darkness of the caverns, and ran into the room.

The creatures screamed now, hissing and bellowing their anger at the intrusion. We fired at will, pieces of the slimy black monsters flying everywhere, gore and blood spraying around, covering everything in sight. It was pandemonium, and under it all, Slate and Magnus lay still on the ground.

When we thought they were all dead, Terrance circled the room, and I ran for our downed friends. Magnus was moving now, his armored suit covered in guts.

"What happened?" He sat up and shook his head. Slate was still in his EVA and hadn't moved yet. Scratches tore through his suit, exposing blood on his skin.

"Slate!" I hopped over Magnus and unclasped Slate's helmet. I tossed it to the side and held his head in my hands. "Slate, buddy. Talk to me," I said as I reached for his arm console to check for vitals. It was damaged beyond repair. One of the creatures must have smashed it with an attack.

"Dean…" Magnus said, his voice weak. He was sitting up, looking behind me. "Dean," he said again, this time a little louder.

"What?" I asked and didn't wait long to find out what he was going on about. The dark monster raced toward me from the edge of the room, long arms pulled back, and it swung at me hard, knocking me backwards. I flew a few yards and landed hard on my back, my suit taking the brunt of the impact.

I reached for my gun, but it was beside Slate. "Terrance!" I yelled, and the creature was on me, flailing away, its fists repeatedly beating my armor. I rolled my head to the side and saw another one of the monsters attacking Terrance.

A beam ripped through the room and narrowly missed my attacker. "Magnus, I don't think they can see in the light. He's fighting blind. Can you distract him from me?"

It was still pummeling away, and I didn't know how long my armor would last. Another blast hit the ground nearby as I jumped around erratically, trying not to get hit by the pulse rifle.

I rolled, escaping the assault, and aimed all of my lights directly at the angry being. It roared, baring the teeth at the top of its head. It was a horrific sight, but Magnus finally found his aim true and hit the screeching monster in the back. It toppled over as he fired again, and

I ran away from the falling body.

Terrance had finished off his assailant and made his way over to our side of the room. "We have to get out of here. Keep the lights on." We heard more cries coming from deeper in the caves, and my skin crawled.

"Magnus, you okay to walk?" I asked, helping him to his feet.

"Yeah, they caught me off-guard." He walked toward the exit, limping.

"Help me with Slate," I said to Terrance, and together we lifted our friend up. We draped his arms over our shoulders and took his weight between us.

More of them roared in the distance, and we hurried our pace as much as Slate's heavy, limp body would allow us. Magnus stayed behind us, limping along, keeping a gun pointed down the hall. Soon we found Rulo where we'd left her, sitting on the ground, her back to the stone wall and her minigun ready to shoot.

"Come on," I said to her, and she got up, struggling along with her injuries. Before we knew it, we were back in the main cavern, the rope still hanging down waiting for us.

"Leslie," I called into my mic.

"I'm here," she said, peering down. "Everyone okay? I couldn't get through to you for a while."

"We were attacked, but we have Slate," I said, bringing him into the light from outside. "We're going to need help getting him up." I pointed to Magnus and Rulo. "And we have a couple of injuries."

Leslie nodded and returned a few moments later with

a large harness. "This was in the lander. Should do the trick."

We spent a few minutes getting the harness around Slate's unconscious body, keeping an eye on all four corridor entrances. Those things could run through at any moment, and none of us desired to see them again.

I was the last to climb up, my arms burning by the time I breached above ground. I lay on my back for a second before joining the others at the lander.

"Let's get Slate to Nick. He needs medical attention." I looked around, grateful we'd found him but worried we were too late. I was done playing Robinson Crusoe. I wanted to take my wife and baby and go home.

―――――――――

"*H*e's going to be fine." Nick came out from the medical room where Mary had been just hours before. She was in crew quarters with the baby and Suma, and I was sitting on the floor in the hall, waiting for word on my buddy.

"Thank God. What's his condition?" I asked, getting up from my sitting position.

"Concussion. He was banged pretty hard in the head, and he has lacerations on his left thigh and abdomen, but they were shallow. I've bandaged him up, and he should be okay in no time. You can go in and see him now," Nick said and opened the door for me.

"Thanks, Nick."

"That's what I'm here for. Glad to be able to help the old crew," he said, smiling widely.

Slate was on the bed, half sitting, half propped up. He was pale, and with his messy blond hair, he reminded me of a ghost. "How're you doing, big fella?" I asked, trying to keep my voice light.

"You should see the other guys." He forced a smile. "I'm assuming. I don't even know what attacked me."

"Did you see me get abducted in the forest?" I asked, wondering how he'd gotten underground.

"Yes. I wanted to go after you, but there were too many. The drones had done a good job cutting their numbers down, but it wasn't enough. When they took you, I tried to go after them, but it was a suicide mission. So I ran." He looked down, as if ashamed.

"Slate, you have nothing to make excuses for. There were far too many enemies this time," I said, arms crossed as I stood beside him. I let them fall to my sides.

"A few of them chased me down toward the lake, and when I got to this rocky area and saw a hole, I thought it was my only chance. At first, it was perfect. The robots were there waiting for me and wouldn't leave. I tried to come up with a plan. I considered collapsing the roof and having the robots fall, hopefully damaging them. Before I could act, I was attacked from behind. I didn't wake up until Nick was standing over me with a needle."

He looked frazzled. I stuck a fist out, and he grunted as he lifted his arm to tap it.

"I'm glad you're okay. We have someone for you to meet when you're up to it," I said casually.

"Mary? Did she…is it…" His unfinished questions came quickly.

I smiled like only a recent father could. "The baby girl's fine… more than fine. She's happy and healthy, and Mary's well. I can't believe I'm a father."

"What's her name?" he asked.

I didn't know. We hadn't given her one yet. Over the last few months, we'd talked about it a few times, but nothing was set in stone. "I don't know," I mumbled.

"You don't know? Then what are you doing here? Go to her. Be with your family," Slate said.

"You're my family too," I said and saw his eyes begin to well up.

"I need sleep, boss. Your wife and baby need you." He closed his eyes, and I knew the conversation was over.

"I'll be back," I promised.

"I'm glad you're okay. I want to hear how you escaped them later," he said, his eyes still closed.

I left him there, glad to have someone so strong and resilient fighting beside me every step of the way.

I wasn't going to miss the planet. We understood its official name was Sterona, at least according to the readings we'd scrounged up. I preferred to think of it as nameless: an abandoned world we'd thought was vacant of sentient life, until we found the underground creatures.

We lifted in the ships, and I stood on the bridge of

our ship, my baby girl in my arms, cooing softly from her warm cocoon of blankets. Rulo was there with more of her kind, running the show, and she nodded her head at me in a sign of acceptance. Everyone was healing from our encounter a couple of days ago, and Rulo looked no worse for the wear. She had a bandage on her cheek and said she would wear the scar as a badge of honor.

The viewscreen showed a lightning storm flashing out over the vacant city we'd called home. This was where Slate and I had first entered the portals; where we'd first met little Suma, and where we'd eventually come back to save Mary from the clutches of the Iskios. I had a lot of memories from here, but I'd be a happy man if I never had to see it again.

"Dean, glad to be going home?" Suma asked, sneaking up beside me.

I put my arm around her and hugged her close. "Yes, Suma, I am. How about you?"

She looked up at me, and then at my baby girl. "Home will be a welcome destination. I look forward to seeing my father."

"Sarlun must be at his wits' end, wondering what happened to you. I hope he doesn't kill me," I said.

Suma squawked a laugh. "You stopped the universe from being eaten by the Unwinding. I think that awards you a little slack."

I looked down at my newborn and said grimly, "Not from the love of a father, it doesn't."

"Did you name her yet?" Suma asked, and I shook my head. Mary was sleeping, and our schedules hadn't allowed for a lot of alone time. I knew we'd come to a decision soon.

We stood watching the lava ocean seethe red and hot in the distance, and soon we were lifting into space. From there, I saw the fleet Magnus had mentioned. Four massive ships hung there, and for a second, I had a flash of the Kraski vessels. I closed my eyes to forget the sight, but saw the Kraski with the scar across its face from my capture. What had a Kraski been doing with Lom of Pleva's robot army?

These vessels were large but rounded, like the landers and other vessels that had come to the surface, yellow and orange over pale gray. Massive thrusters clung to the sides, making them look like disks with two cylinders strapped to them.

"Come on, we need to have a good long talk with the powers that be," I said, knowing ultimately that title always fell back on my shoulders. That was going to change now. Mary and I had been through enough. It was time for a break.

The ships we were in entered the fleet vessel's hangar, and we passed through the containment barrier before touching down on the floor inside.

"See you out there," I said to Suma, and went down the halls to find the crew quarters. Inside, Mary was awake, and already dressed.

"There are my two favorite beings in the universe," she said, coming over to take the baby from my arms.

"We need to name her. I can't keep thinking of her as 'baby'," I said.

"I know. I was thinking about Jules. It was my grandmother's name, and well, kind of fitting, don't you think?" Mary looked down at our baby girl, who was sleeping softly in her arms. She ran a hand over Jules' small head, which had a few whispers of thin dark hair flattened on it.

"I love it, Mary." I moved beside them. "Hello, Jules. I'm your dad." She didn't seem to care right now. "We're inside one of the fleet ships. We can finally learn what happened while we were gone. I'm curious to see how it all transpired."

Mary didn't look up from Jules. "I'm glad they found us, and that she's okay." She looked exhausted. It had been a long six months, accentuated by an extremely stressful birth.

We left the quarters. We had no possessions, so it was empty, save the few tattered clothes we'd had on our backs when we were found. Everything stayed behind. It was time to leave that part of our lives, and to get home.

SEVEN

The "war room" was half empty. We sat around the large table. Alien art adorned the walls, and everything felt so… unfamiliar. It was Rulo's people's art, and they liked clean lines and simplicity, with a flash of color.

Magnus sat across from me, looking casual in shorts and a button-down short-sleeved shirt. It was off-putting, seeing him wearing it in this setting. Leslie and Terrance were together, as ever, beside him, and they both smiled at Mary and me. One of Rulo's people was there, though he was more gray than black, and older, somehow more dangerous-looking.

Slate sat at the end of the table, his head bandaged, but otherwise bright-eyed. He winked at me, making me laugh. Suma was at the other end, her snout twitching uneasily.

"Guys, this is Yope, Admiral of the Keppe. You've met Rulo. They're the reason we were able to get here. Without them, things would have turned out much differently," Leslie said, motioning toward the gray being.

"It's an honor to meet you, Admiral Yope. Thank you for your assistance." I stopped, unsure what else to say. A translator on the table echoed my words, but he remained silent, choosing not to reply to me.

"Yes, thanks for coming to get us," Mary said. Jules let out a small cry.

"It wasn't easy," Magnus said, and now I saw the bags under his eyes, and the newly-formed wrinkles.

"What happened?" I asked him.

"You first!" Magnus was upset. "I mean, the last thing we knew, you were going to see Garo Alnod; the next, Bazarn Five is under attack, and you're telling us you're right on our tail."

"Look, I know it was messed up, but it was what I needed to do." I didn't feel like I had to explain myself, but for Magnus, I would. "I found the Theos."

Magnus' eyes went wide. I glanced to Leslie, who wore a great poker face. "You what?"

"They gave me the power to carry some of them, like Mary was carrying the Iskios. It was the only way I could fight them. It worked too, but when we extracted the Iskios from her, we had to put them into the portal stone, where the Theos inside could fight them. In the process, the stone became useless, trapping us."

It was actually a fairly simple explanation. Magnus' expression told me otherwise. "That is… I don't even know what to say."

"Magnus. We're all safe. Without Suma and Slate coming here, the battle was lost. I used the Shifter, a device Rivo's father was only too happy to part with."

Yope leaned forward, his snake eyes blinking slowly. His smooth words translated for us. "What is a Shifter?"

I didn't know this man, or his people, but he'd gone

out on a limb and fought Lom of Pleva's troops to help save us, so I felt I should be able to trust him. Magnus clearly did. "Garo Alnod created a device meant to shift people, or even a planet, to another dimension, only he hadn't intended it to be used as a weapon. Lom of Pleva did, and he wanted it. That was the reason Rivo was taken by those pirates in the first place."

Magnus leaned back and rubbed his face with a meaty paw. "And the attack on Bazarn?"

"Lom, coming for it. I offered to take it in exchange for meeting Regnig, an ancient bird man who only speaks telepathically."

Magnus let out a deep chuckle. I laughed with him, hearing how ridiculous it all sounded. "I know, it sounds insane, but I swear it's true. Without him, I wouldn't have found Karo."

"Where is this device?" Yope asked plainly.

"Gone," I said, and Yope went rigid. "You might notice the Unwinding is gone too."

"You threw the Unwinding into another dimension?" Terrance asked, speaking for the first time. He looked impressed.

Suma joined in. "Dean was so brave. We didn't think he was coming back."

"Is that so? Suicide mission to stop the Unwinding. Just when I thought I'd seen it all, Dean Parker impresses me once again," Magnus said. He looked over to Mary uneasily. "I'm glad you did make it back. Not that I doubted your ability to remain unscathed when danger calls."

Mary met Magnus' gaze. "How are Nat and the kids?"

The question broke the formality. "They were great when we left. I've been able to keep in touch with them using the communication devices Dean had when he and Leonard went to the Bhlat homeworld."

"Now that's something I could have used," I said under my breath. I'd been so hell-bent on getting to Mary, I'd been short-sighted on a few things. Maybe a lot of things.

"Oh, Leonard's staying at your house, Mary." Magnus smirked at this.

"He is?" she asked.

"It needed someone to take care of it, and he was complaining about the apartment he was in, so I offered him the job. I hope you don't mind," Magnus said.

"Not at all," I answered. "How are the dogs?" I missed Carey and Maggie, and even little Charlie. I knew they'd feel like I'd abandoned them yet again.

"They're great, Dean. Leonard's taking care of all the younger ones for a while, since Nat has her hands full. Carey's by her side night and day, though." Magnus lowered his voice. "That dog's been with us through it all. He loves those kids so much."

"Good. Glad to hear it." Part of me wished I could turn it all back and never leave chasing after Mae. That Mary and I could have stayed and kept Carey with us, a small pseudo-family brought together in the chaos of the Event. But I knew Carey was happy with the way things worked out, and sitting beside my beautiful wife and healthy baby girl, I couldn't help but feel grateful for our eventual path.

"Can we get back to the subject at hand?" Yope asked, clearly annoyed at our personal discussions. "So this Shifter is gone?"

"That's what I said. Eaten up as it transferred the vortex into some unsuspecting alternate reality." I watched Yope; if I didn't know better, he looked relieved.

"Lom of Pleva is not a man you want to anger, but clearly the Alnods have. The accident at the mine left Lom dead, or so we all thought," Yope said. His words flowed like melted butter in his native tongue.

"That was no accident," I said.

"How do you mean?" Magnus asked.

"Garo set it up. Things weren't good between the two of them. Ever since Garo swiped the purchase of some hyperdrive tech company from under his nose, Lom has had it out for Garo. They're two rich titans out for blood. If my perspective is accurate, which I think it is, Lom's on the wrong side of the fence," I said. It was hard to tell sometimes. For all I knew, Garo's lines to me were cold and calculated to have me side with him, while Lom was innocent.

"I knew it," Yope said, slamming a fist on the table. "When I saw his ships and the markings on the artificial army, I'd hoped it was just someone from his corporation stepping in to take control. If Lom of Pleva lives, and his sights are targeted on you, then be afraid."

"You seemed to take care of them pretty easily," I suggested.

"And shifted the target to my back in the process,"

Yope said.

"Dean, the admiral didn't have to help us, but he did," Leslie said.

"What exactly transpired to get us here?" Mary asked the group.

Suma leaned forward, and I glanced to Slate, who was sitting there like a silent soldier, assessing the entire conversation. I looked forward to discussing it with him later.

Leslie started. "We knew where you went, and we left your *friend* with Natalia. He's safely on New Spero."

Karo was on New Spero. That surprised me. I'd been worried about him being left to his own devices on Haven. Who knew what kind of trouble he might get in with a slip of his tongue? "Who else is here?" I asked, knowing Nick was. "Clare?"

"Just us, and Nick. He wanted to come... for Mary," Magnus said.

"Anyway," Leslie continued, "we knew where you went, and told Slate and Suma when they arrived. I thought you might be mad about that, but knew they'd be able to help if you needed it."

"We wouldn't be here without them," Mary said, shooting Suma a smile.

"When Magnus showed up, bringing the fury of hell with him, we had no choice but to tell him what we knew," Leslie added.

"We tried to access the portal here, but the icon was gone. Vanished. We knew that happened to the crystal world when you brought Leonard through with a visiting Iskios, so we assumed there was trouble," Magnus said.

"We waited, Dean. We waited for a week, hoping you'd find a way to come to us, or to New Spero, but nothing. Then we got word from the Bhlat."

I sat up straight. "What about them? What did they want?"

"They won't tell us," Magnus said. "The Empress claims it's for your ears only. Her emissaries weren't pleased when we told them you were incapacitated at the moment. At first they thought we were trying to keep you from them, but eventually, I corresponded with the Empress herself. Thank God she remembered me, because otherwise, we might be screwed."

"What happened?" Mary asked.

"She told me our time was up. That they needed the planet we promised as part of our deal with them," Magnus said.

"What did you do?" I asked, nervous for the answer.

"I gave them a planet."

"Do you have that authority?" Slate asked, getting a dirty look from Magnus.

"Listen, pup, I make the authority when I need to, and I handed the ice world over," Magnus said. "With Sarlun's blessing, of course."

Slate let out a light laugh. "Of course," he added.

The Bhlat were looking for me, and Magnus had given them the ice world where we'd found the first sign left behind by the Iskios. At the time, we'd thought they were the real Theos, guiding us to salvation. "That was the right move," I said.

"It was. But the Empress was still adamant she speak

with you. It wasn't a suggestion," Magnus said.

Leslie took over. "A week passed with no word from you, so we had to start the mission."

"Which was?" Mary asked.

"Finding you at all costs. We knew where the planet was, but we had no way to quickly access it. The portal was down, but most of them are still functional," Leslie answered.

I thought about the Theos life energy faintly thrumming inside the remaining portals. I felt the urge to close them all, releasing the Theos for all eternity. "How did you get here, then?"

"One of the portals opens to Keppe. They weren't the closest race to Sterona," Leslie said, using the name we'd discovered for the vacant world, "but Terrance and I knew of them from the odd visitor to Haven. We went there with Magnus and Sarlun, and pleaded our case for help."

I saw Yope shift uncomfortably in his seat. "And they gave it so easily?" I inquired.

Leslie was careful with her words, glancing over at Magnus. "They accepted our terms."

I decided now wasn't a good time to find out what those terms were.

"They have a powerful fleet, a widespread system of colonized planets. Dean, the Keppe are someone we need on our side. Their ships got us here in two months, and when we arrived, we couldn't believe there were ships already in orbit. Once we realized they were here for you as well, it didn't take long to remove the threat." Magnus said the last after a slight hesitation.

There was something Magnus was leaving out of the conversation. It was written all over his tired face, and his body language was rigid, pretending to be calm. It was off-putting. I made eye contact with him, and the frown he was wearing softened slightly.

Once again, he'd been dragged across the universe, through a few portals, and, after bargaining with the Keppe, onto another alien fleet. He missed his kids, his wife, his life.

"Now that we're all caught up, can we go home? We have Mary, the Iskios are gone, the Unwinding isn't here any longer, and you found us. Let's leave Sterona behind and go home. What I wouldn't give to sleep in my own bed for a while," I said.

"I miss my father," Suma said, no doubt wishing he'd come on the trip to rescue her.

"If there's not anything else, I say we let everyone go and get on our way." Magnus started to get up, but I raised a hand.

I didn't want to say the words out loud, because it would only make them truer. Maybe if I kept it to myself, it could be like it hadn't happened. When I closed my eyes for a second, I saw hordes of Kraski back on the mother ship, vomiting green before collapsing to their deaths.

"When you rescued me, I was being interrogated by someone," I said, catching everyone's attention.

"You were? I assumed you were just being held by them until Lom of Pleva arrived," Magnus said.

I shook my head. "I don't think he was coming here personally. He sent someone in his stead."

Mary set a hand on mine. "Who was it?"

"It was a Kraski."

EIGHT

"*A* Kraski?" Magnus asked loudly. "Are you sure?"

"I am. It was hiding in the room's shadows, asking me questions about my guilt or my decisions. It was going to try me for my crimes against them, I think. I only saw its face when I was being pulled out of the room after you rescued me."

"Then you could be wrong," Mary said.

"No. I'll never forget their faces. Never." I motioned a finger horizontally across my cheeks. "This one was scarred."

"I thought we destroyed all of them." Magnus shared the guilt of our task with me. It bonded us, but also affected us in a way most people wouldn't understand. We thought we'd committed genocide against an entire race, but we'd come to terms with that as best we could. Now, knowing there were more out there, I felt relieved in a small way, but with that relief came the worry of vengeance.

"It all makes sense if you think about it," Mary said. She adjusted a sleeping Jules in her arms and looked around the table. "What do we know? Lom of Pleva created the hybrid technology."

Leslie and Terrance shifted in their seats, and Yope glanced their way, a look of distaste on his face. I saw him and Rulo lock eyes, sharing something between them. It worried me.

Mary continued. "The Bhlat were coming for the Kraski and their system, and when they knew they'd lose the inevitable battle, they fled, taking their Deltra slaves and their hybrid army. Where did they get the hybrids?"

Magnus answered, "Lom of Pleva."

"Right. He sold them to the Kraski," I said. "What did Sergo say on Volim? There's profit to be made in times of chaos. That's the mentality someone like Lom of Pleva would live or die by."

"So they have a relationship. Now the Kraski are using his assets to find the one that destroyed their people. Dean Parker," Admiral Yope said. "I've heard of these Kraski. They were once a feared opponent, before the Bhlat grew so powerful. It seems you've made an ally with one of the universe's most deadly races, Dean. How is that so?"

I wasn't going to get into that at the moment. I was tired of talking already. We'd have two months to discuss things. "I did what I had to do to save my people. Sometimes bartering and talking creates solutions that guns and death cannot."

Yope smiled at this, baring sharp teeth. "You aren't what I expected, Parker. Not at all."

"I've heard that before," I replied.

"So the Kraski are still alive, and hunting you. That isn't good," Leslie said. "We'll put out our feelers when we're back."

"And we'll use the Gatekeeper network to search for news on this," Mary added.

"I am intrigued, though." Yope nodded toward Leslie and Terrance. "If Lom of Pleva created the hybrids, then why do you trust these two?"

"If you were to kill someone, would I look at you and blame your parents for giving you the DNA used to pull the trigger of the gun?" I asked. He smiled again, this time letting out a smooth laugh.

"I like you, Parker. Come and talk when you have settled in. You can learn about my people, and I yours," Admiral Yope said.

I didn't like the way he called humans "my people." It wasn't the least bit accurate, but I left it for the moment.

Yope got up from his chair and exited the room, leaving us alone: a motley crew consisting of four humans, two hybrids, and a Shimmali girl.

"Slate, you've been quiet. What do you make of all this?" Mary asked, beating me to the question.

Slate pushed back from his chair, and his hand subconsciously went to his bandage on his head. I knew he wasn't feeling up to par today, but I also knew he couldn't sleep yet. "I think you're right. The Kraski might be back, and with the resources of this Lom guy, we could be in danger. Don't worry, boss, I'll be at your side to protect you."

"Hard to do that when you're dragged off into a monster's cavern, isn't it?" Magnus asked.

Slate stood, walking over to the big Scandinavian

man. "I seem to recall hearing you were dragged in there by the same creatures as I was."

Magnus stood, and Mary shouted across the table, "What's your problem with each other? Sit down and stop acting like little boys. You're so similar, yet you feel like protecting everyone is your sole individual task."

Magnus looked ashamed in an instant, and his puffed-up chest deflated. "Sorry, brother. I miss the family. And I hate to think there's yet again another old enemy, creeping up from our buried past."

Slate stuck out a fist, and Magnus bumped it. "We'll be ready for them," Slate said.

"That's what I'm worried about." Magnus headed for the door. "If anyone's interested, I'm going to get some food." Then, with a sparkle in his eyes, he added, "Dean, remember that golden syrup drink from Volim?"

I nodded.

"They have it," he said.

I followed him to the dining room.

———————

*T*wo months. Another two months away from the one place I could now call home. Mary and I had wonderful quarters, a far better set-up than we'd had on Sterona, but it still left me feeling cold. We were in the section of the ship for Keppe officers – whom, it appeared, they treated quite well. Our floor consisted of six separate quarters, and with it we had an odd robot taking care of our every need, like it was our personal caregiver. It coddled Jules as if she were the most precious creature it'd even seen, and treated her like a delicate flower, often asking when her armor would grow in.

We were given clothing: thick, colorful robes. At first, it felt like we were being pranked, but we believed them when we saw a huge Keppe man walk by with a pink-hued robe on and a minigun in his hand.

Slate, Suma, and Magnus each had their own quarters, and Leslie and Terrance shared a unit, leaving the other unit on our floor empty. It had been a month now: halfway there.

"You guys aren't going to like this," Magnus said, coming into the dining room. We were all seated together, Rulo and Nick joining us this morning.

I picked up a chunk of precut fruit and let the sweet juices melt in my mouth. The Keppe had some great food. If there was one thing I'd miss about being on this ship, it was the cook's skills in the kitchen. He was the roundest Keppe I'd seen, his body's armor plating stretched around his immense girth. He knew his way around a kitchen, and it showed in his culinary prowess.

"Did you hear me?" Magnus asked after none of us responded.

"We just want to enjoy breakfast. What could possibly be serious enough to ruin the most important meal of the day?" I asked, placing another piece of fruit in my mouth. This one was bright orange with the consistency of a banana, but with a sharp flavor unlike anything I'd ever tasted.

"They're making a detour." Magnus looked pleased with himself when my two-pronged eating utensil fell to the plate.

It was Mary who spoke first. "Detour? What kind of detour?"

Magnus sat down, grabbing some crispy meat slices from the center of the round table.

"Yope said they got a distress call from some system full of a race called the Motrill. They're basically neighbors with them, and they watch each other's backs. One of their leaders' sons was on a diplomatic mission to a nearby system, only he never made it there. All signs seem to indicate the ship went down while traveling through the system."

"Then why don't the Motrill, or whatever they're called, send help?" I asked, angry about the delay.

"We're closer. The Keppe are always out and about, patrolling or exploring," Magnus said.

"What does this mean?" Mary asked.

"It means we're heading for this system and looking for a ship." Magnus grabbed some more meat and chewed it with a smile. "Don't worry. I want nothing more than to get home too, guys. But this isn't our ship, and the admiral's been gracious this whole time. We'd still be trying to find a beat-up ship to fly to Sterona, if it wasn't for him. And by the looks of things when we arrived, Dean would be in the Kraski's hands, and Mary would have been a single mom in the forest, surrounded by maniacal robots."

He had good points. My shoulders slumped slightly.

"How long?"

He knew what I meant. "A week there, another week back. If we find what we're looking for right away, it's at least a two-week delay." Magnus set the communicator on the table. "Anyone at home you want to talk with? Natalia has the other one."

Slate's eyes lit up. So far he'd been listening to our conversation, not being an active participant. I noticed he did that more and more, the larger the group we were in. When it was just the two of us, he wouldn't stop talking. "Mag, can she get the other end to Denise?"

Magnus nodded. "Of course, bud. She's become a friend of Nat's, so they talk all the time."

I knew Slate was worried Denise would have moved on. They'd only been dating a short while before we'd left, and he didn't expect her to stick around while he was off fighting the fight on random planets. For his sake, I hoped she was still in the relationship. He needed her.

Slate pushed his plate forward and smiled at Suma. "Thanks, Mag. Let me know when."

"Suma, what's on your mind?" Mary asked the Shimmali girl.

"I miss my father and my friends, but I love the library here. Did you know that the Keppe trace their roots back twenty thousand years? They had what you referred to as an industrial revolution five thousand years ago, and they do almost all of their manufacturing on the three moons surrounding their home planet," Suma said excitedly.

"That's quite forward thinking," Nick said. "They

have some seriously advanced medical practices as well. I'm working on learning how to translate some cell regeneration processes to work on humans."

"Nick, I think you and Clare may be the two most enthusiastic people about our new lifestyle. Clare using each alien technology piece she can, and you working to advance our health care," I said. I was proud of the two of them and wondered something.

"Are you and Clare ever going to tie the knot?" Slate asked while sipping his beverage, something akin to a coffee.

I laughed. "Did you learn to read my mind now, Slate?"

Nick smiled and ignored our inquiries. "I have an idea as well. I was hoping to run it by you guys." He looked nervous, something I didn't see from him often.

"Go for it," I said.

"Clare and I were talking about having a board, with representatives from different interests. Health and wellness, technology – which would cover a lot of bases, from power generation to space fleet logistics – and of course, military," Nick said, his hands moving as he spoke.

"Sounds like a good idea so far. What's the end goal?" Mary asked.

"With the Gatekeepers' permission, we'd like to seek our allies and other worlds, to have conversations about these specific topics. Share data," Nick said.

"Some of this occurs already. Not all races are happy sharing their secrets, though," Suma added to the conversation.

"It's a good idea," I said. "Magnus, what do you think?"

The large man cracked his knuckles. "We've been meaning to do more of that on the military side. But as Suma said, weapons tech is held close to the chest. Ship technology's a good one, though, as we've seen some really cool things for long-term vessels just being on this Keppe ship journey."

"Then it's settled. Let's make a go of it and see what Sarlun thinks when we get home," I said, and Nick smiled: a silent thank you for the support. I thought of reminding him I held no official title and didn't hold any substantial power, but he would have waved me off.

Jules stirred from her Keppe crib. We were thrilled to learn they had anything a new parent could want on board. The vessels housed five thousand Keppe when fully manned, and three thousand now. It was mindboggling to know that families traveled together on certain exploratory missions. Right now, it was nothing but soldiers, officers, and staff to keep it all running. There were four such ships in the party, heading back home now.

This got me thinking. "Magnus, is there any way Yope will let one of the four ships go back to their world? I mean, do they need twelve thousand Keppe on hand for a search party?"

"You do when the missing man is betrothed to your leader's youngest daughter."

NINE

The ship's drive slowed, and I watched the scene unfold from the bridge of our lead vessel in the fleet. Admiral Yope sat in the captain's chair, with the regular captain relegated to the side as first officer, and so on. They all seemed honored to have the older Yope on board and gave him nothing but deference and respect as he barked commands to them.

"Scanners on full. Check the results from the probes," Yope said, translating into my ear.

They'd released thousands of tiny probes as we came out of hyperdrive, looking for any sign of the energy a ship of that class would output. So far, everything was coming up blank.

"We're checking, Admiral," a fresh-faced female officer said. Her black armored skin was a contrast to the sharp white uniforms they all wore. I was once again impressed with how advanced the Keppe were. They felt like a real crew, unlike the makeshift small crews we'd had over the past few years. I wondered what it would be like to be part of such a machine; a tiny cog in the running of a ship and exploratory vessel like this one.

The system was small; a yellow star burned hotly at

the center of it all. Five planets followed their ellipse patterns around the star, each unique in size. One of the planets was known to have an atmosphere and life, though no advanced life forms were present, according to the Keppe's databases. I wondered if there could be a portal on the world, one from the worlds hidden years ago by the Theos Collective. There was no way of knowing right now, and it bothered me.

"We're picking up something. A tiny number of particles left by a Motrill singularity drive. They have a unique signature, and this has their prints all over it," the first officer said from the side of the bridge.

Yope looked pleased. "Bring us in," he said, and we raced toward the destination, using an in-system FTL jump. One second we were days away from the world; then I blinked, and the planet loomed on the viewscreen only ten thousand kilometers away. I'd read some details on the world with Mary on the in-room computer earlier in the week. It was about half the size of Earth, with four distinct regions.

"How large was this ship?" I asked, realizing I hadn't been given that information yet. It was a need-to-know detail, and evidently, I didn't need to know.

"Class Five Motrill Skipper. Small, made for getting places quickly and effectively, with little armaments," a tall thick officer said off the top of his head, from my right. I stood behind Yope's chair, trying to stay out of the way since I didn't have a station. They'd honored me by even letting a human on the bridge.

"Not really something royalty should be racing

around the galaxy in, is it?" I asked.

Yope shook his head. "We don't know the whole story, but it seemed he didn't have clearance from his father to make the trip."

"Is it common to have arranged marriages?" I asked, hoping it wasn't a slight to them.

Yope answered without emotion. "It's not common, but we're genetically similar and can reproduce. It's said the two races sprouted from one long ago, though we have evolved separately in our environments."

"When was the last time this happened?" I asked.

"Seven hundred years," he said. I'd gotten used to understanding time was different for each of our races, depending on calendars, rotations, and all sorts of things I didn't fully understand, but Suma stated the Yope calendar was close to ours. Eighty percent, so those seven hundred years would be somewhere in the neighborhood of five hundred and sixty Earth years.

My gut was telling me this wasn't an abduction. I bit my tongue and stood back.

"We're tracing the drive to the southern region." A Keppe woman tapped a screen, and a section of the world zoomed in.

It was the tropical region I'd learned about. Something very close to palm trees rose high into the sky; thick vegetation took over, covering everything on the main viewscreen. It looked like paradise, with a green-blue ocean hugging the coasts.

"The signal stops down there," the officer stated.

"Very well. Send the team down. Find Polvertan and

bring him back to our ship. We'll escort him home," Yope said.

It seemed like an easy enough task, and I was getting stir crazy after our first few weeks on board. I knew Mary was going to kill me, but I'd rather help bring this Polvertan back and get on with our trip home than twiddle my thumbs while others set to the task.

"I want to join the search team that goes down," I said, getting Yope's attention.

"Parker, you aren't part of our culture, nor are you a member of my service. Why should we accommodate this request?" Yope asked, looking me square in the face. His snake-like eyes followed me as I moved over to speak in front of him.

"I respect that, but you know how much I've been through. My outside perspective might be valuable. The sooner we get this done, the sooner we get back to your world. Then I can get my baby and wife, along with my friends, back to their homes." I said the words forcefully, but low enough to not come over as arrogant. It seemed to work.

"Very well. I'm already annoyed at this disturbance. Polvertan hasn't been vocal about being averse to the betrothal, but neither has he come across as supportive." The admiral looked around me at a strong woman with a scar on her cheek. It was Rulo. "Do whatever is necessary to bring him aboard, within reason." He paused, and when Rulo smiled, he added, "And don't break anything this time."

I wondered how different their version of "within

reason" was from mine. I suspected they weren't even close. "Then it's settled. Slate and I will join your team." I noticed Yope's face fall just enough to tell I'd irritated him.

"*F*ind him and let's get home," Mary said, and leaned in for a kiss. I bent over and picked up Jules, who was drooling on a toy.

"I'll be back soon, little one." I kissed the top of her warm head and set her back down. "Thanks for not being upset."

"Why bother?" Mary asked. "In any other circumstance, I'd be going with you. Just promise me something."

"Anything."

"The odd time, let me go kick some ass while you stay with Jules."

I laughed. "It's a deal."

Slate arrived at the room, wearing Keppe clothing. Tight black pants and a long-sleeved white shirt fit a little too snugly over his muscled body. "Slate, you look…" I didn't finish.

"Handsome? Herculean?" he asked with a grin.

"Let's go with the second one." We walked down the hall and took the elevator to the lower section of the ship. Level three brought us near the hangars, where fighter ships lined the space, along with some dropships and landers. The rest of the team was waiting impatiently by one of the landers. It consisted of Rulo, the battle-hardened woman who was quick to smile. A huge Keppe man arrived, carrying a pack jammed with supplies. Anything you could think of was strapped to that bag on his back: ropes, a rifle, tarps, tents, something resembling a fishing rod, and a dozen other items of varying use.

Lastly, a thin female Keppe was there. She introduced herself as Kimtra. She was the tracker and had computer devices strapped all down her long, armored arms.

"Is this all of us?" I asked.

"What else do we need?" Rulo asked, her words translating easily. "We have our tracker. I'm here to blow things up if needed, and Hectal" – she jabbed a thumb toward the lumbering man with the supplies – "carries things."

"I blow things up too," he said with a frown.

"Yes. You do. Unfortunately, you hurt yourself as often as the enemy," Rulo joked with him, and I got the feeling the Keppe loved ribbing each other. They weren't so different from humans in that regard. It was refreshing to hear.

"How convenient. I also like to blow things up," Slate said, patting Hectal on his broad back.

"Good. Then maybe you can take this one." Hectal pushed a large pack toward Slate, and he nearly fell back from the impact.

"No problem at all. I'm here to do my fair share," Slate said when he regained his balance.

"What can I do?" I asked.

Rulo answered, "I've seen you in action. You surprise me. Stay close, and I trust you'll come through when it's needed."

The compliment surprised me. She'd been down there when we rescued Magnus and Slate from the underground creatures. I hadn't even thought that I'd earned her respect while doing so. I knew Yope relied on Rulo for his personal missions, and I finally understood why Yope gave me leeway. It was because Rulo vouched for me.

We loaded the lander, and I had to question the amount of supplies we were bringing. "How long are we going to be down there?"

"Always be prepared for the worst-case scenario," Kimtra said. "We're seeing some severe storm activity heading toward the region we're venturing into. It's best to be aware and have shelter and food, but hope we don't encounter any inclement weather systems." She ran a hand over her bald head, turned, and headed onto the ship.

"And the insane number of guns?" Slate asked.

Hectal answered, "Didn't we just say we love to blow things up?"

Slate laughed. I was the last one to board the small lander, and looked to see a few Keppe lingering in the hangar. Life went on here on the exploration vessel as the door closed, and Rulo lifted us up, through the containment field, into the blackness of space.

TEN

The trip to the surface took an hour from this far out, and we sat discussing different away missions that the Keppe had been on. Some of them bordered on ridiculous, and I wasn't sure how many of the adventures Hectal told were made up to impress us.

"Rulo, head this way," Kimtra said, adjusting the map settings on the main computer. Slate and I sat in the back on the pilot side bench, facing Hectal; the huge Keppe was keeping himself busy by checking the charge on each weapon he'd brought.

The sheer number of weapons worried me. What did they expect to find? Were they holding out information from us? Slate looked impassive as he watched the alien man go through his obsessive process.

"The trace amounts of residue end here," Kimtra said, and I glanced out the viewscreen to see ourselves over an immense body of water.

"He disappeared?" I asked, moving closer to the front of the lander.

"Not likely, but he may have cut the engines," Rulo said.

"Why would he do that?" Slate asked.

"Couple things could have occurred," Kimtra answered. "He could have lost power to the ship... or he didn't want someone following him."

"Are you saying he knew you'd come for him, and he wanted to stay hidden?" I wondered just what this Polvertan was up to.

"Kimtra, the Class Five Skipper is fully sealed, right? Even in the thrusters?" Rulo asked slowly, as if deep in thought.

"Yes. The containment fields seal the thrusters from debris and act as a shield in battle," Kimtra said.

"I thought they were a speedy travel ship?" I prompted.

"They are. With few weapons on board, wouldn't you want the best shields money can buy?" Hectal set his last weapon down, smiling at me.

"Good point," I said. "Where does this leave us?"

"Only one place." Rulo let out a yelp, tapped a few keys, and lunged the lander forward, nose-diving toward the water.

"What did we sign up for?" Slate asked as we braced for impact.

The ship cut into the large waves, putting us underwater in seconds. Rulo turned and laughed when she saw the color drained from our faces.

"Always gets the newbies. Don't worry, we visit a lot of water worlds. You'd be amazed at how many civilizations reside under the water."

I thought back to the Apop from our journey to the crystal world and nodded. "We've met some of them."

Rulo looked surprised. She turned back and began to move the ship toward the island we'd seen in the distance. "If he went under here, we'll check the island first. I don't think there's anything under these waters but some deadly leviathans and their prey."

Our ship had an incandescent blue glow around it; a containment shield strong enough for keeping air inside would be robust enough to keep water out.

"Engines?" Slate asked.

"Switched to the propeller thrusters on the side of the ship," Rulo said, as if this was obvious.

The water was crystal clear, and a few schools of speckled foreign fish dived apart as we flowed through the ocean toward the lone island. Kimtra read some data off as the rocky base of the surface grew in the viewscreen. "The island has no details in our databanks. From our scans earlier, it's approximately one hundred and fifty square kilometers."

"That's not very big," I said.

"It is when you're looking for one man," Hectal said stoically.

When we didn't see a ship at this point, Rulo began to circle the island. Eventually, when we'd made it halfway around, she slowed.

"Kimtra, is that what it looks like?" she asked her counterpart.

Kimtra studied the opening and nodded. "We can try here. It's the logical point of entry for a ship or boat, as it were."

The common usage of phrasing among alien races

astounded me. Perhaps it was our translator's ability to turn the phrase to something understood in English. One day, I'd get a better grasp, but I was no linguist.

I broke from my daydream on the Keppe's speech and stood as we turned to face the maw in the rocks. It was like an angry god's open mouth, threatening us with sharp stone teeth.

"I don't like the look of this," Slate said, shifting uneasily in his seat.

Hectal got up, bending to stand in the cramped space. "I do. This is great. I've always wanted to enter an island like this."

I wondered who in their right mind would have ever dreamt of this, and decided to keep my mouth shut. Hectal was at least three times my weight, and I didn't want to offend the giant armor-skinned alien. He grinned at me, as if reading my mind.

"Here we go." Rulo slowly eased us toward the opening, and I could hear the push of propellers on the side of the ship as we moved into the space, rocks surrounding us on all directions. We were essentially in a tunnel now, one that was only four times as wide as our ship.

"The Skipper could fit in here?" I asked.

"Yes, but not easily. He'd have to be careful not to bump the walls," Kimtra said, and we all stood watching our progress as we wound our way deeper into the dark tunnel. The ship had bright white headlights that cast their glow onto the red-gray stone. We moved this way for a few minutes, traveling cautiously. I had a sinking feeling the tunnel would just end, caving in on us from behind and stranding the ship underwater. My skin crawled as I felt the walls of the lander shrinking. Slate casually bumped into me, and I let out a quiet cry of shock.

"You okay, boss?" Slate asked. "You aren't looking so great."

I wiped my forehead with an arm. "I'm fine." I wished I was wearing an EVA so it would cool my flushed skin. Just as the pounding of my increased heart rate was reaching its crescendo in my ears, our lights poured into an open-water pool, the walls widening to give us room to maneuver.

"There it is." Kimtra pointed to the left, and I saw the Skipper. It was a narrow and long vessel, like a spear, and it lingered there like a submarine breaching the surface.

It was in the dark; all power appeared to be off on the Skipper as we approached the side of it. Rulo pulled up beside the other vessel, and we floated upward as she cut the engines.

"Grab our stuff; we're going in," Rulo said.

"Through the water?" I asked.

"Do you have another way?" She moved past me and grabbed a circular device from the wall of the ship. It clipped to her belt, and she tapped it, soft blue light twinkling from its underbelly. "Stay close when we open the doors."

I was going to ask more questions, when I saw the energy field push out from the device and extend past the ship's walls. We were going to go to the surface in a bubble, free from getting wet. I'd have to see if I could procure one of those. You never knew when you needed something like a portable containment shield.

We grabbed as many packs and supplies as we could carry. Slate and Hectal took the brunt of the load, and Rulo opened the doors. I half expected water to come gushing in, but it was held back by the transport vessel's shields. Once through those, we'd rely on Rulo's own. She left the lights on, and we could see the rocky ledge only twenty or so yards away.

"Jump with me," Rulo said and pushed off the side of the ship with her powerful legs. We each followed suit and came in the bubble with her, momentum taking us the short distance to the edge of the underwater tunnels. Rulo was up first, quickly followed by Hectal, who reached down to assist in getting us out of the bubble in the water and to the damp ground.

"That was cool," Slate said, dropping his packs to the rock.

With the shield now off, Kimtra headed over to where the Skipper was docked. "Foot imprints still show up here in the dust." It was damp near the water, and humid, but a few steps away near the wall, a row of dust had settled and stayed over the years. There, a blatant footprint was evident. We followed it a few steps until the dust was gone, and the tracks ended abruptly.

"We know he went this way," Hectal said.

I wanted to suggest it was the only visible pathway out of the cavern, but kept it to myself.

Slate passed me a flashlight and a pulse rifle. I explored the open cave with the lights and found it smaller and more closed in than I'd originally thought. There was a ledge on the other end of the water, over the tunnels we'd floated in through. It made me think of Gollum, hiding in the dark caves, slipping the ring on to appear invisible as he hunted fish. With a shiver, I hoped there was no small creature watching us from the ledge. Slate's gaze was darting around the space, and I worried he should have sat this one out. It had only been a few weeks since his ordeal and near death back on Sterona.

"Are you going to stare backwards your whole life or move forward?" Rulo said as she threw a pack on her shoulder and started down the corridor, which we hoped would bring us to our target.

"How long has he been here?" I asked.

Kimtra answered. "Twenty days."

"Twenty days is a long time. He could be anywhere," Slate said.

"The island's not so large. We'll find him," Kimtra whispered.

I added the weight of the tent pack and followed along behind the rest of the team, watching behind me for menacing creatures in the dark. If there were any there, they didn't interfere with our passing.

We traveled on foot at an upward angle, our elevation increasing with each step. The caves were short. Hectal and Slate had to crouch at most points, and Slate turned sideways a few times to get through the tight passageway. The air was musty, the walls heavy with green moss as we kept moving. When we spoke, the sound was muffled, like speaking in a small, well-insulated closet.

Sooner than I would have expected, we saw light from the end of the tunnel, and my back instantly felt less tension. The heat hit us in waves as we stepped through the opening and onto the side of a green mountainside. Sweat that had threatened to bead minutes ago now flushed to the surface of my skin, dripping down my spine.

The view was one of the best things I'd seen in my life. We were halfway up the hillside; tall palm-like trees rose wildly, the palm leaves shorter and less fan-like, but so similar, they looked natural to my eyes. Round purple fruit hung from the tops of most of them.

Straight ahead, a lush valley extended for as far as the eye could see, hills rising up on either side. In the distance, a body of water sat still, green waves drawing my gaze with its beauty.

"We're in paradise," I whispered, wishing Mary was there to see it with me.

Before I knew what was happening, Hectal was shouting for everyone to get down.

I did without question and heard a pulse pistol go off beside me. Something fell to the ground with a thud nearby, and Hectal was laughing. "I got him first try," he said, stepping over to his kill.

I joined him, and saw the threat lying dead on the grass. "It looks like a mosquito, only the size of a German Shepherd," I mumbled.

"I don't know what either of those are, but this is a big insect." Hectal nudged it with his boot, making sure it was dead. The bug was like a nightmare; its long-pointed proboscis looked powerful enough to pluck out an eyeball.

"Boss, did you remember the bug spray?" Slate asked, laughing nervously at his own joke.

"Keep an eye out for any threats. This island could be full of predators," Kimtra said. She was fiddling with an arm console. "Yes. This world, while mostly unmarked by higher life forms like us, does have a host of living things. A few are cataloged."

I went to her side as she scrolled through a few images on her console screen. I saw everything from huge snake-like reptiles to birds with five-yard wingspans.

"This should be fun," I said.

"It always is. Now do you understand why we have so many weapons?" Hectal asked with a grin.

I couldn't help but smile back at him. His energy was infectious.

"Which way?" I asked, ready to get looking for the missing Polvertan.

Rulo pointed toward the water. "That's an inland water source, fed through these mountains. It will be fresh and untainted. He'll make camp near it."

"Unless there are more water sources like it," I added.

"We'll check the largest first." Rulo was off, quietly stalking through the rainforest terrain. The humid heat made everything stick to me, my shirt already plastered to my chest. With a last look at the epic view, I let out a warm breath and walked after her.

With any luck, we'd have this Polvertan in our possession in a few hours, and we could finally get home.

ELEVEN

At first, I was looking forward to the hike through a tropical paradise. After weeks on a ship, I was happy to stretch my legs and move around on something other than unfamiliar Keppe gym equipment. That feeling lasted less than an hour. My legs burned from the steep decline, and my feet were already soaked. It wasn't raining now, but it obviously did a lot here, and the underbrush held on to the moisture like a greedy sponge.

Everyone slogged through the trees without complaint, but I could see the annoyance in their postures and clipped speech. Twice we were attacked by small groups of the giant mosquitoes, and both times, when we killed one, the rest scattered into the wind.

By the time we reached inland to the center of the valley, where the fresh water was situated, my legs were on fire, and I'd sweated out twice my body weight in liquid.

"Let's take a break," I suggested as we neared the water. It sat there in sight, beyond a slight hill, the trees bending to face the liquid, as if it held an answer to their questions and was whispering the truth with its light ripples.

"We're almost there," Rulo said.

"And you think we won't spend an hour circling the lake looking for Polvertan?" I stopped walking and sat down on a fallen tree, its palm-like leaves browned and dead. Rotten husks from the fruit sat on the ground beside it.

Slate joined me, and we guzzled water in synchronicity. I looked for a spot on my shirt that was dry so I could wipe my forehead, but failed to find one.

"I used to dream of what it would be like to live somewhere tropical. Now I'm glad I chose upstate New York," I said, getting a snicker from Slate.

Slate leaned back. "I spent some time in the Middle East. That was a totally different type of heat. I think I prefer this."

The Keppe stood before us, each drinking water now. Their black armored skin wasn't dripping sweat like ours. "How do you deal with the heat?" I asked them.

"You think this is hot?" Hectal laughed.

"This is like our Schunta season," Kimtra said, the word not translating to English.

"That must be like our winter. Snow falls on parts of Earth," I said. "Or it did." I really had no idea what the damage from the Bhlat had done to Earth's weather patterns. We had snow on New Spero, so I could get my fill any time I wanted it, though it wasn't quite the same.

I hadn't been around for a lot of special occasions on New Spero, and I made a mental note to remind Mary that we should celebrate Christmas with Jules. Continue the old traditions for our daughter, and maybe make some new ones. There was already a New Spero national holiday for the Event. It was a day where everyone remembered the loved ones they lost and celebrated our survival.

I was going to be there in Terran One for this year's celebration, unless I'd already missed it. I truly had no idea what month it was. Things like that didn't seem to make a difference to me any longer. Maybe that was another thing I could bring back once we settled into our old lives on New Spero. Routine was good for babies, and it would be good for Mary and me.

"What's snow?" Rulo asked.

Slate took this one. "Do you have rain?" he asked, the words translating to the smooth Keppe speech.

They all nodded. "Rain. Water from the sky. Of course."

"Areas of Earth and New Spero get below freezing temperature, and the precipitation stored in the clouds comes down in the form of flakes instead of drops. Someone a little more scientific could explain it to you clearer." Slate stood as he spoke, moving his hands around.

Kimtra's eyes were wide. "Flakes? I've seen this. Worlds covered in ice, white ice constantly falling on the ground."

"Back where I'm from, we played in the snow when we were children. We'd sled down hills of snow, ski and snowboard down mountains. We'd make snowmen, have snowball fights, and it was my favorite time of the year. Compared to our hot summers, the weather changes were not-so-subtle reminders of Mother Nature each time they came around," I said.

I doubted they knew what Mother Nature meant to us, or what a snowman was, but they nodded along. "If this isn't hot to you, what are your hot times like?" I asked, not sure I wanted to set foot on their world when we got there. I knew I had to, to get to the portals, but in my current overheated state, I was dreading it.

Hectal took this one. "We have to stay indoors if possible. It's probably twice as hot as this, right, Kimtra?" She nodded, and he continued. "It lasts for one tenth of our year, and we spend it with family, reforming our bonds. If we're there. I haven't been home for it in a few years. The three of us are aboard *Starbound* most of the time."

"Does Admiral Yope spend much time on board these days?" I asked, curious to learn more about their military leader.

"It was his ship for years. I think part of him is bitter he was promoted. He loved leading the charge into the stars. He named the ship. While everyone else was naming their vessels *Duty, Destroyer, Seeker,* Yope named his *Starbound.* He wanted to discover worlds, space anomalies, and spend his days among the stars.

"He did this and made contact with so many races, but after a war, we were left with a hole in our hierarchy. Yope was forced to give up his ship and take over things." Kimtra looked sullen as she told us a little about their admiral.

"Is he married? Children?" Slate asked.

Kimtra shook her head. "No. He said his love was for the stars, and he couldn't share it." She looked away, and I read more meaning in her words than the others did. If I was reading it correctly, she and the admiral had been an item at one point in their lives.

"It's a hard balance. I want to help here right now, but half of my mind is back on *Starbound* with my wife and newborn," I said, and Kimtra nodded.

"What was the war about?" Slate asked, and the Keppe finally started to relax. They each found a spot in the surrounding area to sit and take a load off. Hectal grunted as he let his heavy packs down to the soft ground.

"The Motrill were in a skirmish over a colony world. Some faraway planet, a few years' travel by hyperdrive," Hectal said, and I realized they didn't know about the portals. "This was before the wormhole drives were around."

From my experience, few on each world knew about them. Earth had been ignorant that, for thousands of years, one had sat in Egypt; when a planet had awareness of the portal, only select patrons realized it. Bazarn Five had some traffic from theirs, but only the most wealthy and influential from the universe would be able to travel there by the portals. Otherwise, they were traveling there via space vessel like everyone else.

Kimtra continued the story, taking over from Hectal, as she did when any science was involved. "According to the Motrill, whom you know we have close ties to, the world was fertile, and a ninety-five-percent match for our genetics to colonize. We could grow our crops, farm our livestock, and breathe the air. Finding a ninety-five or up is near impossible, and they'd done it. The world remained nameless and was in its infancy stages. Life was only starting there, so the colony impact wouldn't be intruding on existing environments."

"Sounds like a winner for the Motrill," I said.

"It was. And for us. We were each on the lookout for a colony world to share. It had been a long time since our treaty was formed once again, and we were going to start a community together in good faith. Our people made a marriage pact, the one Polvertan's going to honor when we find him," Kimtra said.

"How long ago was this?" Slate asked.

"Before Polvertan was born. Before his future spouse, Brina Crul, was born."

"So the impact of this colony was a big one. What happened?" I asked, amazed two races would promise a marriage to bring the worlds together before the children were even born. To be those kids, growing up never having a choice, and knowing the whole time that you were forced into a marriage? It had happened on Earth for countless years in many cultures, sometimes with good results, others quite terrible.

"The Motrill found the world and left behind a base camp. This camp was only a hundred Motrill. They would be responsible to start building shelters, surveying the world with drone mapping. Crops would be planted, and the basic livestock carried aboard the colony-searching vessel would be acclimated to their new world. The journey is long, but they have communication capable of traveling the distance with only a few days' delay. Things were great at the start; messages came through as the vessel headed back for Motrill to get the second phase of supplies and colonists." Kimtra stopped, took a drink of water, and looked down to the ground.

Rulo took over. "The attack came in the middle of the night. One hundred colonists burned away while they slept. One escaped, made it to the communication tower, and sent a message. The invaders landed after dropping a bomb on the village, and found Trem alone in the tower. He saw the invaders and relayed the message, which the ship got on their way back home. It had been a year since the Motrill landed."

I was on the edge of the log, almost slipping off as I listened with intent. "Who were they?" I asked, the words a whisper off my lips.

"His last words were this: 'They're here, the Kraski are here'."

TWELVE

I remembered the look on Admiral Yope's face when I told them I'd seen a Kraski. It was fleeting: the flickering anger of a man who was used to hiding his true emotions. It had been enough for me to catch. Now I knew why.

I was standing but didn't remember getting onto my feet. "The Kraski killed the colony?"

"They did." Hectal walked over to me. "You know of them?" He looked ready to attack me, like I had a connection to their enemy.

I looked to Rulo, who'd been with us in the room when I told the others about seeing a Kraski on Sterona, right before being rescued. "You didn't tell them about my history with the Kraski?"

Rulo stood, set a hand on Hectal's shoulder, and whispered something to him. He sat back down, seething. "What history?" he asked.

I wasn't sure if I had the energy to get into the Event. "How much time do you have?"

"We can talk and walk," Rulo said and picked up her gear. "Yope told me a little, but not much. I know you've had a run-in with the Kraski before, and now you don't live on Earth. I'd also heard a rumor they were dead, but

I figured the Bhlat had something to do with that."

It was almost funny, because the results were accurate, but the details weren't.

We moved toward the lake, and I crouched by it as Kimtra dipped a sensor probe into the calm waters. I scanned the water's surface, looking for signs of life that would undoubtedly be in there on this lush island. I saw air bubbles break the surface in a few spots, and shuddered as my imagination pictured a huge creature thrashing below the calm face.

I slipped my water bottle into a pouch on the side of my pack. "Tell me what happened with you first."

"What's to tell? The Kraski killed the Motrill's colony. They took the world as their own. When we learned what occurred, we sent a fleet after them. We didn't expect five of their warships there, thousands of Kraski vessels in total. The battle didn't last long, but both sides had far too many casualties. In the end, the Kraski kept the world. We pulled out," Rulo said.

I tried to piece it together. This couldn't have been more than twenty years ago, probably less. Everything I'd heard said the Kraski took over worlds, while enslaving some and murdering the rest, like they'd done with the Deltra. Then the Bhlat came in, a bigger, more powerful race, and forced them to evacuate their home system.

"The Kraski came for Earth, our homeworld. We're infants in the space race. We didn't have the technology to travel FTL. We held no colonies, and though there was always talk of trying, it would have been an epic endeavor that would most likely have ended in disaster. They beamed nearly everyone off the planet and stuck us in the very vessels they'd intended to bring themselves to Earth in. The Bhlat had won their war.

"They limped in, a small number of them now. The Deltra, an enslaved race of theirs, outsmarted them. They'd placed a Shield, the Kalentrek, on Earth centuries earlier. They had a plan to free themselves that took that long to come to fruition." We were walking along the water's edge, and everyone was listening with rapt attention at the tale I told.

"I've heard of the Deltra," Kimtra said solemnly.

I nodded. "Now I know more about the whole picture. The Kraski used what we call a hybrid, a being created out of human and Kraski DNA. It was the only way they could get the beings to survive, a technology I've since learned was created by Lom of Pleva."

"This is getting too strange for me," Kimtra said.

"It gets better. The Kraski planted these hybrids, only they couldn't shut down the device that would kill anything matching their DNA without succumbing to its power themselves. So they sent them to infiltrate us. I was married to one." I averted my eyes when Rulo stopped and turned to me. "Magnus and his wife were there too, as well as Mary. Janine, my wife at the time, had been dead for a few years when it happened. The Deltra had turned her, and she set out a plan to have us not only keep the shield on, but to kill all the Kraski in space in the process, setting the Deltra free." I hadn't told the story in a while, and it felt good to go over it, especially now that I knew there were ties to my current situation. Everything was connecting. Lines were slowly being drawn over the random dots, and a picture was emerging.

"You fought the Kraski? And won?" This from Hectal.

"We tricked them, but we did win," I said.

"What about you?" Hectal nodded to Slate.

Slate looked at the ground. "I was one of the unlucky humans beamed up. Tried my best to help up there, but I'm ashamed to say I didn't make a big difference."

"I'd be dead without Slate, about ten times over, so he's a real hero. Believe me," I said, and he met my gaze, standing up straighter. "We brought the Shield up in a Kraski ship. Boarded the warship and turned it on. They disintegrated from the inside out." I paused as Hectal let out a strange whooping noise.

"I knew there was something special about you, little man," Hectal said.

I didn't love the term he gave me, but compared to Magnus and Slate, I guessed I would seem like a small human. "Once they were gone, the Delta thought they had us. They could leave our ships to fly into our star, snuffing our world's population in quick order, and take Earth for themselves."

We were standing still again, everyone too wrapped up in the conversation to move.

"What did you do?" Kimtra asked.

"Mary came on board and kicked some ass. We escaped and blew a few ships up in the process of it all. Then we had to convince the brainwashed hybrids to do the right thing and work with us. A lot of people died that day. A lot," I said.

"We are brothers, then," Hectal said. "Both our people have suffered loss at the hands of the Kraski. We will seek revenge."

"Truthfully, I'd rather leave them alone and have peace."

"Peace? We're in a universe with no peace. Believe me. The Keppe are an old race. We have seen many civilizations rise and fall, just the same. Tell me, did you have peace on this world of yours? Internally?" Rulo asked.

I got her point. "No." I didn't elaborate.

"You impress me, nonetheless," Rulo said. "A planet-locked race fought off not one but two invaders and lived to tell the story."

"Three," Slate said.

"Three what?" Kimtra asked.

"We fought off three, if you count the Bhlat," he said.

"The Bhlat?" all three Keppe members of our entourage echoed together.

"We didn't fight them off," I said, hating the attention. "It wasn't like that. We lost Earth that day."

"But we turned them into an ally," Slate said.

"You're in a treaty with the Bhlat?" Hectal asked. "I've never heard of that happening before."

"Are they really as terrible as everyone says?" I asked, hoping the Keppe didn't take my relationship with the Empress as a negative connotation.

"We've been blessed to have stayed clear of them, but many haven't been so lucky. They're powerful. If they want something, they get it. Looks like you made a deal, but they still got what they wanted out of it, didn't they?" Rulo asked.

"They did. But we live." I started to walk, the group following behind.

"You live, and that's what impresses me," Rulo added. "Come, let's not waste any more time."

The sunlight was waning as we pressed on, and I judged it would be dark in another hour. I really didn't want to be out in the open, easy prey for whatever creatures were lurking behind the trees or under the water.

We kept moving, and I answered a few more questions, then diverted a few more, before letting them know I was done talking about the Kraski and Bhlat for the time being. Hectal looked admonished.

"Look ahead," Rulo said, swiping her minigun from her back holster. Her strong arms flexed as she held the heavy gun and swung it around, looking for a target.

I spotted what she'd seen: a shelter about a hundred yards from the waterline. It was tied to four bases of the tall trees and was very basic in nature. Polvertan hadn't been looking for comfort; he'd been looking for lightweight and ease.

Rulo tapped her earpiece. "*Starbound*, we've found our target's nest. Will proceed with caution and report back." Her face scrunched up, and she looked to the darkening sky as she listened to the reply from the vessel in orbit. "How far away? Got it, thanks," she said, and tapped the earpiece again.

"What is it?" Hectal was looking to the sky now too.

"Storm's coming in. Looks huge from the radar.

Should hit the island sooner than I'd like." Rulo started for the sparse camp.

I didn't like her lack of information. "What kind of storm, Rulo?"

"A big one. Winds already at ninety kilometers an hour."

"A cyclone's headed for us? Should we leave?" I asked.

"We're here to find our target. Plus, we won't be able to evacuate in time." Rulo stepped to the shelter and lifted the canvas material. It was nearly empty inside. A bedroll sat on some sort of field generating from a small box to the left.

Slate saw it and nudged me with an elbow. "Boss, check out the inflatable mattress. That's cool. How many times could we have used that?"

"Do we set up camp?" Hectal asked as the wind began. At first, it was a light breeze, a slight reprieve in the sweltering heat. Soon it was buffeting the trees, and one of the purple fruits fell beside me with a bang.

"No time. See that cliffside?" Kimtra pointed in the distance. "We go there, look for an entrance. Somewhere to take shelter."

I wasn't going to argue, and I turned my gaze upwards, making sure to not stand under one of the hard fruit clusters. I warned the others as well.

We walked fast, and when the water started pouring from above, we ran for the cliff in the distance. The skies darkened, and as the sun set, it became hard to make out the looming outline of our destination. We arrived in less than an hour, drenched and exhausted. Even Hectal seemed winded as he threw the packs down on the ground at the cliff wall. It cut the wind, but I was still worried something would fall down the mountainside and crush us.

"I'm concerned about rockslides." I had to yell to be heard.

"Over here." Kimtra was heading back. She'd disappeared for a few minutes.

Rain still dropped on us in buckets. The sound of wind tearing at the trees was terrifying and powerful at the same time.

We ran along after her, and I expected to see an opening in the rock face. When we turned away from it, I saw the glowing device some twenty yards away. "What is that?" I asked.

"I saw the light a while ago. It's a locator, used by hikers or explorers. They mark their position in case something bad happens to them. He had to be down there," Rulo yelled into the wind.

"Down where?" I asked, and she pointed toward the wet ground. We were surrounded by thick palm-like trees, and another of the dense balls of fruit smashed into the ground beside me. It looked like we were on Polvertan's track, and just in time. "Let's go."

THIRTEEN

The crevasse was only three yards wide and three feet tall, but we lowered into it one at a time, using a thick tree trunk as our anchor. I went second to last and stuck my flashlight into my belt as I climbed down the rope, carrying an extra pack. We were making sure Hectal didn't weigh more than the maximum capacity of our thin rope. The locator device hummed, shooting a thin blue beam into the sky. It was hardly noticeable from most angles, and now I understood why we hadn't seen it earlier.

It was wet under the opening, but otherwise, the ground was bone-dry around us. The rope hung twenty feet up, and I watched Rulo make quick work of the descent as soon as my feet touched down.

Tree roots stuck out of the ceiling before bending to go back underground. Moss clung to everything, and I spotted a few mushrooms growing along the far wall.

"We have no idea what's down here. Slate, are you okay being here?" I asked him, remembering his recent mishap with the monsters on Sterona.

"I have to be," was his answer.

"We'll be home soon. Then your days of crawling around underground are over, I promise," I said, hoping it was one I could keep.

Slate nodded and followed Rulo's lead deeper inside.

Hectal pointed to footsteps in the direction we were heading. "He was here."

"What's the heir to Motrill doing alone on this island in the middle of a cyclone?" I asked, knowing no one had the answer.

"You'll have to ask him when we find him," Kimtra said, smiling at me in the bright flashlight beam.

I could still hear the storm blustering above us, but it all stopped in a heartbeat as we crossed the room.

"Did you notice that?" I asked the group.

Kimtra stopped in her tracks, raised a finger to her mouth, and stepped backwards. "I hear the storm now. Do you?"

I shook my head and joined her, two yards behind the others. The sound of wind thrashing trees about echoed to my location. We stepped forward, and nothing. It was like we'd passed through an invisible sound barrier.

"I've never heard of this specifically, but there is something that could do this. A portal field." Kimtra walked away and headed for the wall. I followed her, and so did the others.

Kimtra ran her hand along the wall, and I noticed the variation along the dirt. The right edge was darker than the left. When I stepped to the left, I could hear the storm again. "I think we passed through a barrier. A portal to somewhere else," she said.

"A portal?" I asked, confused. We used portal stones, which took you somewhere, but this was unlike anything we'd ever seen.

"Embedded in this room, there's a device that stretches across the walls, making us think we're still underground in the same cavern. But clearly the wall is different, and the storm is gone. Theoretically, of course." Kimtra ran to the other side of the wall and found the same thing.

"Couldn't it just be a sound blocker?" Slate asked.

"I don't think so. Those are common enough, but they don't change the pattern of a dirt wall like this," Kimtra answered.

"Are you saying we're not underground on the island any longer?" I asked nervously.

"We might still be on the island, but I don't think so," Kimtra said.

"To what end?" I asked.

"That... I don't know. Let's continue and see what we find. Polvertan went this way, so do we." Kimtra started to walk, and we went after her. The cave still seemed dank, but now that I knew there was a difference, I could swear the smell was off, the moss a different shade. It was eerie to think we'd traveled somewhere else. If technology like this existed, then what need did the portal stones serve any longer? We could free the last of the Theos locked away inside and let them rest for eternity.

The end of the room was a dead end. "Now what?" Rulo asked as she lowered her minigun. "No doors."

"Oldest trick in the book," Slate said. "Make a fake room no one will notice. Hide a doorway so anyone who comes here turns around and leaves."

"Unless the storm was going on, we would never have noticed the sound difference." I got close to the walls, looking for a secret doorway. "Come on, there has to be an opening here."

We spread out along the walls and searched high and low before ending back together, exhausted.

"So much for the oldest trick in the book." Hectal shot an angry glare at Slate, who ignored the jab and took a drink from his water bottle. I joined him.

"What other purpose would this serve?" Rulo asked.

That was when I saw it. Standing up, the light didn't cut through, but sitting on the ground, resting my weary legs, a sliver of light hit my eyes. "Over here!" I yelled, rushing over to the dirt wall. Even up close, I lost the line but quickly found it again. "It has to be what we're looking for," I said, running my fingers along the rough edge of the crack.

"We don't have time for this." Rulo motioned for us to step back, and she grabbed a pulse rifle from Hectal's pack. When we were clear, she fired three quick shots below the hole. When the dust settled, we had our doorway.

"Guess that was faster," Slate said. "That's what I usually do."

When Rulo stared blankly at him, he added, "Dean, tell her that's what I always do."

I walked by him and patted his arm, before taking the lead through the pulse-made opening. It passed into a hall, but not a dirt one. The walls were some type of resin-based substance, designed with slight detail and color.

They were light gray with red border lines painted on. Computer screens sat inside them every few yards, an indecipherable language written under each, labeling them.

"What have we found?" Hectal asked as we all stood there, looking around at our surroundings. The lights were off, and his voice echoed down the corridor.

"I think this is a ship," I said as I took in the surroundings.

"A ship? I think you're right," Kimtra said, taking the lead.

She was a few yards in front of me when I saw a red glow emanate from the floor ahead of her. She was looking back at me, and my body sensed the danger before my mind did. I ran to her. "Stop!"

She kept moving, but I reached her just in time to grab her, pulling her back, covering her with my body as a grid of red beams shot up from the floor to the ceiling. It was a booby trap, clearly meant to prevent unsuspecting visitors from getting any further.

"How did you know?" Kimtra asked as I rolled off her. Hectal, Rulo, and Slate all stood with guns at ready, looking for an unseen enemy.

"I didn't. I saw a red light and assumed it wasn't there to greet us." I stood up, helping Kimtra to her feet before going up to the red grid of light blocking our way in the corridor. It covered the entire space from wall to wall, floor to ceiling.

Kimtra was already attempting to get into the closest computer. "I'll see if I can deactivate it."

"If there was one trap, we can expect more," Rulo

said as we watched Kimtra activate the screen. She tapped away at it, somehow accessing a program in the unknown language.

"Do you recognize the language?" I asked her.

Kimtra shook her head. "No, but the mathematical base of it is enough for me to find the back door." She kept typing away, and within minutes, dim lights glowed in the halls. Another five breaths, and the red grid of death dissipated into nothing.

"Suma's going to want to meet with you later," I said, knowing how much the Shimmali girl would like to learn from Kimtra.

"Consider it done." Kimtra picked up her pack, and we moved down the hall, Hectal taking the lead now. We moved much more slowly, looking for signs of other traps, but didn't encounter any. We were indeed on a ship, or something like one, but none of the small empty rooms we entered along the way had windows or viewscreens.

"We could be on a different planet," Slate said, touching the wall.

I thought about the Bhlat outpost's similarity to this, so he was right, but my gut was telling me otherwise.

The corridor ended, and a larger doorway sat closed. "Step out of the way," Rulo said, raising the pulse rifle again. I stepped around her and smiled.

"You never know," I said and tapped a button on the side of the door. It slid open with ease, and a lift rose to greet us.

"Show-off," Rulo said, but she smiled back, her sharp

teeth seeming a little less threatening than usual.

We piled inside the elevator hesitantly, and there was just enough space for all of us to stand with our supplies.

Kimtra messed with the console and found what she was looking for. "There appear to be six stories, but which one do we check first?"

"Can you see where the lift just came from?" I asked, wondering if it could be that simple.

"Great idea. It shows the lowest level. We're on the highest now," Kimtra said.

Rulo said it again under her breath. "Still a show-off."

The door slid closed, and we proceeded downwards. In seconds, the door opened, and we were no longer in a corridor. It was a large room, crates upon crates piled high to the twenty-foot-tall ceilings. Some were locked metal boxes, others wooden, yet others made from unfamiliar materials, all in different shapes and sizes.

"What is this?" Hectal asked, stepping into the room with us all spreading apart, looking for signs of danger.

Something fell from the far corner and slowly rolled toward us. A being followed it, looking down to the ground as it walked. It muttered something I couldn't make out and stopped when it picked up the object. It looked up, meeting our gazes. Rulo and Hectal had guns up, ready to fire if necessary.

The man had dark gray armored skin, was bald, and had the same snake eyes as the Keppe.

"It looks like we've found Polvertan," I said quietly.

The Motrill raised his arms in the air and gave us a rebuked grin. "Don't shoot?"

FOURTEEN

"We're here to bring you home immediately," Rulo said, walking toward our target. He stumbled backwards, gripping the object that had rolled toward us.

"You can't do that," he said, this time with authority. It was as if he'd suddenly remembered his rank and power.

"And why is that?" I asked, my foreign words translated so he could understand them.

"Who or what are you?" he asked, squinting in the dimly-lit room.

"My name's Dean Parker, and this is Zeke Campbell," I said, motioning to my friend.

"Slate, call me Slate," he said, rolling his eyes at me.

"Polvertan, we are ordered by your father to bring you home safely. What are you doing here?" Kimtra asked, her voice softer than Rulo's had been.

"Call me Pol, please. Only people that hate me call me Polvertan, which would include my parents," the Motrill prince said. He wasn't as thick as the Keppe, but you could tell they were cut from the same cloth. Yope had said they could reproduce together, and their story of sharing a new colony added up now that I saw the two races side-by-side. It made me wonder if New Spero should expand to a second colony, somewhere like Haven, to live among other races. A handful of humans already lived there, but not on a permanent basis.

"You didn't answer her question. What are you doing here?" I asked, asserting myself.

He looked at me and hesitated. "Dean, is it?" I nodded, and he continued. "I can't tell you. How did you possibly find me? I did everything to keep my location hidden."

I pointed at Kimtra. "She's the brains. Tracked your engine residue all the way to the water and knew there was only one way to go, which was down. It was easier than I expected," I said, making it seem like we did this every day, all day long. "Also, you left a location tracker outside the crevasse above."

Pol's straight back loosened then, and he slouched forward, his hand going to his face. "I found it. I seriously found it, and now you're here." He sat down on a crate, and I walked over to him, sitting on a nearby wooden box.

"What did you find? Where are we?" I asked, genuinely curious. Part of me was in a rush to grab him and drag him out of here, but we seemed safer here while a hurricane was going on outside on the island.

"We're a hundred thousand light years from home, that's where we are," he said, and Kimtra took a quick sharp breath.

She hustled over and knelt beside the Motrill man. "What do you mean?"

"Have you ever heard of Fontem before?" He asked the simple question, and I shook my head. The others did as well, except Kimtra.

"Sure, but only in passing references. Wasn't he some famed collector from a few thousand years ago? Terellion, if I'm not mistaken," she said.

"I'm impressed. Not many have heard the tales of Fontem. He wasn't just a collector, he was *the* collector. He had artifacts from every single race to ever exist," Pol said, his hands and eyes animated as he spoke.

"Even the Theos?" I asked casually.

"Even the Theos. I found a crystal in his catalog said to be from their homeworld." Pol stopped talking, probably wondering if he'd said too much.

"Where? Here?" Kimtra asked, getting to her feet.

The crates around us started to make more sense. "Are you saying this is his collection?" I asked, looking around.

Pol smiled lightly and adjusted some metal bands on his forearms. "It is."

"How did you find it?" Kimtra asked. The need to know burned through her question.

"I've spent over a decade trying to track it down. And I did, and now you're here to take me away, back to the life I don't want. Do you have any idea how hard it is to be someone you're not? To step into someone else's shoes and deal with things you have no desire to deal with?" Pol's eyes were large and glossy as he asked the question of the room.

I answered. "I do. I know exactly how that feels. And

you do it because you have to. Because they need you to."

"I suppose you're right. Is there any way you can let me go through the rest of the catalog before we leave? I have to find it," he said, but I didn't believe his words. He'd given in far too easily.

"Find what?" I asked.

He wouldn't answer me. "Something I need."

I didn't like the sound of this. Was it a weapon he was searching for?

Rulo smiled faintly, and a shiver shot down my spine. "I suppose we have some time," she said, running a hand along a stack of metal crates.

I stood at the end of the room, looking out the now-activated viewscreen at a vision that was far away from home indeed. We were in a ship, a cloaked one, hidden from any sensors or eyes, according to Pol.

"Have you ever seen anything like this?" Slate asked me quietly.

"No. No, I haven't," I said, in awe of the colorful glow among the distant stars. A planet was close, only twenty thousand kilometers away, with three moons around it. Oranges and pinks danced on the edges of the moons, and I had no idea what kind of anomaly we were seeing. Kimtra wasn't even sure.

I left the viewscreen, feeling sick to my stomach that I was so far away from my family. Mary and Jules were in orbit around the small world where an island was under threat from a storm, and we were one hundred thousand light years away, on a two-thousand-year-old ship.

Kimtra was working closely with Pol, searching through the records.

"Did he expect someone to come looking for it?" I asked, knowing nothing about this Fontem the Terellion.

Pol shrugged. "I'm not sure. The clues weren't easy to find. The last clue came from the library on Bazarn Five."

"I've been there," Slate said casually, and Pol's eyes widened. "Dean didn't make it. He went to see the real library while we were there."

Pol stood. "The real library? What are you speaking of?"

"The real secrets are held under better security. Obviously, you didn't need it."

"I may, because the manifest is under a code of some sort. Why would he go to all this work to hide the artifacts, then not allow access to someone smart enough to find them?" Pol asked.

"Maybe he figured someone with enough resources to find his secret cache would have done so with credits and not honor. He was protecting the universe from whatever's in here," I suggested. "What have you found?"

Pol sat back down, deflated. "Fontem has a lot of cool things. I found the portal web, like the one used when you enter the cave." He pointed to a section of shelving he'd set items on in a specific order. I walked over to it, seeing the small devices clipped together.

"How does it work?" I asked.

"One side is placed at the destination. It sends out an invisible beam until it touches any surface. The entire wall becomes a live portal once the other side is activated in the same manner," Pol said. "Trick is, you have to manually add them to each spot," he said dismissively. He wasn't worried about something like that; he had bigger fish to fry.

"What else?" I asked, sensing value here. I swore I was done when I got home. Done with saving the world, done with endlessly traversing through the universe by portals and vessels. But deep down, I knew that wasn't going to happen. The Kraskis' return was too much to ignore. They knew I was alive, and they had the backing of one of the most powerful men out there, Lom of Pleva. I wasn't going to get the early retirement I wanted.

Whatever happened, I'd keep Mary and Jules safe. If there was anything in this room that would help ensure that, I was taking it with me.

"Voice changer. Simple technology that's been used for years, but this one is a translator too. I've seen them as two plug-ins before, but not in one," Pol said. "Worked with my existing system."

"Where's that one?" I asked.

"Second shelf. Small black box."

I grabbed it, opening the container to see a button. "How does it work?"

Kimtra came over, and in moments, she had it functioning. "It will work in your EVA."

"Mind if I…?" I asked.

"Go for it," Pol said dismissively.

I slipped it into my pocket. "What else?"

———————

"*I*t's time to go," Rulo said. Almost every crate had been opened. Some were marked with dangerous symbols, and Rulo had the most interest in those. She and Hectal piled those to the side. They seemed to have no interest in anything that wasn't directly related to weapons.

I did. I took various tools, things that could give me an edge, instead of weapons that could accidentally blow me up.

Pol glowered in anger, frustrated he hadn't found what he'd come for. "It has to be here. I know it is. He hid it among this junk. But where?"

It had been a full day, and I was getting anxious to get word back to *Starbound* that we were okay.

"If you tell us what you're after, maybe we can help," I suggested for the tenth time.

"I can't. It's too dangerous," he said.

"Pack it up, Polvertan. Time to bring you home." Hectal flipped out something from his cart. It unfolded to a flat frame. When he tapped a button on the end of it, the center of it glowed green, and it hovered. It was a portable dolly. He began stacking the found weapons on it, the cart not lowering from the added weight. I'd been wondering how they were planning on transporting the crates out of here. I wasn't about to carry them.

119

"Boss, this feels off. Anti-climactic," Slate said.

"I agree, but since they didn't seem too interested in most of this stuff, I'm glad to take it." I looked at the shelf, seeing the portal webs still sitting there untouched. I didn't have my Relocator from Kareem any longer, since I'd traded it to Sergo. I considered taking both ends of the portal, but there was something in the way Pol spoke about the mysterious device that had me intrigued.

"Ready to go?" Rulo asked from the doorway.

Pol looked back at the room wistfully. "Don't tell anyone about this place," he begged.

"We have what we want. Yope will be pleased. No need to bother him with the details of where it actually came from," Rulo said.

The elevator door opened, and everyone piled in. With the cart, there wasn't enough room for all of us. I grabbed Slate's arm and held him back.

"We'll take the next one," I said and stepped back as the door closed and they lifted.

"What's this all about?" Slate asked.

"There's something inside here that we may need. Pol's so dead-set on getting it. I bet Regnig will be able to tell us what this Fontem guy was really all about." I ran to the shelf, grabbing the portal device, and noticed a second one behind it. I grabbed that too and detached the two pieces, setting one down on the ground and activating it at the far end of the room, near the now-inactive viewscreen. It hummed as the barrier glowed and hit the walls and ceiling. When it covered the space, it vanished, hiding from the world. "Now we can come back, secretly."

Slate looked impressed. "Glad I thought of it," he joked, and we ran back to the lift just as the doors slid open. Rulo stood inside, hands on the rifle. She looked past us, eyeing the room suspiciously.

"Come in. We're done here," she said, and we obeyed. When she turned, I slipped the second piece of the portal into my pocket.

FIFTEEN

*H*alf a day later, we were finally aboard *Starbound* with our target, Polvertan, in our possession. My fatigued legs plodded across the hangar floor, leaving the Keppe to deal with their new guest. The far door opened, and I saw the silhouette of a human. It was my human, Mary, and with renewed energy, I jogged over to her and Jules. The baby was wriggling in Mary's arms, and I reached out and took her after setting my pack down.

"Dean, can you promise this is the last time you'll run off for a while?" Mary asked, her voice serious.

I hugged her one-handed and kissed her on the lips, fully aware of what I must smell like. "I'm all yours."

"Good. Now how about a shower?" she said, finally cracking a smile.

An hour later, we sat in our quarters. Jules lay on her back in the middle of the bed, eyes closed, drool softly falling from her mouth.

I told Mary about the room, and being so far away on a hidden ship. It was hard for me to believe as I told the story.

"Are you sure it wasn't just a fake image on the viewscreen?" she asked.

"It could have been, but I don't think so." But if this guy went to all this trouble to hide something in that room, he might have added a fake viewscreen, showing stars and space out the window that weren't really there. "Either way, I got some cool stuff. We'll have to see what Regnig thinks…"

"Dean." Mary cut me off. "What are you doing?"

"What do you mean? If there's…"

"If there's what, Dean? If there's *what?*" Her voice grew in volume, and I knew I'd messed up.

"I'm sorry. Forget about it," I said.

"We said we were going to try to be *normal*. A normal family. Remember those three months on Sterona? Every day, we talked about going home. Spending time in our house, letting Maggie lick our baby's face so they could grow up best friends. Letting us bond together again as husband and wife, not as partners in a space journey. I need us to be normal, Dean. I can't do it anymore. I've been through too much. *We've* been through too much." Tears fell down her cheeks, and I knew what to say.

"You're right. I get so caught up, it's hard to turn off sometimes. We'll put it behind us, and live our life for ourselves. Let's get home." I stretched my hand across the bedding and found hers, squeezing it lightly in my grip. I sat there trying to convince myself that I could be happy without all the drama and conflict. I even half believed it.

"Thank you," she said, and we both lay down, Jules sleeping soundly between us. "It's time for us to be a family."

---

*T*he next couple of weeks went by without incident, at least for us. I stopped going to any meetings and did my best to relax. Sitting in on bridge meetings about *Starbound*-related matters was the last thing I needed to be doing, so Mary and I spent the time together with our baby.

We often ate meals with Slate, Nick, Leslie, Magnus, Terrance, and Suma, though we also integrated with the crew a lot. The Keppe were a strong people, but fun to be around. While they could be serious and fearsome when needed, most of them had a playful energy, Hectal most of all. He and Slate used the strange workout gear almost every day, and after I tried to join them once, I decided I'd stick with walks up and down the immense ship's halls.

Mary and I would push Jules around in the stroller-like apparatus we were given. We found the Keppe weren't so different from us. It was refreshing to be around them, but the feeling of being homesick never left my gut the whole trip.

I'd been running around the universe searching for Mary, and she'd been with the Iskios during that time. Add in the time spent on Sterona, and the period searching for the Theos before that, and we'd been away for almost six months. That was a long time to be away. When we arrived at Keppe, I was so anxious to head straight for the portal that I could hardly contain myself.

"Dean, we have to do the right thing," Magnus said, setting his meaty hands on my shoulders. Jules lay sleeping in the stroller beside me.

"I know. What? Do we go to the surface and kiss some alien's ring or something?" I asked jokingly.

"Be serious, Dean. These guys answered my call. You don't know how lucky you are," he said, and he was right.

"Sorry, Mag. We know you did everything you could to get us back, and just in the nick of time." I'd woken up from a few restless sleeps drenched in sweat, wondering if my arms were shackled to the wall, a Kraski with a scar standing in front of me. "Thanks for always being there."

"Since the moment I saw you and Carey walking down that dirt road in South America, I knew I had to put you under my wing. Natalia probably would've left you behind." He guffawed at his own joke, and I joined him.

Mary entered the hangar with Suma and joined us. "What are you two talking about?"

"How I always need rescuing, and how Magnus has made it his personal mission to get me out of trouble," I said.

"I know the feeling. We all need someone to save us, right, boys?" she asked.

Suma bent over and pulled Jules' blanket up. "Everyone ready to get to the surface? I hear it's hot down there."

"Jules won't need that blanket long," Magnus said as the rest of the entourage entered the hangar.

Slate was with Hectal, Rulo hanging just behind them. Admiral Yope joined us and grimaced when he saw me. I didn't know if he had something against me personally, or if it was more of a "humans in general" thing.

Pol was beside him, his head still hanging low. I'd spoken to him a couple times, trying to decipher what he'd been looking for in that cache of technology, but he wouldn't budge. He kept saying he'd go back and make it right. I didn't press him on it.

Once Leslie and Terrance came in with Nick, we were ready to go. We got into a large transport vessel, three times the size of the one we'd lowered to the small planet a couple weeks ago. The viewscreen was huge, and I watched with interest as we headed out of *Starbound* and toward their world. It was interesting, with dark red sand tones, and far less water than Earth, or even New Spero. The star was yellow, at least twice as large in the sky as the sun we'd grown up with.

"No wonder it's hot," Slate said. "I'm already sweating."

We lowered through the atmosphere and zoomed down, then across some grassy plains. The fields were dry, brown stalks of unknown vegetation. It wasn't long before we arrived at a city among the desert. Tall blue glass buildings rose from the ground; white streets snaked across the city, many above ground: a series of overpasses. I watched with interest as hovering trains flew by, our transport vessel flying up and above one as it raced toward us. I could see the heat haze emanating from everything outside and hoped the air-conditioning was working at our destination.

"What do you think?" Rulo asked Slate behind me.

"I think it looks pretty cool. Magnus, maybe we should see about getting some of those trains. Would be a lot easier for the colonies to maneuver around Terran locations," Slate suggested.

Magnus nodded. "That's a great idea. I'll mention it. We could bring one piece-by-piece through the portal stones, if needed."

I hadn't shared my new portal barriers with anyone but Mary. It would get too many questions, and I had a feeling I was going to need them eventually.

Slate was one hundred percent right. As New Spero expanded with the incoming Earth population, things were being built, but it was still tight. We needed to expand to more Terran sites and grow our existing ones. While some locations specialized in manufacturing, we still didn't have great interstates set up for transporting goods or people.

I was curious to hear what plans were in the works for logistics like this. I was so far removed from the colony, and I wanted to integrate myself into my home more when I was back. Mary had suggested I apply for mayor of one of the sites, but I didn't see myself as a behind-the-desk kind of guy any longer. When I'd told her I was too young for the gig, she'd laughed at me, saying I was forty and had already lived a lifetime.

"I'll make sure you meet anyone necessary," Yope said. "I think we'll have a long relationship now, and the Keppe look forward to trading and learning from one another." He turned from his front seat and looked me straight in the eyes when he spoke. There was something about the tone of his voice that made me uneasy.

I still didn't know what the trade-off had been to get their help. Magnus said I'd know in due time. I looked at Jules and hoped it wasn't some sort of Rumpelstiltskin deal. She started to cry, waking up in an unfamiliar setting, and I picked her up, feeling her warm body against my chest as I cuddled her close. I kissed the top of her little head and smelled it in the process. She was mine. It was hard to believe, but I loved her with every ounce of my body. A baby. Amidst all the chaos of our lives, somehow Mary and I had created something so perfect.

"Thank you, Admiral," Magnus said, breaking the silence. I realized I should have answered him, but I was lost in my own contemplation.

The ship carried on, down to the far end of the sprawling city. There were a lot of high buildings, but also miles of housing units, not unlike our suburbs. At the end was a large rounded building with a landing pad half a mile from it. That was our destination. We passed through an energy field before nearing the ground.

"Welcome to Oliter, everyone," Yope said, standing as the transport ship touched down lightly. The Keppe pilot had done this a million times before, judging by the soft touch he displayed.

The doors opened, and the heat instantly enveloped us. It was like the time I'd flown with some friends to Phoenix in the summer, but twice as bad. For a second, I struggled to find my breath, and I noticed the other humans, and even the hybrids, with the same look across their faces as me.

"Come," Rulo said, waving us out of the vessel and onto the white landing pad. A few other ships hovered on the hard surface nearby, some resembling the Keppe ships we were getting accustomed to, others looking completely bizarre.

A bus hovered toward us, and soon we were piling into it, the room-temperature air inside feeling like a cooler compared to the heat outside. In a matter of minutes, we were stopping at the front entrance of the rounded building. It was a rusty orange color, nearly matching the sand around us. Ornate windows sat in the structure every few yards, and I counted them vertically, seeing there were twelve stories to the building.

It reminded me of the White House in a way, only in stature, not design. It was clear this was where the leaders of Keppe resided. A shield domed over the area, its blue energy visible if you looked closely. Dozens of large Keppe guards were close by, and I noticed a few on the roof, as well as some walking the perimeter of the building.

"Expecting someone?" I asked, and Yope looked back at me.

"Wait until you see inside. And believe me, what you think we have for security out here, multiply that by ten." Yope smiled, and I peered around, wondering where they could be. Cloaked?

We exited the bus one at a time and let Yope and the others lead us into the building, up a short flight of stairs, before entering the wide double doors into a grand foyer. Everything was white inside, and it looked to be made from a smooth stone substance, something like marble or quartz. The floor, the walls, some pillars, all the same design. No art or ornaments adorned the walls.

It was cooler inside, but the Keppe clearly didn't like to run too cold. Their bodies were used to the heat, so they didn't need to shock them. I guessed our seventy degrees Fahrenheit would be like a winter day to them.

We went by a handful of tall black-armor-skinned Keppe, each with vests on and guns strapped to their waists. They were imposing, each nearly as big as Hectal, the women even bigger than Rulo. They each tapped their right shoulders with their left palms as their admiral walked past them, and when we'd passed through the room, he turned and returned the salute.

I wasn't sure what I'd expected, but it wasn't this. We were ushered into a room at the end of a wide-open hall. A few Keppe walked around, these not carrying weapons. They wore more formal outfits, instead of the vests and functional military-type gear like the ones with us. The men had cream-colored shirts on, their bulk still evident under the thin fabric. They each wore pants reminiscent of capris, coming below the knee but only halfway down their shins. The women adorned themselves with similar garb, but they wore brown.

I'd seen more color on board the ship, but here, they stuck with uniforms, or at least a dress code. "I don't want to work here," Mary whispered in my ear, and I laughed out loud, clamping a hand over my mouth.

A few Keppe looked toward me and I put a serious face on, looking around as if to seek the culprit. The doors shut behind us, and I noticed not all of us had entered the room. Rulo, Kimtra, and Hectal had stayed out in the hall, their services no longer needed for the time being.

"My lord, we have brought young Polvertan back safely," Admiral Yope said, and I glanced to the end of the room, where a Keppe spun around in a hover chair. He was behind a simple wooden desk, the top resting on four thin pillars made from the white marble seen everywhere. A tablet sat there, and he was tapping on it idly, not even bothering to look up at us.

He was a dark gray man, older, but still very imposing with his thick armored skin. "Very well." He finally regarded us, and his bright orange snake-like eyes caused me to step backwards.

"Mr. and Mrs. Parker, and the others, meet Lord Eren Crul, our supreme leader, bless his family name. They have ruled our people since the first dawn of memory." Yope said the words, standing proudly.

"And these are the humans we spent so much energy to retrieve?" Crul asked. He seemed to have a bad taste in his mouth as he spoke.

"These are," Yope answered.

"They don't look that valuable," Crul said. The lord stood up now, crossing the tight space to stand before Mary and me. Slate and Suma flanked us, and Crul looked at the Shimmali girl with interest for a moment before locking eyes with Mary. "They are small. Soft."

Jules took that moment to start crying from her stroller behind us, and Crul's eyes widened.

"Sorry," I said, picking Jules up. I bobbed up and down with her, and soon she was giggling. She often woke up afraid, as if she'd been having a bad nightmare. I wondered if this was residual effects of being in the womb while her mother was under the Iskios' control.

"You have good friends," Crul said.

"We know that, Lord Eren Crul," Mary said firmly. "We humans don't leave friends behind."

"Is that true?" Crul asked. "I've done some digging, and I've heard a lot about your race in the past couple months. If I were you, I'd consider this Kraski attack a blessing to you."

"And why is that?" I asked quietly, still looking at Jules smiling toward me.

"Because you were on the brink of self-destruction. Sometimes it takes a catastrophe to bring a people together." Crul said this like he had experience on the subject. "I suspect your world wouldn't have lasted long, the way you were going."

I couldn't deny it. He was probably right. "That may be so, but losing half our population in the process doesn't seem like a win."

"Could have been worse. Oh yes, with the Kraski, it could have been worse. Dean Parker. The name being whispered in a lot of corners of the universe. The human who not only stopped the Kraski invasion, but killed the lot of them. You also ended the Deltra's betrayal. That one surprised me, because the Deltra always seemed unusually cunning. Some of the best inventors I'd ever met."

I thought of Kareem, and how good of a friend he'd become. "They only did what they thought they had to do to free themselves. I can't fault them."

Crul nodded, still content to discuss the topic. "And the Bhlat? I hear you bargained with the Empress herself. Quite the surprise. I've never been able to meet with her, yet you managed to be in a struggle with them and come out on top."

I shifted from foot to foot nervously. I didn't like the way he was looking at me now. "It was my turn to do what I needed to do."

"Give away your planet. That's a new one, but a good solution. Too often, everyone defaults to violence. Too often, we have heavy losses when diplomacy may have worked better. You have done both. Which way do you prefer?" Crul asked.

"I prefer to not be in a struggle in the first place," I answered.

"We are always in a struggle. Always. Humans were in a struggle with themselves before this and may end up that way again if you're not careful. Believe me, we know. We've been around a long time. You may not have an enemy at your doorstep now, but you will. Oh, you will." Crul turned and walked toward his desk. Yope stood by his side, listening closely.

"We'll deal with it when we get there," Mary said.

"What have you done, Mrs. Parker?" Crul asked.

Mary started to speak but stopped when Yope whispered something to Lord Crul, whose eyes widened. "You were the one? All of that destruction by the Unwinding? I heard the tales, but didn't believe it until I saw the feeds."

I stepped forward, Jules still in my arms. "Back off, Crul. She didn't do any of that. It was the Iskios." I spoke in a low growl.

"Yes, the Iskios. Tales of them snatching children from their beds if they were ill-behaved are still used to this day. Maybe now they'll work once again." Crul dismissed me with a wave and stared at Mary. "Impressive. And this threat is over?"

"Yes," I answered.

"Let me guess. The great Dean Parker had something to do with it?" he asked.

I didn't answer, but Suma spoke, startling me. "Dean Parker is a great man. He helps anyone in need and cares about everyone so much. I'm proud to know him, and even more proud that he gives me attention and respect. Don't belittle him and don't take him for granted. It won't do you any favors."

My heart melted as the small girl spoke about me. She was a great part of our team, and it was almost embarrassing to have her speak of me like that.

"And who are you?" he asked.

"I am Suma, daughter of Sarlun the Gatekeeper," she said proudly.

"The Gatekeepers. An honorable group."

"Mary, Slate, and Dean are members of them too," Suma said, and now Crul laughed, a smooth throaty sound that filled the room.

"Of course they are. Of course they are. Why

wouldn't they be? What are we going to do with you all?" He looked past us toward the hybrids and Magnus. "Magnus, we may have to change our agreement."

Magnus folded his large arms over each other at his chest. "I don't think so, Crul. We made a deal, and that's the one we're sticking with."

"What's the arrangement?" I asked, still unsure what Magnus did to receive their help.

"Your large friend here has agreed to captain one of our exploratory vessels for a while." Crul looked amused as he spoke.

I turned to look at Magnus. "What's a while?"

He glanced to his feet. "Three years."

"Three years!" I shouted, and Jules began to cry. Mary reached for her daughter and took the small baby from my chest.

"Dean, what was I supposed to do? They wanted new blood. A new ally, and when I talked about my history and leading our fleet back at New Spero, he suggested this was a reasonable transaction. I took it. Would you rather we left you on Sterona? Things weren't going so well for you. Remember the Kraski and the robots?" Magnus asked.

"What did you say?" Crul asked.

"Which part?"

"The Kraski. You said the Kraski." Crul strode over to Magnus, getting closer to my large friend than most men would have.

Magnus defiantly stared around Crul toward Yope. "You didn't tell him? I know you have communication with home from *Starbound*, so why didn't you tell him?"

Yope paled slightly. "Lord Crul, I was waiting for the right moment to tell you."

Now it was Yope getting Crul's anger. "To tell me what?"

"Dean was captured on Sterona right before we arrived. We arrived to find ships of an unknown origin in orbit, and when they fired on us, we destroyed them all," Yope said.

"And what of this Kraski?" Crul asked.

"They took me, separated from the others," I said. "I think it was Lom of Pleva's robots. At least, one of his companies manufactured them." I paused while Crul turned to me, eyes wide. "I was talking with someone in the shadows of the room I was chained inside, and as I was pulled out by the rescue team, I saw him. A Kraski."

Crul was leaning against his desk, looking smaller than before. "Are you sure?"

"I'll never forget what they look like, Lord Crul."

"Very well. Leave us. We have a lot to discuss," Crul said.

"Can we go home?" I asked, reaching over and grabbing Mary's hand. Slate locked eyes with me, a worried look on his face.

Crul waved us away as he sat down behind his desk. "No. Not yet."

SIXTEEN

"Where's the portal room?" I asked Magnus after we were escorted to some quarters at the rear of the building. The rooms were sparsely decorated, favoring function over style. The few of us sat in a common area in the center of the dormitory-style rooms.

"It's under this structure, but there's no way we're getting there without a fight." Magnus leaned back on the uncomfortable bench. He ran his hands over his face and let out a deep sigh.

"Three years being a captain on a Keppe ship? What the hell, Mag?" I asked. I was angry he'd make that bargain, but compared to what they could have asked, it didn't seem that bad. I knew I'd have to swap with him. There was no way I'd let him be apart from his family for that long. Mary looked at me knowingly, reading my mind like only a spouse could do. She shook her head slightly, not enough for anyone else to notice.

"I had no choice."

Slate rose and poured some liquid from a pitcher they'd left us. He filled seven glasses and handed them out to our group. "This Crul is quite the character, hey?" he asked.

"He's something," Mary said under her breath.

"He's got an attitude, but I don't think he's that bad," I said. "The Keppe and Motrill have had a hard time, no thanks to the Kraski. I think they want allies. That's why they helped us, and that's why they're asking a human to captain a ship. And think of it this way. We get the Keppe on our side, and we get their cousins too."

"Throw in the Shimmali, and even the Bhlat to an extent, and we're starting to get a little team going on out here," Slate said, and Suma nodded beside him.

"Haven is happy to help where we can too. We have some connections," Leslie said, and Terrance agreed.

"Don't forget about your new friends on Bazarn, Dean. Garo Alnod isn't to be taken lightly," Mary said.

I suddenly thought about Karo, wondering how he was adjusting to life on New Spero. He was the last living Theos, and that had to be hard on anyone. I was looking forward to getting home for many reasons, and talking with him was one of them.

"You guys are right. Maybe this new relationship is of value. We'll have to make another deal, though. Magnus, you can't do this." I took a sip of the liquid and found it bitter. We'd had this on board *Starbound*, and I usually stayed away from it. Hectal said it grew brain and muscle tissue, but all it seemed to give me was a sore throat.

"What's done is done. I've already talked about it with Natalia, and she's going to join me, with little Dean and Patty," Magnus stated.

"Seriously?" Mary asked. "Nat went along with it?"

"She did." Magnus took a drink and grimaced. "She

understood it was the price to pay to get you four back safely."

I couldn't believe it. We had friends that would sacrifice so much for us. My eyes began to well and I turned away momentarily, hiding my reaction.

"Plus, three years on a cool ship like *Starbound*? Exploring space like a real captain from a TV show? Tell me that doesn't sound a little bit fun," Magnus said.

Slate shrugged. "If you look at it that way, then maybe."

"I think you're an honorable man, Magnus," Suma said, and Magnus smiled at her.

"Thanks, Suma. Let's just hope the mission is a safe one, free from space battles and drama. Plus, I think it will be good for the kids to grow up around the Keppe. They're a strong and good-humored bunch who work hard, but still have close families," Magnus said.

I still felt bad, but seeing Magnus light up at the prospect of doing something like this put me at ease.

We broke for the night, heading to our rooms. An hour later, we were settled in, Jules slumbering near our bed in a Keppe crib.

As soon as my mind shut off, and I drifted into a dreamless sleep, I was shaken awake. Rulo stood at my side. She spoke in a whisper, but I didn't have my translator on. I got up and followed her out, grabbing my earpiece in the process.

"What is it?" I asked, worried.

"Lord Crul would like to speak with you," she said.

"I'll get the others," I said.

She shook her head. "Just you."

I had the urge to wake Mary, to let her know where I was going, just in case, but seeing her sleeping so soundly, I couldn't bring myself to do it. I threw on one of the Keppe robes hanging on my door and cinched it around my waist.

I followed Rulo to a room across the building, and it took a few minutes to get there through the deserted halls. We barely spoke, and when we arrived at the destination, Rulo opened the door, motioning me inside. She turned and stood there at guard. So this was to be a private conversation, late at night, with Rulo, someone Crul trusted, at the door.

The room was dimly lit, and I was surprised by the setting. Compared to the plain white of everywhere else inside this place, this room was the opposite. Black floors were accented by colorful furniture made from exotic woods covered by smooth patterned fabrics. Artistic shapes danced slowly across long screens on the walls.

"Have a seat," Crul said. He was wearing a muted robe, and I didn't know if it was a formal garment or a dressing gown.

"What can I do for you in the middle of the night?" I asked, hoping the words had enough edge to them. I didn't want him to think I was cowed by his power. It would take whatever trace of the upper hand I had away from me.

He didn't seem taken aback by my comment. "I wanted to talk." His smooth words translated into my ear, and I nodded.

"Okay, let's talk."

"You seem put off by me," Crul said plainly.

"I'm stuck on your world when all I want is to get home. It's been far too long, and my wife and I have been through a lot. Not to mention my exhausted friends, who are constantly sticking their necks out for me." I sat down on a chair, surprised that it was more comfortable than it looked.

"I understand," he said.

"Do you?" I was getting tired of talking with him. "Can we get on with this?"

"Dean? Do you mind if I call you that?" he asked.

I shook my head but said, "Be my guest."

I wasn't sure if the phrase translated, because he gave me a blank stare before continuing. "I despise the Kraski. Our war with them over the colony was something every Keppe will remember for a long time. The way they killed the first settlers in their sleep, the suicidal advances they made when we brought the fight to them. They were merciless, and we lost a lot of good people. A lot."

I leaned back, trying to let myself see it from Lord Crul's perspective. I was beginning to understand him a little better. "I hate them too," I said. "I hate them for what they did to my people. I hate them for enslaving the Deltra and making them turn on their own values. I hate them for creating the hybrids and brainwashing them to their will. I hate that I was married to one of the hybrids, and that I actually thought she loved me.

"I hate that the original hybrid I fell in love with didn't die from sickness on Earth. She lived on, and I found out when we chased her across the galaxies to a Bhlat outpost. I had to watch my brother Slate shoot her like a target, as he was trained to do. I hate that every time I see him, I think of that moment." I buried my face in my hands but kept talking.

"I hate them for everything they've done, and it all led to Mary and me being on a crystal world, where the idle Iskios sat, waiting for someone worthy to come and set the Unwinding free. I hate that Mary was taken, and it all started the moment the Kraski came for Earth."

Crul smiled in a pained, understanding way, meant to comfort me. "I see we are not that unlike one another, Dean. Why did they come for you on Sterona?"

"I don't know. I honestly don't know how they found me either. The one spoke to me about regrets. He wanted me to atone for my misdeeds, I think." It felt good to confide in Crul.

"How does Lom of Pleva play into this?" he asked, and I was unable to tell if he recognized the name.

"I don't know that either. I've never seen the man, just heard the name whispered around me behind closed doors. He's like a ghost. Garo Alnod thinks he's after him," I said.

"You know Garo Alnod?" he asked.

I nodded. "A few months ago, I saved his daughter from a robot pirate ship that was marked with Lom of Pleva's trademark."

Crul laughed. "You seem to be at the center of everything. I've read of people like you, Dean."

"A Recaster?" I asked, seeing surprise well in his eyes.

I wasn't sure if the word translated properly.

"Yes, a Recaster. Few know of them, and fewer have ever met one. I now think I have. Where did you earn that name?" he asked.

"You wouldn't believe me if I told you," I said, thinking about the two-foot-tall bird man, who only spoke telepathically.

"If you say so, but I feel at the center of something big here. The Keppe have stayed to the side of a lot of conflicts over the centuries, until the Kraski forced our hand. I want to bring the fight to them. I want you at my side." Crul leaned back.

"No." I didn't hesitate to say the single word. It was the easiest response I'd ever made. "I can't. I have a family. A home. I need to be there, with them. I'm sorry, but the fight isn't mine anymore."

"They're after you, Dean. They'll come to you," he said, and I knew then that he was right.

"Then they will find a very pissed-off enemy when they do." I hoped my bravado carried over, but inside, I was worried he was right.

"Good. Think on it. I don't need an answer today. You can go home tomorrow. Rest now." Crul smiled again, this time baring his sharp teeth.

"You're not as bad as I thought," I said, grinning at him.

"Neither are you, human." He said the last with a laugh.

"While we're so chummy, can I change your mind on Magnus coming aboard for three years?" I asked, crossing my fingers mentally.

He shook his head. "A deal's a deal. He'll be safe. I think it's a good exercise, and one we've never extended to any other race outside the Motrill."

I nodded. "Fair enough. What will happen to Pol?"

"Polvertan is a kid. He's so angry about losing his mother in the Kraski war, he has this insane idea he'll find a time-travel device and bring her back. He wants to stop the war. Time travel isn't possible, Dean. Young Polvertan won't accept that." Crul lost his smile. "Rulo will show you to your room."

"Thank you. Have a good night, Lord Crul." I extended my hand. He looked at it and did the same. I grabbed his and pumped it twice before turning to leave the room.

As Rulo and I silently walked the halls towards my room, I couldn't help but think about the time-travel device Pol had been looking for in the secret cache we'd been inside.

SEVENTEEN

*T*he breeze was cool as we exited the tunnels outside Terran Five. I took a deep breath, the New Spero air filling my lungs. I closed my eyes and took a few more breaths before pushing the stroller down toward the waiting landers.

Magnus took off toward the first lander, and I saw why. Natalia was there with their two kids. We watched as his son jumped into his father's arms, and soon Magnus was holding Patty, one arm wrapped around his wife. It was a touching moment.

"She's here," Slate whispered, and he ran down to the landers, approaching his girlfriend, who was wearing a New Spero police uniform. He picked her up and spun her around, kissing her when they settled to the ground.

Suma had jumped home, and I could only imagine how happy Sarlun would be to see his daughter. Leslie and Terrance had gone back to Haven, saying they'd check in on us soon. The team was being broken up, but we all lived in different places. It felt strange to not have Suma with us. We'd all grown so close during the three months being stranded together, and then another two plus months on board *Starbound*.

Mary was wiping tears away as we watched everyone's reunions, like voyeurs in these private moments. Nat waved at us, and I pushed the stroller down to meet with everyone. Clare was there greeting Nick. They looked at each other with love in their eyes, sharing a welcoming kiss, not caring that we were right beside them.

"Mary!" Clare realized her friend was there, alive and well, and she proceeded to hug Mary like she'd never let her go. "I'm so glad you're all right." She looked over to me. "Dean, you did it. I'm so proud of you. Wait… who's this?" Clare looked toward the stroller, and unabashed tears fell down her face. Natalia arrived and joined her, the disciplined woman showing a softer side.

"Mary, get over here," Nat said, hugging her for a long time. Magnus arrived, holding his two children close.

"Nat, is it ever good to be home and to see you." Mary broke the hug when Slate and Denise arrived.

"And who's this little one?" Nat asked, leaning toward the alien stroller. Jules was awake, small and inquisitive.

"This is Jules." Mary looked so proud of our little girl.

"Jules? As in Verne?" Denise asked.

I glanced at Mary to see her reaction. We talked about how many times she'd hear that, but honestly, it was a strong name, and she would be proud to carry her grandmother's name. She'd been a pilot and the main reason Mary joined the Air Force.

I took charge. "Jules Verne did write some of the best exploration stories of the nineteenth century. Plus, Mary's amazing grandmother had that name, and it only makes sense to honor those we've lost and love."

"I think it's the sweetest name for the sweetest girl," Denise said, her index finger wrapped by Jules' little fingers. She was pulling Denise's hand toward her slobbering mouth.

"Denise, is it good to have Slate back?" I asked, and I saw the woman's smile break across her face.

"You have no idea. I've been waiting for this moment for a long time. Thanks for taking care of him," Denise said, her hand reaching and squeezing mine.

I laughed. "If you think *I* take care of *him*, you're kidding yourself. He's saved me more times than I can count."

Slate puffed up a little bit, unconsciously. He wasn't that proud, though. "Don't tell her about dragging my body away from the monsters."

"Monsters?" Denise gave Slate a look that demanded answers once they were alone.

"Anyway, it's good to be home. Can we get out of here and get home?" Slate asked.

Everyone agreed, and we piled in to the landers, heading back to Terran One.

---

*L*eonard was in the kitchen making coffee when Maggie arrived with Natalia. I felt so bad for leaving the dog again, but she ran over to me, and instead of acting hurt at how long I'd been gone, broke my heart and whimpered sweetly. I couldn't help but scoop her up close to my chest and get a series of dog licks as a prize.

"Maggie, I'm so glad to see you," I said, setting her down. She rubbed her face into my leg before lying down with her chin on my sock.

"What's been going on around here, Leonard?" I asked the young man who'd stayed at our house, watching over it while we'd been away. He'd been so happy to see us home safe and sound, and he took an immediate liking to Jules.

"I put the comics on hold," Leonard said, and Natalia came inside, sitting around the table with us. We poured coffees, but the simple gesture felt so out of place.

"How come?" Mary asked.

"I've been working with the government. I had a little notoriety, since the comics gained so much popularity. It doesn't hurt that I've been on missions with Dean. My efforts in the Bhlat conflict haven't gone unnoticed, and I'm on the Terran One council now." Leonard took a sip of his coffee, as if this wasn't a big deal.

"Leonard, that's great, buddy," I said. "I heard rumblings of other Terran sites being erected."

"There are twelve Terran sites, and most of the originals have expanded quickly. We basically have Terran 1.1 all the way to 1.9 now. With three billion people, we didn't have room, and the temporary structures built after we moved from Earth were becoming slums. With a little hard work, and efforts from each Terran site, we've created homes for everyone.

"Sure, some families still share a house or apartment,

but hardly anyone is on the street or living outdoors any-more," Leonard said, and I loved how he used the word *we* in his discussion of it. He really was a part of it now, and we needed more minds like his involved.

"I can't believe there are twelve Terrans. Mary, we should do a tour in a while, see what's going on out there," I said.

"We will, Dean, but we've only been home for a day. Can we relax and enjoy it first?" Mary smiled at me and picked up Maggie, who settled in for a sleep on her warm lap.

"Can you tell me about the sites?" I was curious about them individually.

"Terran One is our capital, as you know. We house the main military force here, and the government house, Dalhousie Tower, is here. While most of the manufacturing is still done in Terran Three, that's starting to spread to other cities, since logistics aren't great here. We have automobile manufacturing in three cities," Leonard said.

"The Keppe have a hover train we're trading for," I said, and Leonard looked excited by the prospect.

"Do we have anyone in negotiations with them?" he asked.

"Not yet, not that I know of," I said. "Magnus was leading the charge at the time. I'm sure we can get you involved. Are we still against a single leader for the colony?" I knew some people wanted it, while others hated the idea of our whole world under a single ruler. I was on the fence.

"We're using the term 'mayor' for each site, though

our populations are larger than most countries. It works, though. Twelve mayors now, each with a group of ten to twenty councilors, depending on population. We're getting things done and moved," he said.

Natalia was staying silent, and I wasn't sure where she stood on the way things were progressing. I'd ask her later. "And we're full-blown capitalists again, aren't we?" I asked him.

"It's split down the line. A lot of people still need social assistance. Do you know how hard it's been for a village from Namibia to acclimate while being thrust into a city of Irish, Israeli, and Canadians? It was pandemonium for the first year, but things are getting better," Leonard said.

"And have these cultures tried to forge their own way? Start a village or a town for themselves?" I asked.

"A few have, but the government basically says they have no control over you, and you'll get no assistance from them. They really want to keep everyone safe and integrated among each other. By merging and mixing all our cultures, they're trying to prevent the old conflicts from Earth, but I'm not sure it was the best solution."

"And how's that going?" Mary asked. "I'm sure thousand-year-old grudges don't end overnight, even after the Event."

Leonard nodded along. "You're right. They've had to deal with a few skirmishes, but nothing like they'd expected at first. And yes, we're using a national credit system for money."

"A lot of jobs to be had out there during a rebuild," I

suggested.

"There are. Far more than we have able bodies, it seems at times. If you know anyone looking for work," Leonard joked.

Part of me longed for that life again. Maybe they needed an accountant, but there was no way it was going to happen. I could feel it.

Natalia finally broke her silence. "I don't think Dean Parker will be seen driving a forklift at the docks any time soon."

Leonard set his cup down on the wooden table. "Dean, the mayor asked to speak with you when you were able."

"Do you know what it's about?" I asked.

"He didn't tell me. He looked serious, though. As soon as he heard you two were okay and coming home, he called me in right away," Leonard answered.

"I'll see him this week. I don't believe we've met before," I said, looking to Natalia. "Nat, what's with the Bhlat? Have you heard anything else from them?"

"*Da*. The Empress did make contact again. I had the other end of the communicator they used to speak with you. Magnus didn't want to bring it, in case something happened to him. He thought they might take a lack of response as a sign of war. She's adamant she talks with you."

One day. I'd had one sleep in my own bed, and already I was supposed to meet with the mayor of New Spero's capital and try to communicate with the Empress of the most powerful and dangerous race out there. Good thing she was on our side. For now.

As much as I was trying to complain about it to myself, I actually found I was thriving on it. This whole time, I'd wanted to get home to relax and recharge, and give Mary time to heal after the traumatic ordeal. But I needed more, and I knew she did too.

"We're leaving in a month," Nat said, and I broke her gaze and looked into my cup.

"I'm sorry. We didn't mean to have your family turned into bargaining chips," Mary told her friend.

"I think it might be good for us. Magnus is always under so much stress here. Out there, maybe he can lead the vessel like he's always wanted to. Less red tape to wade through each time he tries to implement a military process. I think he's secretly looking forward to it," Natalia said.

"And the kids?" Mary asked.

"The kids are young. Patty's a baby, and Dean will be fine. He's not even in school yet," Natalia said.

"How about you?" I asked her.

"I love adventure. This is another one I get to go on. While all of you have been chasing the stars, I've been stuck at home, for the most part. Don't get me wrong, I love that we had a family, but I need more." Nat's thoughts mirrored my own.

I sat up straight, realizing that I'd forgotten someone important in the whirlwind of getting home. It had only been a day ago that I'd had my talk with Lord Crul about standing beside him in a war with the renegade Kraski.

"What is it, Dean?" Mary asked, sensing my mood

change.

"Karo! Where is he?" I asked.

"Don't worry about Karo. He's still with us." Nat waved a dismissive hand in the air. "He's been a godsend. He cooks for me every night."

I let out a laugh, imagining the tall ash-colored being with long white hair fussing over boiling pots in Natalia's kitchen.

"He did like pizza," I said with a smile.

"He makes it twice a week." Nat threw a hand over her mouth, and we all laughed about this.

"Can I see him?" I asked.

"He's all yours when we leave. You can see him anytime," Natalia said.

I hadn't thought about that. Karo would need a place to stay. I glanced at Mary, who knew what I was thinking. "Of course he can stay with us. I like pizza too."

EIGHTEEN

"*D*ean Parker. I was beginning to think you were ignoring me." The Empress spoke in clear English. I pictured her swirling red eyes boring into mine, her thick black braids hanging down her back.

"I wouldn't do that, Empress. I was… incapacitated," I said.

"I heard all about it. Bravo. Saved the universe from the Unwinding, and protected your wife and child at the same time. What a sacrifice you made. You didn't expect to return from that, did you?" she asked, and I wondered how she'd gotten this detailed intel. She always seemed to be a step ahead of the competition.

"I didn't, Empress. I thought I was a goner." I wasn't sure what else to say.

"Thank you for the ice world's location. We have already begun our trek there. Your contract is completed for now." I didn't like the way she paused before the last two words.

"What can I do for you?" I asked.

"Are you alone?" she asked.

I was on my back porch steps. Maggie sat beside me, tired from her morning walk. It was cooling off outside, the sun's red light casting a strange ominous glow over my yard today. "I'm alone."

"Good. I've heard some rumors," she started and stopped.

"What kind of rumors?" I asked.

"Lom of Pleva is angry."

"What's new?" I asked, trying to make it not sound like a big deal. The truth was, I didn't want anything to do with the guy. He was bad news. As much as I didn't think the monotony of colony life was suited to me, I'd rather do that than fight anymore.

"What do you know of him?" the Empress asked. I listed the very few facts I had on him, then delved into the hearsay, which was a much longer list. She listened, saying nothing.

"Your turn," I said when I was done.

"The Kraski are a nuisance. I honestly thought we'd had all of them when we took their world over. We knew some escaped, and those were the ones you met back in what you call the Event, but we didn't care. Now we learn there's a planet of them. Multiplying and vengeful," the Empress said.

"Vengeful against whom?" I asked.

"You and I, Dean Parker."

"You mean the Bhlat and humans?"

"No. I mean you and I, personally."

"Why?" Not that I didn't know the answer already.

"My Admiral Blel attacked their home, killing billions of them. They wouldn't surrender, and we took what they wouldn't give. You killed the rest of them. Later, we learned they had a plan in place to take Earth with the use of the hybrids, bought from Lom of Pleva."

"Did he use these hybrids often?" I asked.

"No. It was a new technology, tested for years before he perfected it with the human DNA. At least, that's another rumor. We have spies, but not all information is accurate. I fear Lom of Pleva has become sympathetic to the Kraski cause," she said.

"Why? Why now?"

"Because of you. You stopped his hybrids. You gave them a home." As the Empress spoke, I realized it was so much more than that. I'd sided with Lom's nemesis, Garo Alnod. I'd stopped the Unwinding, which could have been profitable for a man like Lom, and I'd taken the Shifter device Lom of Pleva wanted more than anything, and used it. He had every right to be very upset with me, and he likely was. But what did that mean for me? I was beginning to worry for my family and for New Spero. With the wealth he possessed, he could bring a fleet unlike anything we'd ever encountered.

"What do we do?" I asked her, hoping she had some guidance. I wasn't sure if I could trust the Bhlat, but since that day on board Admiral Blel's vessel, I'd had no reason not to trust the Empress. She'd been nothing but true to her word.

"We'll protect you if you need it. Bring your friends to Earth," the Empress said.

"Earth?" I was shocked. "Why Earth?"

"That's where I am."

"What are you doing there? I thought you were using

it for resources." I stroked Maggie's head, scratching her behind the ear.

"We changed our mind. Earth will be another outpost world for us. We have nothing close to this system, and it will act nicely as a colony planet."

I seethed at her words. After all that, the Bhlat decided to kick us off and take the planet for themselves. I took a deep breath and tried to push out the anger. Truth was, I'd handed it over. What business of mine was it what they did with it? "You want me to come there? It would take a couple of months."

Mary and I had seen to that. We'd blasted the corridor under Giza so no one could access the portal room. Now I was regretting it.

"Come. We'll discuss what to do with Lom of Pleva. Bring your friend with you," she said softly.

"What friend..." I started to ask, but it all came clear. They'd heard about Karo. How? Did they know that he was a Theos?

"Come, Dean. Come back home." She was trying to lure me back using emotions, and it was working. What I wouldn't give to be back on Earth again, to walk the streets of my neighborhood one last time. Only, it wouldn't be the same any more. They'd all seen to that.

"I can't," I said, my shoulders slumped as the words spilled from my mouth. "We've had enough. We're safe here."

"For how long?" the Empress asked.

"I don't know. Thank you for your concern." I left out the fact that I knew it was for selfish reasons. These leaders knew I was special. Lord Crul had even named me a Recaster, and that didn't sit well with me. The Empress probably knew there was something different about me too. Where I went, strange things happened, and she saw value in my being at her side.

"Consider it. I'll still be here for a few of your months. We're rebuilding."

"Where are you?" I wondered what area they'd settle.

"Your people call it Egypt."

Why would they go to Egypt, of all places? The answer came to me quickly: the pyramids. The portals were there beneath, and that whole area had an immense energy to it.

Something about what she said struck me that moment. "My people? Have you talked to humans there?" I asked, knowing we hadn't been able to transport everyone that fateful day.

"Of course we have. They're everywhere," she said.

Everywhere. Humans were everywhere. The air was breathable. The ones we left behind hadn't died after all. Relief flooded my mind and body. I picked up Maggie and held her close. She licked me and wiggled around excitedly when I set her back down.

Maybe I should go to Earth, then. Give them the option of coming to New Spero. "I'll discuss a visit with Mary and the others. I'll be in touch."

The Empress' voice was soft now. "You know how to reach me."

"Thanks for the concern for my friends and family," I said.

"We're allies, Dean." The call ended, and I sat there in the afternoon sun for a few more minutes before venturing inside. Mary was at Natalia's, helping them prepare for their trip back to Keppe. Karo would be coming back with her, and I'd finished setting up his room. It felt odd to be making a bed for the last of the Theos. He was ancient, yet we were treating him like a normal house guest.

When I saw him for the first time since Haven, he'd embraced me like family, stating how much he'd missed my company. Leonard had moved out to an apartment in the city, near Dalhousie Tower, so he could be close to work.

"Well, Maggie. It's time I visit the mayor and get this over with."

I walked downtown Terran One and gawked at the advancements like a tourist from the country. High-rises stretched upwards toward the heavens. So many projects were on the go, with construction noises constantly bombarding the streets.

I was a stranger in my own world, my home city that had changed so much lately, and even more so in the past few months. Things were progressing quickly. With the added knowledge shared through our Gatekeeper network, we now possessed technology unlike anything we'd ever seen before. Drones and robots created structures at all hours of the day, never stopping for bathroom breaks or to talk about the weather over coffee.

Even so, Leonard still said we had more jobs than people. Starting fresh on a new world took a lot of effort. Most colonies, from what Sarlun had explained to me, started with a few hundred of their kind and slowly built on that number, adding necessary pieces as they went. We'd dropped another billion onto an already thinly-stretched planet, and were still trying to accommodate for the changes. Considering all of that, I was impressed. We had some great minds working on it, and it was nice to see.

I walked down the sidewalk, with Dalhousie Tower casting a long shadow down the road. Cars drove by, a few people honking as they recognized my familiar face. I'd never get used to the attention. Soon I was in the lobby of the government building named for our previous president, Patrice Dalhousie. She'd been American, and I knew there were some people against using her name on the New Spero office tower, but the vote had passed almost unanimously among New Spero's council members, according to Leonard.

"Can I help you?" a guard asked. She was idly looking down at a tablet.

"Yes, I'm here to see Abdul Patel," I said, clearing my throat first.

"He's on the thirtieth floor. Who may I say is coming up?" The woman looked up, and her eyes went wide. "I'm sorry, sir. Right this way." She lightly clasped my arm. "Hank, cover for me. I'm bringing Mr. Parker to see Mr. Patel."

"Thank you" – I craned my neck to see her name sewn into a patch on her New Spero military badge – "Shelley. How long have you been doing this job?"

She bristled with pride as she tapped the elevator button. "I've been in this posting since I came here with the initial wave. Well, I didn't work here, per se, but with the base up until the tower was built. I knew Patrice Dalhousie."

"I did too," I said softly.

"Now I feel stupid. You knew her better than most of us," Shelley said.

I set a hand on her shoulder. "I was only around her briefly. She was with you all for more years on Earth than with the first big wave to New Spero. Many of you spent a lot of time with her. I wish I could have."

She smiled sadly at me. "You and Mary Lafontaine are amazing."

"Mary Parker," I said, and Shelley laughed nervously.

"I keep forgetting. I apologize."

"Nothing to apologize for." The elevator lights showed we were at floor fifteen. Halfway to the top. "Shelley, are you married?"

"Yes, sir."

"Kids?" I asked. She looked about thirty.

"Two girls, sir."

"Just Dean. You don't have to call me sir. Do you like living on New Spero?" I was out of touch with the regular residents of our world. I needed to get that normalcy back.

"I love it. We're part of something new, something

important here. It's our second chance. Thanks to you and the other Heroes of Earth, we have new life breathed into us," Shelley said. We were facing each other in the elevator, and it was strange to hear her say that name given to the few of us from the Event.

"Do you think we have what it takes to thrive here? Honestly?" I asked, unsure how she would reply.

She waited a moment, and a few floors zoomed by. "I do. I think we're resilient and resourceful. We've made it through a lot and will continue to do so."

"Good. I'm glad to hear that." The elevator beeped, and the doors slid open. Shelley led me down a hallway, and to a reception desk.

"Mr. Parker is here to see Mr. Patel." She turned to me. "It's been an honor accompanying you. Thanks for taking the time to speak with me."

"Anytime," I said, and she walked away. "Shelley," I called down the hall.

"Yes, sir?" she asked.

"Would you and your husband like to have dinner with Mary and me this week?" If I wanted to know what was happening in New Spero, what better way than to discuss it with two regular citizens?

"We'd be honored," Shelley stammered.

"Bring the kids," I added as the secretary motioned for me to enter the mayor's office. I left Shelley bewildered in the hallway. I would never get used to the notoriety my fame brought with my own people.

Mayor Abdul Patel's office was surprisingly simple. Everything about Dalhousie Tower was basic. Resources were limited, so it was made from cheap alloy metals, as well as hard resin materials. The designers still ensured it was all comfortable and safe, and I didn't mind the simplicity of it all.

Wide windows overlooked the water for several kilometers, and the military base could be seen in the distance. Mayor Patel stood from behind a simple desk and crossed the room to meet me as I entered.

"Mr. Parker, so pleased to make your acquaintance. We met once before in Washington, years ago, but you wouldn't remember that," he said, his accent thick.

I smiled, indicating I might have remembered him, but the reality was, I didn't. I'd met a lot of faces and heard a long string of names in the weeks after the Event. Not many of them stuck in my memory of a time that wasn't much more than a blur for me and the others.

"Thank you for the invite. You have no idea how nice it is to be home," I said.

"Where were you?" he asked, and I let out a laugh, which I covered with a cough. Of course he didn't know what craziness was going on with me and Mary. He had a city to run and a world to help steer.

"Off-planet for a while. Anyway, what can I do for you?" I asked, changing the subject.

"Come, Mr. Parker. Take a look with me." He walked back to the window, and I joined him.

"Quite the view," I said, taking in the widespread city below and beyond. I hadn't realized how far Terran One spread out now, and it was impressive. To the west, endless skyscrapers stood; to the east, row upon row of dwellings. I couldn't imagine the sheer amount of energy needed, or the amount of waste this many people in one area would create.

"Do you know how many people live in the boundaries of Terran One?" he asked.

Clearly I had no idea, and I shook my head.

"Over one hundred and fifty million people." He was looking outside and didn't see my jaw drop. I knew the population was huge, but hearing that number was absurd.

"I didn't know," I said.

"The Shimmali people have gifted us renewable energy sources, allowing us to never worry about power again. Sewage is transported to the next barren world over. Things we could never dream of before are now possible. Health care is so easy now that most of it's done by a robot. Cancer, gone. Birth defects, gone. Old age will become a thing of the past." Abdul kept looking outside as he spoke. "Our population was decimated by the Event, and then we lost a lot more after the Bhlat took our world. But we're still going to grow exponentially. Without war or illness, we'll populate and populate. As people become happier, they'll fall in love and have children, and the cycle will continue."

"That's a good thing," I said.

"Yes. It can be a good thing. We have the space here. The planet can accommodate a lot of people. Pollution is a thing of the past. With our new manufacturing technologies in place, we'll never kill this world. But we *will* need leaders, Mr. Parker. I can only do so much, as can the rest of the mayors and their councilors. We need people to help improve conditions at a fast pace."

I had a feeling I knew where this was going. It seemed a lot of people were in need of Dean Parker these days. "Look, my wife and I have been through a lot. We need some time for things to get back to normal."

He turned to me and smiled thinly. "Everyone here has been through a lot. We don't have time to wait for things to happen. We need structure for our people. We need leadership." He sat down and motioned for me to take a seat in the chair on the other side of his desk. I obliged.

"From what I hear, you guys are doing a good job. Leonard can't talk to me without singing your praises," I told him.

"Yes. Leonard is a friend of yours. What a lucky boy he is. Good head on his shoulders too. Terran Thirteen is going to break ground soon, and we need a mayor there. I'd like you to take that spot, Dean. It's in the southern region. Fertile soil, a lot of fresh water, and potential for so much. It would be a great place to raise a family."

"I have a great place to raise a family," I said.

He steepled his fingers. "Consider it. Talk to your wife. Talk to Magnus about it. He would love you to take on a leadership role. He told me himself."

I doubted this mayor knew Magnus as well as he was claiming. "I will. Thank you for thinking of me." I got up to leave, and he stood at the same time.

"Dean. The people of New Spero can use a leader. Eventually, when everything is ironed out, we'll need a single person in charge. Terran Thirteen would be a stepping stone for that. For you to become New Spero's president, or emperor, or king, if you wanted to be. No one would question Dean Parker, the man who single-handedly saved our race."

I wanted to laugh in his face, to tell him how crazy he was being. King Dean Parker. Then I wanted to yell at him for ever saying I single-handedly did anything of the sort. But it wouldn't help, so I shook his hand and left the office, all with a bitter taste on the tip of my tongue.

NINETEEN

*J*ules' cries woke me, and I got up first so Mary could stay sleeping. I left the warmth and comfort of the bedding, my bare feet cold against the wooden floors. Jules' room was beside ours, and I entered, seeing my little girl flailing about, pumping her tiny arms into the air.

"What is it, honey?" I asked her. She kept crying, and I picked her up, smelling one possible reason for being upset.

I quickly changed her before carrying her into the kitchen, where I prepared a bottle filled with her mom's milk. I saw a reflection and spun, worried someone had invaded my house. My first thoughts went to the gun I kept in the cutlery drawer, but they vanished when I saw it was Karo. The tall Theos was sitting on the couch, his hands wrapped around a mug.

"Good morning, Dean," he said quietly.

"Hi, Karo." I sat opposite him, Jules laid across my arm, taking to the bottle with closed eyes.

Karo smiled as he watched Jules curiously. "What a miracle. A spark of Dean Parker in a tiny package."

"What are you doing up?" I asked.

"I don't sleep much."

"Anything you want to talk about?" I prodded.

He looked up at me, and I saw sadness in those bright green eyes of his. "I'm alone."

"We're here with you, Karo." My words sounded empty.

"Not like that. I'm the last of the Theos. There are no more of my kind."

"Hasn't it been that way for a long time?" I asked, not trying to diminish his feelings.

"Yes, but then I had a purpose. I was the last, the one to wait for a need. You stopped the Iskios, and now I have no function." Karo stared into his empty cup.

"I'm sorry you feel that way. I'm looking forward to getting to know you better," I said, meaning every word. I couldn't imagine what it must feel like to be the last of your kind.

"Thanks, Dean. And thanks for taking me in. If anything, it's been interesting to learn about humans. They're not so different than we were at this infancy stage."

"I'm glad to learn we're only in our infancy, and that we have nowhere to go but up as a people. We're heading to Terran Thirteen today to check out the progress. Would you come with us?" I asked.

Karo leaned forward, his posture a little better. "That sounds like just what I need."

"Do you miss staying with Natalia?"

"They were a delight. I hope their travels bring them what they want," he said.

"So do I." Magnus had left last week with Natalia and their two children. He'd also taken Charlie and the older

Carey with him. I'd wanted to ask if I could keep Carey here, but they were too attached to him. He slept beside little Dean each night, and I couldn't take that away from them. Carey was getting his second chance at racing around in a spaceship. Three years was a long time, and I knew the chances the wonderful dog would be alive when they got back were slim to none.

Maggie woke up, and I could hear her shake her body on the bed before jumping down and joining us in the living room. "Do you want to come for a walk with me and my girls, Karo?" The red morning light cast through the windows; just enough light to go for a walk out here in the country.

Karo got up in answer and stretched. He was tall and had had custom clothing delivered to our house last week. It was in our styles, but he looked out of place, with his dark gray skin and long white hair, in jeans and a hoodie.

Soon we were outside, the air fresh. Smells from neighboring crops accented the breeze, and Maggie ran ahead as I pushed a sleeping Jules in her stroller.

"How are you finding being on New Spero? From what I hear, you haven't spent much time at home," Karo said.

I thought about the question long and hard. "It's been an adjustment. I feel like a stranger among my own people. I walk down the streets of Terran One and I don't recognize anything anymore." I needed to get up to Terran Five for a visit with Isabelle and James soon as well. We'd talked over teleconference, but not in person since I'd been back. Isabelle was so excited to be an aunt.

"I understand that better than anyone," Karo said, idly kicking a rock as we walked.

"Take your time and figure out what you want to do," I said. "If you want to hide out here forever, you're welcome to, or you can spend time with Sarlun on Shimmal. Maybe even Bazarn Five, or back to Haven. Whatever you want."

"I'll have to see what's left for me."

After a few more minutes, we turned around, heading back home. Today, Terran Thirteen awaited us.

---

*T*he lander trip took three hours. Terran Thirteen was much as Mayor Patel had said. I beheld vast sprawling lakes as we lowered, and farming already started; squares of different crops colored the landscape below us. Otherwise, there were only a few buildings up so far. We landed near the construction, and as the doors opened, I felt the warm afternoon air envelop me.

I took the stroller out, and Mary propped Jules into it. We were bringing her everywhere with us, and I was getting used to pushing a stroller. This was my new reality. At times, I felt a longing for something more, but when I looked down at my four-month-old baby girl, I snapped back to the present. She needed me with her. Mary smiled as we started toward the waiting hosts. Denise walked behind her, in uniform. Slate had urged we bring her as backup. I thought he was being a little too overprotective, but we liked having her around regardless.

"This might not be so bad," Mary whispered in my ear before kissing my cheek. Since I'd told her about Patel's offer, she'd been excited. I knew she'd get bored after a year on the acreage as well, though she claimed it was the life we deserved. Mary always had a driving force that needed to be filled. I did agree that she needed some time after her ordeal to get back into normalcy.

Karo got out of the lander, wearing a baseball cap with his long hair tucked underneath. He still stuck out like a sore thumb, but no one here knew he was a Theos, not that the word would mean anything to most of them. He went and stood beside Denise, who glanced up at him and smiled.

"Welcome," a short woman in a pantsuit said as we neared the small group. She shook our hands. "I'm Sharon, and I work with Mr. Patel. This is Francis, and Bart." She gestured to the two men beside her.

"It's a pleasure to meet you all," Francis said with a French accent and shook our hands. His gaze lingered on Karo in awe.

"We're happy to be here," Mary said. "Where do we start?"

Bart took the lead. He was an older man, nearing sixty, with a shaved-bald head and a white goatee. "This is ground zero. We're building the first residence for the construction crew, though as you know, we primarily have robots doing the grunt work now." He pointed at the structure behind us, and when I focused on the building, I saw them. Dozens of small drones hovered around the edges of the building, some soldering frames, others lifting and dropping supplies into windows.

"Then we're creating the basics for a city. We start with a health care facility, schools, and food-processing plants. Once we have shelter, health care, education, and nutrition taken care of, we expand to the rest of things, like recreation, entertainment, and of course businesses for everything in between. We've done this with seven Terrans since the initial five were created, with a much sparser population," Susan said, ticking the areas off with finger counting.

"How long does all of this take?" I asked.

"In four months, we'll be able to accommodate ten million people."

I nearly choked at the response.

She continued, "In another six, we'll house fifty million."

"That's ambitious," Mary said.

"We don't have time to mess around. We're overpopulated. Things aren't getting better in the outskirts of our existing colony cities. We need to spread out on Proxima B," Bart said.

"You mean New Spero?" I asked.

"Yes, New Spero. I almost forgot, we also set up fire and police in the first stage. Most of the fire protection is built into the structures now, with fire suppression drones. Those came via Shimmal, and have stopped half of Terran Seven from burning to the ground," Bart said.

"How is crime?" I asked.

Bart looked over to Denise, as if to pass the baton to

her for this question. "It's getting worse. We're mixing many nationalities together, and tensions get high. We preach that we're one race, against a thousand others who'd take what we have from out there." She pointed to the sky; my gaze followed her finger. "Drugs are bad in areas too."

"Drugs? How?" I asked. We'd left in such a hurry, that amazed me.

"People will look for any way to survive. Some of it comes from things as simple as someone bringing marijuana seeds with them. Others are chemical. Sometimes we've seen a complex chemical drug traced back to a faraway world where it's prevalent." Denise wasn't shying away from the questions.

"And how does it get here?" Mary asked.

"We don't know. We have limited trade with partners across the universe now," Susan answered, then looked to me, as if giving me credit for that, or blame. "Someone's sneaking it in. We're trying to be diligent at the 'borders'," she said with air quotes, "but once the recipe is found out, the dealers are cooking it themselves."

"Other crime? Murder?" I asked.

Francis answered this. "We've had a total of five hundred murders in the last twelve months. Considering our population, we consider this a huge win, but it's still too many."

It stung to know we were still killing one another. Even after everything, we kept the mentality and capability of murder. I tried not to think how many lives I'd personally snuffed out.

"I heard you might transfer here if we move out this way," Mary said to Denise. It was the first I'd heard of that.

"Slate too?" I asked.

"Of course. Do you think Slate would let us live three hours from him? He wouldn't be able to protect us then, would he?" Mary laughed.

Denise nodded, adding, "We want a new start together. This could be a good place to do that."

"You're right." I didn't have the heart to tell Mary there was no way I was going to accept the mayoral job. We'd discussed it a lot, and she'd ordered me to consider it before answering. I'd thought long enough and didn't think it was for me. "Plus, I'd miss having him over three times a week for dinner."

"If you'd like to get in, we can show you the rest of the area," Susan said, and we followed her to a modified passenger van. It sat taller than most, with enormous windows, twenty-inch tires rounding it out.

We loaded Jules into the mounted baby seat. One point to them for being prepared. Before we knew it, we were heading down the rough road, past miles of land where ground was being tilled, dug, and prepared for the immense city that was to be. Only a few humans were around, and those did maintenance or used tablets to control the drones and robotic machinery doing the heavy lifting.

"We have twenty different neighborhoods planned, each with more than enough amenities to allow our people to thrive. With each new Terran site, we're relieving the stresses of the other cities. Within five years, we'll have enough set up to be optimized," Bart said proudly.

I wanted to ask what human optimization looked like, but refrained. They did seem to have things under control, and I was happy to see it. People really were stepping up to create this new world. Once again, I thought about sharing colonies with other races. Haven already had a human settlement, and they were looking to expand on it. Sarlun wasn't open to the idea yet, but the Shimmali were happy trading with us. Suma claimed they would change their minds once we'd been around a while.

The Keppe might want to share a colony, perhaps with the Motrill as well. With the goodwill earned between us, and having Magnus and Natalia among them, I could see this happening. I was thinking larger than New Spero. There was so much room out there among the stars. I was drawn to it, like a moth to a flickering flame, but I couldn't tell Mary that. She wanted to plant roots, and I wasn't sure what I wanted for our little family. As long as the three of us were together, it didn't matter to me.

"We're approaching where the military base will be located. We've already begun construction," Francis said from the driver's seat. He slowed so we could see the wide frame of the base building. A few Kraski-style ships hovered on a rough landing pad.

"Who's that?" I asked, squinting at the ships.

Bart grabbed a tablet and tapped it a few times. "Looks like only one ship's scheduled to be here. Interesting."

I looked out the window and saw the familiar logo of the New Spero military on the leftmost ship. The one on the right was bare, missing the identification markings.

"Something's wrong," I said, my gut sinking.

"What do you mean?" Mary asked.

"That ship isn't ours," I said. My voice was tense and low. "We need to get out of here."

Denise lowered her hand to her hip, touching her pulse pistol.

Susan spoke out. "That's absurd. Surely it's just…" The road in front of us exploded, sending the van backwards as the windshield shattered.

Francis let out a scream as the glass cut into his face. I managed to turn and pull Mary down at the same time as we flew back. Jules was facing behind us, and she let out a cry as we landed, skidding to a halt.

My seatbelt was undone in an instant, and I reached behind the seat where the stroller was folded. I grabbed a shield dome from inside a pocket and activated it. The shield had been my idea. With Jules around now, I couldn't be too careful, especially after I'd found out Lom of Pleva and the Kraski were coming for me. I'd expected Mary to tell me I was overthinking it, but to my surprise, she hadn't.

Karo grabbed a pulse pistol from a hidden holster, and I was pleased he'd taken it. I had one tucked under my jeans leg on my shin, and I grabbed it while Karo steadied his hand on the van's side door. All of this took place within ten seconds of the blast coming.

Francis remained screaming in the front, and my gaze

darted from side to side, wondering where the attackers were. Could we risk getting out? Would they fire at the van next time and kill us all? The shield that surrounded us would only withstand so much force, and it didn't stretch to the front seat. Susan was in the middle row beside Karo and she was white as a ghost, a continuous cry growling from her closed lips.

"Dean, over there!" Mary pointed out the passenger side window, and I could see two shadows around the edge of the military base's corner frame.

Denise wasted no time. She burst out of the van and ran behind it, firing a few pulse rounds toward the enemy. Karo followed her. I got out the driver's side, my own gun tight in my grip. I ran to the front of the van, ducking low. The front end was damaged, metal digging into my back as I pushed against it. Karo fired more shots, and I realized Mary and Jules were still inside, the shield dome with them.

I needed to draw any potential attacks away from the van. Karo fired from the back of the van again, and I took my chance as he distracted them. I ran forward to the far edge of the construction site. I didn't get any fire at my feet as I crossed the hundred yards. My back pressed against the metal framework, and drones buzzed above me, soldering joints. I looked behind me, toward the two ships at the landing pad, and saw two bodies sprawled out on the ground, likely dead New Spero military personnel. Had this been a trap for us?

I kept hidden from the Kraski vessel as best I could, trying to determine how many enemies we were up against. I made for the back of the site, ready for anyone to jump out against me. No one did, but I almost tripped over a man at the far corner of the building. I knelt at the limp man's side, feeling for a pulse that wasn't there. His hands held a blinking tablet, and I removed it gingerly. The screen showed viewpoints of ten drones, each doing different tasks.

After a few moments, I figured out how to control one of them manually, and I had it fly around the perimeter of the building. There were five assailants. Three appeared to be the same type of robots I'd now encountered twice before. The other two were clearly Kraski, tall and thin in their shiny uniforms, like the ones I'd found when we first rose into space aboard one of their vessels.

They were firing at Karo, Denise, and the van. "Get away from there, Karo," I whispered to myself, not wanting my wife and daughter to be fired upon. I watched a feed from the drone, seeing the robots send a blast of red energy toward Denise's gunfire, the impact sending the van sideways. I almost shouted for Mary but bit my tongue.

There wasn't time to waste. I had to stop them.

I ran around the building and dropped a drone from the sky toward the two Kraski. It had a welding torch, and I turned it on with the touch of an icon, cranking the volume of the gas up to max. A flame shot forward from the hovering drone, and I flew it directly into the pair of Kraski. They ducked for cover, and Lom of Pleva's robots began to fire back.

It gave me enough time to rush them. I looked up to

see Denise and Karo coming to assist me. We fired at the Kraski while they were distracted, felling the first one with ease. Denise took out one of the robot enemies, while the second Kraski fired in my direction. I jumped out of the way, but the beam hit my left arm, sending a jolt of pain through that side of my body.

I fell to the ground hard and tried to roll back to my feet, but overshot it and landed on my stomach. My pulse pistol miraculously stayed in my hand, and when the Kraski approached me, gun at his side, I spun to my back and fired a series of shots. His eyes widened as the blasts took him in the chest. As he fell, I saw two robots behind him, each with red blazing eyes.

One of them sparked as Karo snuck up from behind, hitting it in the back of the neck with a close-range shot. The other fired at me, and I narrowly rolled out of the way. I shot it in the chest at the same moment Denise blasted it in the back of the knees, and it exploded in a pile of bolts. I threw my hands over my head as the shrapnel rained down on me. It had to have a self-destruct feature, because our pistols didn't hold that much punch.

I was breathing heavily, scanning the surrounding area for any signs of the enemy.

"Are you okay?" Denise asked as she lowered a hand to help me to my feet. I got up, my left arm hanging limp at my side.

"Nothing a little modern medicine won't be able to assist with." I'd kept my streak of bad humor while in terrible situations alive. "Is that all of them?"

"I see no one else," Karo said, and I turned my attention to the van.

Running across the space, I saw Susan climb out and stumble a few steps before stopping.

"Susan, get inside the shield!" I called out as we approached the overturned vehicle. She looked at me, and then upward, her mouth in a surprised O.

It was too late to warn them. The Kraski ship was emitting a green beam: the same one they'd used during the Event. It plucked Karo and Susan from the ground, lifting them into the sky and into the ship. My pendant burned against my chest. I still wore it as a reminder of that day, of our survival. The beam blinded me for a moment, and I blinked hard, trying to see the others inside it.

I shouted in anger at the ship as it moved, standing on the packed dirt road. I uselessly fired at the vessel with my pistol as it started away. The beam glowed out of the ship for a second longer, and a body emerged from the vessel. When the light cut out, the figure fell the few hundred yards to the ground. Susan's corpse was twisted on the dirt forty yards in front of me.

Denise stood beside me, and we watched as the Kraski ship raced away with Karo inside.

TWENTY

"*H*ow does that feel, Dean?" Nick asked, stepping back to admire his work.

I flexed my arm, bending it every way I knew how. My fingers danced as I moved them around, and I nodded to the doctor. "Just like new."

"Can you tell us again what happened?" Slate asked.

"How many times do I need to go over this?" I asked. We were tucked away in Clare's research facility, away from prying ears and eyes. Mary was holding Jules close. Both of them were unscathed after the ordeal, and Mary was taking the whole thing a lot better than I was. I'd come close to losing them today, and I could hardly keep my mind from reeling. We were attacked at home. "What I want to know is how a Kraski ship got through to the surface."

Slate sat beside Denise, who'd changed from her uniform into a plaid shirt and jeans. Nick and Clare were the only others in the room with us. "I talked with the base." Slate pointed upwards, indicating the station we had orbiting New Spero. Any incoming ships had to clear with them; otherwise, I was told, we had five pulse cannons tucked away in various locations on New Spero, ready to pulverize anyone attacking or arriving without authorization.

"And?" I said impatiently.

"The ship had clearance," he said.

"How the hell is that possible? They were clearly an unmarked Kraski ship. We let a Kraski ship land on New Spero! They took Karo!" I was standing, my voice close to a yell.

"They say it had a valid ID number. It scanned through," Slate said.

"Then someone hooked them up. We have a mole on New Spero." I sat down, running my hands through my hair. I examined my arm and saw it was still pink and slightly raw. Nick had said it would be a few days before it was fully healed.

"Who would possibly have contact with the Kraski? It doesn't make sense," Mary said as she patted Jules' back after feeding her. My little girl let out a small burp.

"I don't know, but we need to find out. Clare, can you get the ID number from Slate's contact? Maybe you can go to the station, and see if we can reverse-engineer this code thing. I want to see footage, and records of the Kraski ships interactions with our station. Slate, we need to get Karo back," I said, glancing at Mary.

"How are we going to do that?" Mary asked me. "We have no idea where he went."

"Why would anyone want this Karo guy so badly? Were they trying to get you, Dean?" Clare asked.

"I suspect they would have been happy with both of us." I pulled out the green stone pendant at the end of the chain that hung around my neck. "I was wearing this. Never take it off, and it's a good thing."

Mary was wearing Bob's old ring around a chain on her neck, so she would have been safe too, but our child had no such protection. We'd have to remedy that.

"And why Karo?" I asked. "Because he's the last living Theos."

Nick's and Clare's jaws dropped, and I noticed Denise's fell a moment after. Slate must have told her before.

"The Theos? I thought you said they were all dead," Clare said.

"I did, but a lot happened while we were gone. I don't want to get into that now. We know who took Karo, and we know who hired them to do it," I said.

"We do?" Slate asked.

"Sure. This whole thing stinks of Lom of Pleva." I sat down on the bench beside Mary. "Let's take the facts. Lom of Pleva helped the Kraski years ago, before the Event. He created human and Kraski hybrids, a decade before the Event occurred. They've been in bed with each other for at least that long. The same robots that Lom sent to get the Shifter from Rivo's ship came to Sterona to get me.

"When they captured me, a Kraski was there interrogating me. We escape, get home, and now a Kraski arrives on New Spero with more of Lom's robots, and they take Karo."

Slate leaned forward. "That doesn't mean Lom of Pleva has anything to do with it. They could have bought the robots off him years ago, in the same deal as the hybrids."

"He's right, Dean," Mary chimed in. "We might be barking up the wrong tree."

"No. It's him. I know it," I said.

"Then where do we find him?" Slate asked, looking from face to face for an answer.

"I don't know, but I know who does." I caught the look on Mary's face as I said it.

"Dean, you can't do this. We have a family now," she said.

"Mary, they came to our home. Attacked our family in broad daylight on New Spero. If we don't bring the fight to them, what chance do we have?" I asked.

She looked tired, resigned to my decision.

"You and Jules can go to Shimmal for a while," I said, expecting a fight over it. Instead, Mary peeked down to our beautiful baby girl and nodded.

"I think that's for the best," she said without looking at me. She'd been through enough. The ordeal with the Iskios had taken a lot out of her, and with a small child, she was constantly being pulled from anything she tried to do. I knew she didn't have the energy to come with me, and for once, I was glad that she and Jules could be safely tucked away under Sarlun's protection. I had half a mind to ask Slate to stay with her, but I couldn't do that. Selfishly, I needed him at my side.

"Then it's settled. Slate, we go with Mary to Shimmal in the morning, then to Bazarn Five for a quick visit with Rivo and her father." I ran a hand softly over Jules' head and kissed Mary on the forehead.

"Now let's figure out just how we can outsmart this Lom of Pleva." I went to find a coffee pot. This was going to be a long night.

"Be careful, Dean. You're not messing with just anyone here." Sarlun stood at the other side of his office, arms crossed over his pristine white suit. "I've done more digging on him since our last visit. He's got his hands in a lot of bad stuff. Even more than I knew about."

Mary was beside Suma on the small loveseat opposite Sarlun's desk. "Do you agree with Dean's assumption that Lom is involved in Karo's abduction?"

"I do. Lom's best known for his genetic obsession. If he knows Karo is the last living Theos, who's been alive for thousands of years, then he'll want that man's DNA. I suspect he wants this secret elixir of life the Theos had. Perhaps he wants to find a way to store his own mind into a stone, until there's a way to transfer it back to a new body without complications," Sarlun said.

I'd been so frazzled, I hadn't put it all together. Sarlun was right. Lom of Pleva definitely was behind this all. He wanted me dead, likely as payment to the Kraski for helping get Karo to him. Only that end of the bargain had failed and I was still open game. My decision to have Mary and Jules stay on Shimmal was even more justified now.

"They still want Dean," Mary said matter-of-factly.

"I suspect so," Sarlun said.

Slate stood like a pillar in the corner. His jumpsuit was fresh, his short blond hair recently trimmed. My hand ran to my own thick beard, wondering if I should finally shave it. He looked every bit the devoted soldier. "Sarlun, do we have any idea where Lom is these days?"

"I don't. I sent some encrypted messages out to the other Keepers, but no one knows. Lom is a ghost. Always has been. When Garo Alnod tried to have him killed in the mines years ago, everyone thought he was dead, but clearly, that isn't the case." Sarlun scratched his head; his snout twitched lightly. "We don't even know what he looks like."

"Rivo will be able to get that for us," I said it, hoping it was true. "Mary, who do we still trust on New Spero?" We'd been through this, but my exhausted brain wanted to have someone else help me with something.

She listed the few names off. "Clare. Nick. Denise. Leonard."

"That's not many, is it?" I asked.

"Oh, and your sister and James, of course. We all have some distant family out there. I have some cousins in Terran Four."

"Where's the Kalentrek?" I asked, referring to the large Shield used by the Deltra to prevent the Kraski from coming to Earth for a few hundred years. It was the same device Magnus and I had carried into the center of the Kraski mother ship, killing them all before dealing with the Deltra's betrayal. I hadn't seen it in a long time, but with an impending war against the Kraski, I wanted to have it handy, just in case.

Slate shrugged. "I have no idea. Magnus would know."

Mary chimed in. "Magnus has to know. Patty would have stored it somewhere safe."

I pulled the communicator out of my pocket, the one that would allow me to speak to Magnus live, no matter how far away he was. Clare was still having trouble copying the technology. I tapped it, and the device came to life. "Magnus, come in, over," I said into it, repeating the phrase a few times before getting a response.

"Magnus here," he said, sounding tired. "Is everything okay?"

"We're fine. Karo's been taken by the Kraski." I cringed as I told him. "They beamed him off New Spero."

"Are you kidding me? I'll have their asses!" Magnus yelled into the communicator, and I could picture his hair a mess, neck cords straining in anger.

"We need to know where you stored the Shield, the Kalentrek." I waited for a response.

"Dean, are we safe to talk about this in present company?" he asked quietly.

"Suma, Sarlun, Slate, and Mary are in the room with me. We're on Shimmal. Go for it."

"It's underground in a bunker, east of Terran Two by seven miles," he continued, giving me the coordinates. "We didn't want it to fall into anyone's hands, so we tucked it away where no one could find it."

"We might need it," I said. "Magnus, do you have direct access to Lord Crul?"

Magnus took a second to reply. "I do."

"Can you send him a message for me?"

"Sure. Let me get my tablet."

"No need," I said. "Just tell him I'm coming to see him. I don't know when, but soon."

"Anything else?" Magnus asked.

"No, that's it."

"What are you planning?" he asked, a nervous twinge cutting through his usually confident voice.

"Something big."

"Be careful," Magnus said. "Stay safe, brother."

"You too. Thanks. Over."

The call ended.

"We need to leave," I said. "Suma, can you go to New Spero and work with Leonard to track down the Shield? Bring it back here."

Sarlun looked like he was ready to deny me the right to bring the weapon onto his world, but he sighed and nodded.

"You got it, Dean," Suma said with a smile.

"Take care of yourself here, Mary. Sarlun's vacation home is the safest spot for you two right now." I hugged Mary tight. We'd spent last night in each other's arms, and I could still feel her pressed against me when I closed my eyes.

"We'll be fine here. It's you we have to worry about," she said.

I smiled widely at her. "I'm Dean Parker. Accountant extraordinaire."

"You're something, but finding a flaw in Lom of Pleva's bookkeeping isn't going to win us a war."

I separated from our hug and picked up a happy Jules. She smiled at me as I made a face, and I nuzzled in close, feeling warmth emanate from her soft cheeks as I stood there holding her. She'd changed everything. I had to be more careful now. I had to protect her above everything else. I had to make it home to be a father to this tiny girl. "I'll be back. Then we can stop worrying about everything. Once and for all," I said.

"It feels like we'll never be able to relax," Mary countered.

I didn't reply. Slate was waiting for me in the portal room, and I left Mary after a final kiss goodbye. It stung to leave her there, but we had no choice.

I entered the large white portal room, passing two guards who stood still as I walked to the stone where Slate stood, pulse rifle strapped to his large back. He was ready for action.

I clapped him on the back. "Glad you're on my side, Zeke Campbell."

He grinned at me. "No other side I'd rather be at, boss."

I keyed in the icon for Bazarn, took one last look around the room, and tapped the screen.

TWENTY-ONE

*W*e arrived, and the massive guards at Bazarn Five raised guns to us. They had sleepy looks in their eyes, as if no one had come through the portals in a long time.

I raised my hands in the air. "Dean Parker. Here to see Garo Alnod."

The lead guard stepped toward me. "I remember you," he said and motioned to the missing table along the wall. "You broke our furniture last time you were here."

"Sorry about that. I was having a bad day." I didn't want to spend time explaining the Theos icon that was disappearing from my mind as I thought of it. I'd had to break the table apart to draw the shape so I could re-member it and find the right place to travel to. It had worked, because shortly afterward, I'd met Karo.

"Right. A bad day. We've had a few of those since you were here last. There's no chance you had anything to do with our planet being attacked last time you were here, is there?" The second guard held his large gun up, a snarl on his oversized face.

"That had nothing to do with me. Ask Alnod," I pleaded.

"Fine. I'll see if we can track him down for you,"

Guard One said. He turned and tapped at a small console on his wrist. He stepped away so we couldn't hear what he was saying. The other guard stood somberly, watching us under hooded lids.

"Not much for small talk, hey, boss?" Slate muttered to me.

"Hands where I can see them," Guard Two said gruffly.

The lead guard turned and motioned us forward. "Garo Alnod will make himself available for you. He's sending a ship now. Meet it at the northwest corner of the promenade."

They walked us through the ornately gilded room. I ignored the luster this time, not caring about Bazarn's opulence any longer. I had bigger fish to fry. We exited the portal room and walked the familiar distance to the steps that would transport us up to the promenade. We were alone in the room, the steps clear of other beings like we'd seen last time. A pair of guards walked the perimeter, glaring at us as we crossed over to the stairs and up through the energy field.

We found ourselves in the promenade. Last time we'd come, it had been packed, scents of food trucks and sweat thick in the air. Now it was quiet. Empty. Dark outside. It was night, and we traversed the open space in utter silence, save for the sound of our footsteps across the stone ground.

"What happened here?" Slate asked, his voice loud in the quiet night.

"I guess an attack on Bazarn was enough to keep

tourists away for a while," I answered.

A ship lowered to the ground right where we were told it would be, and the doors opened as we approached. A Molariun pilot sat up front in the small transport vessel, and she lifted a hand in greeting. She was small and blue, wearing a bright yellow vest.

Without a word, she lifted the ship, and we rose into the sky. We couldn't see much, other than the odd lights from the empty resorts below.

Slate and I sat in silence for the trip, and eventually, we lowered onto the floating island Garo Alnod called home when he was on Bazarn Five.

The doors hissed open, and we exited. I went to say thank you to the pilot, but the doors were already closing, the ship lifting away. No one was there to greet us. The large bright moon hung overhead; thousands of pinpricks of light were painted in the expanse of space. I took a moment to look at the beauty that was our universe before blinking and jogging to catch up to Slate, who'd walked ahead.

"Quite the house," he mumbled, looking at the nearby palace.

Someone was coming toward us, and I saw Slate reaching for his rifle. "Don't. It's Rivo," I said.

"Dean!" She wrapped her arms around my waist, and I gave her an awkward hug back. She'd filled out a little since her captivity by Lom's robo-pirates, and I was happy to see she was looking healthy. "I was not expecting you." She said the words in English, and I was surprised.

"You're speaking my language," I said, tapping my

Adam's apple.

"Father made me get the implant. Said if I was going to take on more responsibility, I needed to do it. I'm happy with it. Makes my life a lot easier," she said.

The wealthy had a way to implant a language modifier into their brains. I wondered if I'd consider doing the surgery, or if it even worked on a human.

"We're here on some serious business. Can we come inside?" I asked. Slate was glancing around like a cat hunting in a field of birds.

"Come in. Father is waiting."

"I hope we didn't wake you," I said, trying to be courteous.

"Father doesn't sleep much. He was up," Rivo said.

We followed them through the entrance of the palatial home, and up the same stairs, then down the familiar hallway until we were at Garo's office. Slate looked around with wide eyes.

The door opened, and Garo was in the same spot he'd been last time. "Dean Parker. Come to return my suit?"

"Uhm, I think it's beyond repair. But it did save my life out there," I said. Garo had loaned me his spacesuit, which had built-in thrusters. I'd needed those after being blasted away, after using the Shifter to send the Unwinding to another dimension. It had only been six months, but it felt like a lifetime ago.

"I have more. What can I do for you?" Garo asked, straight to business.

"I see Bazarn isn't the same place. How's recovery?" I

asked, diverting his question for a moment.

"We fought off the invasion. Clearly sent by Lom of Pleva. We've been rebuilding since then. We thought it best to close the world from tourists until it was back to normal," Garo said.

Slate and I took offered seats in the chairs across from Garo. Rivo stood at her father's side.

"How do you know it was Lom? Was he here?" I asked.

"No. It was a mixture of five different ships. We took some prisoners, but none of them would fess up what they were doing here. The closest we got was from a Luppo. Said they were paid to show up, and followed orders," Garo said.

My throat was drying up, and I looked around for something to drink. "Were there any Kraski here?"

Garo's eyes narrowed. "Yes. There were Kraski. What are you doing here, Dean?"

"I need your help."

"Then ask for it," Garo replied.

"I need to know where Lom of Pleva is," I said.

The room stayed silent for a few moments before Garo began to speak. "We don't know exactly where he is, but we've been trying to track his movements."

"How do you do that?" I asked.

"Spies. I have them in every corner out there, and I pay some high-level informants within his organization," Garo said.

"Then you shouldn't have any problem getting the information you need." It sounded simple enough to me.

"If only it was that easy." Garo looked tired. The last few months of rebuilding had taken a toll on him, and even Rivo looked stressed. "He's gone dark."

"What do you mean? Even his own people don't know where he is?" I asked.

Garo nodded in reply.

"He has to be somewhere," Slate said. "Are we one hundred percent sure that he's still alive?"

"He's alive. He left me a private message when we were attacked. Before our defenses obliterated the invasion, my personal communication matrix was hacked. When I got back to this office, a message awaited me." Garo tapped a screen on his desk, and a message started to play. "I'll have it translate to English for you."

I raised my eyebrows at Slate, and we both leaned forward as a voice began to talk. "*Garo Alnod. Your attempt on my life took guts. You took quite the risk, attempting to end me at my own mine. Your actions mutilated forty miners and their families. So next time you look at your reflection, and you think you see an honorable face staring back at you, think about those people and their children.*

"*We've come for your dimensional shifter. Give it to me… personally, and your people will not be killed.*"

Garo paused it now. "We don't know if he meant those of us on Bazarn or our homeworld." He pressed play, and the translated message continued.

"*Your life is now forfeit. Regardless, you will not live to see your daughter's next birthing day. Tell her I'm sorry her betrothed had to die. I'm told he went down without much fight.*"

I glanced over at Rivo from the corner of my eye and

saw her clench her jaw in anger. She had a firm resolve in her posture that I'd only seen hinted at. She looked like someone I didn't want to mess with, even if she was only four feet tall.

"*I've left traceable contact details in this transmission. Respond to them if you weren't killed in this attack. You've made a poor choice once again, Garo. We could have been partners, but instead you chose to betray me.*"

The message ended.

"Did he expect you to show up and give him the Shifter while Bazarn was under attack?" I asked.

"I think so," Garo answered.

"And the contact details he supposedly left you?" Slate pitched in.

"Didn't lead anywhere. Maybe he had a timer on it. Either way, we haven't been attacked again, and Lom of Pleva's own people don't know where he is."

I had an idea. "I don't think the contact is gone. I think he's getting the messages but coding it to make you think he isn't. He wants information and doesn't want you to think he got it. Can you tell me how to reach him?"

Garo looked uncertain. Rivo nodded from beside us, and I saw her father taking her advice. "Sure." I unclipped a tablet attached to my forearm, and he tapped something onto it. "There. It's in your contact list under LOP."

"Thanks." I took the tablet back and reattached it. "I have a feeling he'll reply if I send him a personal message."

Garo looked around nervously. "You didn't bring the Shifter with you?"

"It's gone," I said.

"Gone? How do you mean gone? Hidden away?" Garo asked, seeming relieved it wasn't back in his office.

"Gone as in, I used it, and it's gone."

He stood up quickly, his back rigid. "You used it? On what?"

"The Unwinding. A vortex made from the energy of the long-dead Iskios. They were destroying whole systems, one at a time. I had to flip them into another dimension to stop it."

"Did you find your wife?" Rivo asked, her small blue hand suddenly on my wrist.

"I did." I smiled at her, and she returned it warmly.

"Good," she said softly.

"Then you don't have anything to worry about. The Shifter is gone." I hoped Garo would be pleased. Instead, he looked at me blankly.

"Then I have no bartering tool left. He will kill me." Garo slumped in his seat.

"You fended off his attack once," Slate said. "Who's to say you don't again?"

Garo's four eyes narrowed as he looked at us. "You don't understand. Lom of Pleva doesn't let things go. He'll do anything to see me dead now."

"I'll tell him I took the device. I'll send him a message and take the heat off you," I said, a bit too quickly. Did I want a bigger target on my back than the one I had already? I thought about the Kraski taking Karo and formed an idea. "Garo, we're going to war. The Kraski are back, and we need to end this once and for all. I'm working with the Bhlat and the Keppe, and we're going to bring the fight to them. They've taken over a small world, where they battled the Motrill and Keppe twenty years ago."

"I know of that battle. Many lives were lost on both sides," Garo said.

"Then help us, because the Kraski are working for Lom, and it would be one step closer to taking him down at the knees," I said.

"I don't think you understand. The Kraski are but a tool of his. He won't care if you destroy them. He'll use another." Garo sat back and thought about what he was going to say next. I could see his mind racing. "Did you say the Bhlat? They're going to work with you?"

"They offered us sanctuary, at least. The Empress told me that Lom of Pleva is angry with her as well. It seems he has a lot of enemies. While I don't fully trust the Bhlat, they have a lot of firepower, and if they want to side with me, I'll take it in a fistfight," I said.

"What will you do if you find Lom?" Garo asked.

"I'll reason with him." I had nothing else.

"Not good enough. We need a plan," Garo said, and I liked that he'd said *we*. I needed power and resources on my side. With the Keppe, the Bhlat, and the Alnods, there was no way we could lose. I needed to get Karo back.

"The Kraski just took someone from New Spero I need to get back. What do you suggest?" I asked.

"Gather your forces. Utilize your relationships. Take

it to their colony world and demand your friend back."

"How do I get them to give him to me?" I asked, eager for advice.

Garo looked at me with a smile on his face. "Trick them. It's rarely failed me yet."

I remembered the portal devices in my pocket, and a plan formulated.

"Can you send Regnig a message for me?" I asked Garo, and smiled at Slate.

TWENTY-TWO

"You want me to what?" the Empress asked over the communicator. We were outside Garo's palace, and his ship waited for us.

"Under the Pyramid of Giza is a portal. Mary and I blew the tunnel to it, so no one could use it again. We thought we were done with Earth… you know, since we bartered it away and assumed it was going to die anyway." I heard a noise from behind, and I spun to see Rivo running toward us. She stopped when she approached, and her pack and outfit implied she didn't want us to leave without her.

The Empress continued, and I could almost picture her red swirling eyes calculating what a portal was. "Just what does this portal do?"

I didn't want to give her all the details about it, since the Bhlat weren't aware their own homeworld had one. "It's a bridge between New Spero and Earth," I partially lied. I didn't love that I was giving her access to New Spero, but she wouldn't know how to use it properly, if at all, so I made the gamble.

"We'll clear it out. Does this mean you're coming to see me?" she asked, her voice almost hopeful. I still didn't understand her fascination with me. I guess I'd appeared in her office building and attacked, taking her and her daughter captive. No one ever made it into that secured building before Leonard and I had, and I think it still impressed her to this day. Most people would have been angry with me forever over it, but the Empress was even friendlier. The Bhlat were an interesting race.

I remembered the first time I'd seen one of them, on the abandoned station where Kareem had given me the location of the smaller shield device. They were so large and imposing, I'd been terrified of them. I had ended up killing him, but Mary, Slate, and I were a little banged up after that adventure.

I realized I hadn't answered her yet, and she said my name again. "Yes. I'm coming to see you. We'll be there in a while. Please expedite the portal opening. I don't want to get there and end up in a stone coffin."

"Very well. It will be done," the Empress said, and the call ended.

"Slate, are you ready to go home?" I asked.

"We're going to Earth?" he asked with a smile. "I have a favor to ask."

"Anything for you, Slate."

"We need to stop and get Denise first. I promised her I'd bring her if I ever went back. Now's the time to cash it in." Slate's hands rested on his hips, as if he were ready for an argument.

Denise was a police officer with training and a good head on her shoulders. Not only that, she'd proven her value against the Kraski and robots outside of Terran

Thirteen. Who was I to not take extra help when offered? "No problem. We'll make the stop quickly."

"I'm coming too," Rivo said.

"Fine. Let's make it a party."

I sent a message to Mary as we stood in the portal room outside Terran Five on New Spero. We were heading back to Earth. I needed to get the Bhlat's forces to help us.

The portal table lit up, casting a glow against my face as I searched for Earth's icon. Rivo was in the room with me, and W, our robot pilot friend, was also there. I'd asked him to come with us to perform part of my plan, and he happily accepted, still thinking I was his captain. Captain of what, I wasn't sure. He'd been staying with Clare at her research facility, and she'd been happy to have the resourceful robot around.

Slate and Denise held hands as I tapped the icon, light covering us before we appeared inside the portal room on Earth. It was musty, but fresh dirt and rocks had been excavated from the doorway. It seemed so long ago that we'd traveled there with Leslie and Terrance on a mission to bring the hybrids back to Haven. Without that mission completed, we never would have succeeded in saving Earth's population, and the Bhlat would still be our enemies.

Lights flashed toward us, and a few broad-faced uniformed Bhlat entered, causing Slate to reach for his pulse rifle. I set a hand on his forearm, warning him away from it. They were unarmed. They separated, making way for the Empress. She walked into the portal room and scrutinized the dusty space. I couldn't tell if she was unimpressed or not. I agreed it didn't look like much, but her gaze lingered on the hieroglyphs on the walls before she spoke.

Her hair was still done in long dreads, and she had a striking face, her red eyes mesmerizing as always. "Dean, how good to see you." She didn't step any closer, and she eyed the others with me casually.

"Come. Let's get you out of this hole and up to my home," she said, turning to lead us out. The Bhlat stayed still while we strode past them, following the Empress. We moved down the familiar corridor and up the stairs we'd excavated to allow streams of our people to access the blocked-off portal during our mass evacuation.

Before I knew it, we were outside in the middle of the day, the sun high in the sky. I took a breath, finding the air perfect. "What did you do? I thought your machines were killing our atmosphere."

The Empress spoke as she walked. Her words translated into my earpiece. "We decided to keep your world as an outpost. It made no sense to waste it, since you had so much infrastructure built. Most of it was so old and decrepit, but it was… quaint."

I'd been so busy looking to the sky, I hadn't noticed the changes around the pyramids. Stations and structures were erected everywhere, and hundreds of Bhlat milled about, each set to a particular task. Some of their small vessels traveled up and across the clouds. It wasn't what I'd expected.

"Where are my people?" I asked.

She waved a hand in the air. "They're everywhere. They stay clear of us, though we've had a couple of altercations. They banded together at one outpost in your France and tried to overthrow our facility. We stunned them and moved them into the country. They woke up with headaches, and much less motivation to try it again. We taught them a lesson that day by not harming them. They know we're here to stay, and that we don't care if they are too."

"Do you have any idea how many humans are here?" Slate asked.

"We've run sensors for your type, and the results show around one hundred thousand. Give or take." The Empress was being flanked by at least ten armed guards, but they stayed far on either side, not getting in her way. I suspected she was smart enough to be wearing a shield dome. She trusted me, but that didn't mean her advisors had to as well.

Slate let out a whistle, and Denise's eyes were wide. We knew we hadn't gotten everyone, but Patty's estimates had been around ten thousand living people, not one hundred thousand. Compared to the three billion we had on New Spero, it wasn't a lot, and with them spread around the world, with no contact with one another, there were probably hundreds of small settlements all thinking they were the last remaining groups.

We walked across the range, and I took my time to remember how special the pyramids were for humans. The Sphinx sat like a contented cat, an amazing wonder of the world. Even now, having seen countless planets, the awe of seeing mankind's early monuments was enough to send goosebumps down my arms.

Some of the buildings were on the ground, while others floated like small space stations, surrounding the zone. We arrived at one of those hovering ones, and a remote lift arrived. The Empress stepped on it, and two guards joined her now, getting closer than they had before. We all fit with room to spare, and the elevator pulsed under us, lifting everyone to the floating structure.

Inside, we were greeted with rows of Bhlat standing at attention. A single robed figure was leading them through exercises. We walked directly down the center of the lines of soldiers, and I felt a nervous drop of sweat bead down my chest.

After a few minutes, we ended up in a large amphitheatre. The guards stayed at the doorway, and we were ushered in.

"Sit," the Empress said, motioning to a specific row. She walked to the bottom of the room and stood behind a lectern, like a professor about to drop some knowledge on a hungry college classroom.

W sat down heavily, the seat creaking under his immense weight. Rivo looked around nervously, like she was in the middle of a spider's web. Denise and Slate looked impassive, and I tried to emulate them.

"What do you need?" The Empress' voice was loud,

firm.

I stayed sitting, looking around. "Can we talk freely?"

"This is my personal space in Bhlat territory. You have nothing to fear. My people don't betray their own." Her eyes were fierce, and I hated how she called Earth her territory.

I bit my tongue and spoke. "They took Karo. You know what he is, it seems."

She didn't seem surprised by the news. "Yes. Theos. How very interesting. I was looking forward to meeting him."

"We have to get him back," I said.

"Who took him?" she asked, and I wondered if she knew already, and if this was just part of the show.

"The Kraski. But I know Lom of Pleva was behind it," I said. My gut was sinking. We'd had word from Leonard that the Kalentrek was gone, dug up, and the space filled back in with fresh soil. I'd had the idea to use the smaller shield device that Kareem had gifted me. For that, we needed Kraski DNA to be uploaded into it. I'd asked Denise to get the DNA from the bodies I'd shot down outside Terran Thirteen, and she'd told me the bodies were gone. Disappeared. "We have a mole somewhere on New Spero. They were able to access our ID codes and get to the surface with ease. Other things have occurred as well."

The Empress shook her head, as if implying I'd failed somehow. "What are you going to do about it?"

"About Lom? I want to ask a boon of you." I cleared my throat. "We need to send a ship to the Kraski colony world. That must be where they'll end up. I need you to trade with the Volim to get one of their wormhole capable ships. W here will pilot the vessel and get there quickly."

She nodded as if understanding my plight. "All unnecessary."

"Why?" I asked, my heart racing.

"If they have Karo and it's for Lom, they won't bring him to their homeworld," she said.

I sat forward. "Garo Alnod's contacts say Lom is in the dark. They have no idea where he is."

"Then it's a good thing I have my own contacts. I know where they're meeting." The Empress looked doubly impressed with herself.

"But how…?" I asked.

"Dean, we may have a history with the Kraski, but do you think any good leader wouldn't have kept contact with some of them? I know where they're meeting Lom of Pleva, just like I'd heard they came for you on Sterona."

"You have Kraski contacts?" I was shocked. "Why didn't you warn us?"

"They've proven valuable. I reward them well, and I only heard after the fact." She tapped a screen on the lectern, and an image appeared in the center of the room in three dimensions.

"What is this?" Slate asked.

"This is where they're meeting." The image zoomed in to reveal a large, clunky space station. It was circular; each section looked to be built by a different architect, pieced together over centuries. Dozens of ships were anchored to it, sticking out like tiny fingers from the edges of the station. In the backdrop was a huge moon, gray and empty from the looks of it. As the image zoomed more, I spotted glowing signs all over the place. It was like Las Vegas in space.

"Doesn't look like a military base," I suggested.

"This is Udoon. A station for trading, gambling, drugs, and any other seedy thing you can think of. It's run by no race in particular, and there's only one rule: all are welcome, without bias. It's been a haven for smugglers and criminals for years. This is where Lom of Pleva will meet Kinca," the Empress said.

"Who's Kinca?" Denise asked.

"He's the one Dean met on Sterona," the Empress answered.

I raised a hand high in the air. "About this tall, scar on his face?"

She nodded. "The very same."

My whole plan had been decimated in a few moments, but I now had real substantial hope for our situation. A new plan formulated, one that could actually work with fewer unknowns.

"Do we know exactly where and when they're meeting?" I asked with a grim smile.

The Empress smiled back at me and nodded.

TWENTY-THREE

*E*arth. It was surreal to be back. I watched as the drones and robots worked on building the room we'd provided specifications for. I really hoped this plan worked. The construction was coming together nicely, but we still had some time to kill. A day, at least. This left me with enough time to take a trip down memory lane.

"I have to do something. I'll be back soon," I told Slate.

"Boss, what is it? I'll come with you," he said.

"Stay here and make sure this room gets done exactly as we need it. There can't be any room for error. We need to have the upper hand on this guy." I'd already had permission to borrow a ship from the Empress, and it was close by, waiting for me to take it for a spin.

"Sure thing. Watch yourself out there," he said. He didn't ask where I was going, but I suspected he knew.

"W, do you mind piloting this thing? I wouldn't know where to begin." The robot was standing beside me, silently watching the construction.

"I would be happy to, Captain." W turned slowly and started toward the waiting ship. It was unlike any of ours. This one was small and boxy, not made for looks. It could haul heavy equipment with ease and had no visible weapons, which told me the Empress might trust me, but not fully. She didn't get to live as long as she had by being imprudent.

We got inside, and I found the interior seats roomy, built for the bulk of a Bhlat. W found the pilot's seat and sat down, me beside him. There was no viewscreen, but a console allowed us to see the outside view through live camera feeds.

The doors shut, and the console's lights glowed against my face. "Where to?" W asked.

"Home."

———————

*T*he ship parked in the middle of my street. Each side landed on opposite sidewalks, taking up the entire width of the road. W took out a few light posts in the process, but it didn't matter. They weren't being used any longer. Nothing over here was.

I stepped out into the warm morning air. As I looked at my old house, it was as if I was in a dream. I heard birds chirping, and I closed my eyes. For a second, I was back in time, back when I was nothing more than an accountant, doing bookkeeping for local small businesses. Helping friends file taxes each year. Watching the Yankees play when I could on the flat screen in high definition. Life's ambitions were small, frivolous, but important.

I tried to grasp hold of that version of Dean, but I couldn't. He slipped through my hands as I opened my eyes to see my dilapidated house. Paint was peeling off the window panes, the driveway had more cracks in it than before, and the yard was a disaster, nature taking over.

"This is your home?" W asked in his monotone way.

"It was," I answered.

W stayed put at the end of my driveway as I stepped toward my house. I walked down the long driveway that led to the back yard. My young trees were much larger now. Everything was overgrown, but I was okay with that. It wasn't mine any longer. This house was just somewhere I'd parked for a few years in a different lifetime.

I tried the back door, but it was locked. I went to the small pile of rocks to the left of it, and fished around for the fake one on the bottom that held a copy of my keys. I could have broken in but didn't want to desecrate my old home in such a way.

The door unlocked with ease, and I slipped into the back of my house. My entrance was small, and I saw my old runners sitting under a thin layer of dust. I stepped over them and into my kitchen. Everything was as Mary and I had left it. My fridge held magnets from different places I'd visited in my life. I almost laughed when I saw them, memories of each occurrence flooding my mind.

I kept moving, not sure what I was looking for. Closure, I told myself, but it was more than that. I needed grounding. I headed up the small flight of stairs to the bedrooms, looking to the vacant guest room. When Janine had died, I'd emptied it of her old furniture. I couldn't bear to see it. The furniture sat in the storage facility where I'd also placed the pendant that now hung around my neck.

Next was my home office. The blinds remained open, and a plant had withered away in the corner. My old laptop was on the wooden desk, and file folders were stacked in the organized chaos that was my signature filing system. I choked back a tear as I recalled my old life. Emotions crashed over me as I crossed the hallway into my old bedroom.

Suddenly, I missed Mary and my baby girl with such ferocity, I thought I was going to fall. I sat on the foot of the bed, cradling my head with my hands. I had to get Karo back. I owed him far more than that. I had to stop Lom of Pleva and the Kraski from coming for me. I needed to give my family a safe place to live, one free from the constant worry of attack. Right now, that wasn't the case.

I sat there, hoping my plan was going to work. It had to.

I wiped a hand over my face and stood up, straight-backed. The trip home had given me the fuel I needed to go on. I pictured Jules' sleeping face and smiled. I'd be back to them soon, and I'd be so attentive, she and her mother would grow tired of seeing my mug.

I exited through the front door, leaving it unlocked. There was no one around anymore. There was nothing left to pillage, anyway.

"Everything good, Captain?" W asked, still on the sidewalk.

"Yes. We just have to make a couple more stops," I said with one last look back at my old house.

Ohio was hot. I stepped off the ship and onto my parents' acreage. The huge garden was overgrown with weeds. This was likely the last time I was going to be in America, and I wanted a trip down memory lane. I laughed out loud, thinking of my mother telling me to pick those weeds. Some of them were as tall as I was. My mom hadn't made it through the Event, and my dad had passed long before. I suddenly missed them like I hadn't in years.

For the most part, the house looked as it always had, just a little more weather-worn, in need of serious maintenance. My mom had sold the place prior to the Event, taking Isabelle with her to the coast. I missed coming back to it for holidays. Somehow, visiting my mom in her condo hadn't held the same comfort as coming back to our large farmhouse.

I walked the periphery of the property, taking a breath of fresh air. The Bhlat had done a good job restoring the atmosphere. The air was more suited to them now, but it was still safe for a human's physiology. After I visited the house, checking out my old bedroom and the family room where I'd watched Ninja Turtles on the small

TV for hours as a kid, I meandered back to the ship, where W was waiting patiently.

"Where now?" he asked, somehow computing that I wasn't done yet.

I had him lower in Central Park, on the west side of the Lake. I exited and took it all in. The sun was low in the west, almost behind the buildings lining the park. I was in a post-apocalyptic movie. Parts of the park looked burned down long ago, while others were thriving with green. New York had gone through some heavy riots after the first batch of colonists left.

Then, the government had been in a state of flux, and the people were uneasy. It hadn't taken much for some idealists to throw a match on the gasoline. Sections of the city were torn down: Greenwich Village was burned from its east borders to the water.

I stepped onto the long grass and surveyed the landscape. It felt damaged and sad here, instead of happy like my old homes had. I was only a hundred feet from the ship, and I turned to head back. This wasn't for me. I didn't need the influence of a dead Manhattan circling my head.

I raised a hand to W, letting him know I was coming back, when a gunshot rang out. I stopped in my tracks, scanning the distance, looking for the trigger puller. Another shot echoed across the way, this time striking just beside my feet. It was time to run.

"W, get the ship…" My words were cut off as I tripped hard. My hands jutted out, but too late. I hit the ground hard, and everything went dark.

———

"*H*e's gotta be one of them. The damn hybrids come back to kill us," a voice said.

I blinked my eyes and tried to rub them clear, but my hands wouldn't move. They were behind my back, and I found myself in a sitting position.

"He's comin' to," another voice said, this one from a woman. Her voice was gruff, like she'd smoked two packs a day since she was in grade school.

I shook my head from side to side and could make out their forms in the dimly lit room. "I'm…" I started to say before my tongue stuck to the roof of my mouth. "Water?" I croaked out.

"We ain't gonna waste water on the likes of your kind," the man said.

I forced the words out of my sore throat. "I'm not what you think."

"Then what are you? You come down in one of them space ships from the sky. You think we gonna believe you ain't one of them? We seen those ships before." The woman was coming into focus. She was old, gray hair hanging limp over her shoulders.

"I borrowed it. I'm a friend." It sounded fake, even to

me.

They looked at one another and both smiled, exposing rotten teeth. The man spoke. "Way I figure, you have the means to help us. We gonna get your help one way or another."

"Are you two alone?" I asked.

"We ain't stupid. We gots twenty more men in the other room," the woman said, but I could see the lie in her eyes. She was scared. Hungry and scared. Was this what the left-behind humans were resorting to? They did need my help.

"I believe you." I cleared my throat. "I'll help, but you need to untie me and give me some water." I tried my best to seem innocuous.

"Beverly, give 'im a sip of water. Not the good stuff," the man said. I was worried what the bad stuff was comprised of but accepted the gray liquid as she tilted a cup toward my mouth. It tasted foul, but I took enough to clear the dryness from my throat.

"The hands?" I asked, hoping I could press my luck.

"Not just yet. How are you going to help us?" Beverly asked.

"You're right about something. That's a Bhlat ship. But I assure you, I'm human. My name's Dean Parker." I hoped using my real name was going to help. With these two, I wasn't so sure, so it was a gamble.

"Dean frickin' Parker?" The man laughed now, a throaty laugh that ended in a series of hacking coughs.

"Yes," I answered.

"The same Dean Parker that stopped those bastards

from killin' us all, eh?" he asked.

I nodded slowly.

"Then you abandoned us… disappeared while the world went to hell. When you came back, you gave away our planet. I wished you let 'em burn us away. Anything's better than fighting for scraps." Beverly leaned against the grimy wall, her sallow face staring daggers at me accusingly.

"That's not…" I knew reasoning with them wouldn't work. They had the look of feral dogs. "I'm sorry. I really am. I can help you now. I can make it better."

"How?" the man asked, his voice a low growl.

"You can come to New Spero. I can bring you there."

The pair looked each other in the eyes and then back to me. "How can you do that?"

"Untie me, and I'll show you."

TWENTY-FOUR

"So this is where you live?" I asked, rubbing my hands as we left the small room I'd briefly been held captive in.

Old Bill, as he'd called himself, led me down the halls of the Upper West Side complex. It was one of the nicer ones, the kind that housed a dozen five-million-dollar units back when they still had any value. It looked like they tried to take care of the interior, but things were breaking down, repaired with improper materials.

"How do you eat?" I asked. It had been a couple of years since the last batch of humans had left Earth now, and that meant food supplies would be running low.

"We gots livestock and farms in the northern parts of the park. Big community up there. Everyone from the area came to New York City when they were left behind. Only problem is holding on to it with the raiders," Old Bill said as we walked down a hall and out the complex's lobby.

"Can you show me?" I asked.

"You still bring us to this New Spero?" Beverly asked, her gaze locked on me from the side of her face.

"Sure. If you want to go, I'll make it happen." We stepped outside into the muggy evening.

"Wait here," Old Bill said, and he galloped past the building, down an alley. A few minutes later, I heard the truck before I saw it lurch out of the side road. It was shooting some black smoke from the muffler as he threw on the brakes, stopping right near us. "What are y'all waitin' for? Get in."

I looked at Beverly dubiously and walked around the truck. The slender woman got in, sitting front and center in the old pickup truck. I sat shotgun, rolling the window down.

"How's the fuel situation?" I asked, knowing it had a shelf life.

"Not great. We got wise after a while. Worked hard to store as much as we could, usin' them stabilizers and whatnot. Someone smarter than me came up with that. Paul. You'll like him," Old Bill said.

The truck pitched forward, and I clasped my seatbelt on. It was one of the old kinds with no shoulder strap, just the one you wrapped around your waist. It dug in, and I loosened it, wondering if I should even use it or not. The way this old codger was driving, I didn't feel safe without it on.

He turned down Central Park West, heading north. He drove in a one-way for a while, then on the wrong side of the road. Most cars had been cleared, and nothing sat in the way any longer. He had free rein of the city. We traveled at a slow twenty miles an hour for a while, then he urgently turned a sharp right, as if he'd remembered the corner too late. We skidded, and entered the park.

"Welcome to the Newer York. Please have yer passports ready for the ticket lady." Old Bill laughed like he'd made the world's funniest joke, then ripped toward bright floodlights. The sky was dark now, and the lights cast an explosive white blast across a fenced entrance. I couldn't see anything past the lights and squinted to make out a few forms in towers at each end of the large wooden gate.

The truck parked to the side, and I let Old Bill get out first. If these people had guns, which I was willing to bet they did, they were pointed at me right now, and I wasn't going to give them a reason to fire.

"It's okay, boys. This is a friend of ours," Beverly said as she got out on Bill's side of the truck. I counted to five and got out the passenger door warily. I still couldn't see under the lights, but the gate began to slide open, and two figures walked toward us.

"Old Bill. Haven't seen you in a while. Did you see the ship in the sky a while ago?" a man in brown coveralls over a green sweatshirt asked. He had a thick beard, not unlike my own at this point, and he wore an old baseball cap, half hiding unruly curly hair.

"I sure did. That's where we found this fella," Old Bill said.

"Is that so?" The man in coveralls walked over to me, still holding an old rifle. He appraised me from a few feet away, and I figured I'd take the chance to introduce myself.

"Dean. Dean Parker," I said, sticking my hand out to him slowly.

"Is that so?" he repeated. He stared at me for a few more seconds before meeting my handshake. His grip was strong and quick. Two pumps, and he let go.

"It is," I answered. "This looks like quite the place you've built up here. What's your name?"

"I'm Paul. Can't see much under these lights. Why don't you come inside, and we can talk? I'd love to chat with *the* Dean Parker." His voice told me he was skeptical of who I was claiming to be. I was okay with that.

He led us inside the gates, and now my eyes began to acclimate to the light. We were inside a fortification within Central Park. Storage containers had been moved here, along with some log cabins built within the high metal chain-link fences. It was impressive. LED solar string lights were everywhere, wrapped along the inside of the fences and over dozens of trees, casting enough light to see by. More garden lights were staked along the grass in walkways, illuminating the paths so you could see where you were going by night.

"How many people live here?" I asked, trying to guess, but not having any real clue.

"Not a lot inside the fences. Not much room, but we have those we trust living around the city that come to barter, or do work and receive their share of the food," Paul said.

"You see a lot of trouble?" I followed him further inside the fortification and could smell the pigs and cattle more clearly now that I was inside the fenced area.

Paul's face hardened as he turned to look me in the eyes. "We see enough trouble. There's always someone trying to earn our trust, but more often than not, they fail us in some way. Then there are the groups that come with the idea of taking us over. We've lost some good people."

I glanced back to the gate, where the guards held semi-automatic weapons, and understood why. "The world's a dangerous place, especially when everyone just wants to eat. What happened back when they were gathering people to bring to the portals? You didn't make it to the rendezvous points for pickup?"

Paul let out a sharp laugh that indicated there was nothing funny about it. "You mean those half-assed attempts at telling us to be picked up to go to some distant world? We didn't even know if this Proxima really existed. For all we knew, the aliens were getting everyone to go through a portal and into a slave farm for them."

I hadn't thought of our own people not believing our government about New Spero. I'd been so naïve. No wonder we still had this many people on Earth. Would I have blindly trusted their word on it? I could have been one of these people, living in Central Park, farming cattle for sustenance. I suddenly felt a kinship toward Paul. "I'm sorry, man. I didn't know. It's real. We have our issues, but it's real."

Paul staggered backwards, as if he'd been struck by something heavy and hard. "You're telling me I was wrong?" He sat down on a park bench, and in the darkness, I could see tears glimmer in his eyes. "It's been so tough. Trying to start over again. Two years, Dean. Two years!" His voice came to a shout, and others were gathering now. I saw a mixture of people, all hard-working men and women. Children ran over, a boy and a girl, giggling at each other.

They'd built a real home here, and I was proud of them. I saw love and hope in their eyes as they looked to Paul, sitting on that bench right then.

"You've done an amazing job." I cleared my throat and spoke up. "Hello, everyone. I'm Dean Parker, and I'm here from New Spero. I can't take you there tonight, but I can get you there soon. You've all been through a lot, and New Spero is still a work in progress. But no one goes hungry. We have law. We have police, we have advanced medical stations."

A man wrapped his arms around a thin woman. Dark bags hung under her eyes. She was clearly sick. She could be saved now.

"Why didn't you ever come back for us, Dean?" someone called.

"Why did you give our world away?" a teenage girl asked.

The rumors of my part in the bargain with the Bhlat really had gotten around. "It was the only way for peace. I didn't know so many of you were here. I didn't know the Bhlat kept the world intact." I said the last phrase under my breath, but they still heard me.

More of them began talking over one another, and Paul stood, raising an arm. They fell silent in an instant. "Dean isn't to blame for any of this. He's a hero. He's done more for humans than anyone. If he says he can help us now, we listen to him. I, for one, am not sure I want to leave my home."

"There's another option," I said.

"I'm listening," Paul said.

"The Empress doesn't seem to care that there are humans here. As long as no one bothers them, they won't bother you. Maybe we can take part of the world back. We can send assistance. We have technology that you wouldn't believe. You can have order and safety back again." I looked at the emaciated woman and smiled grimly. "And health. You can have stability again."

They chatted among each other, and Old Bill clasped a hand on my shoulder. "Sorry about tying you up and all. You understand, right?"

I shrugged. I did understand. They were afraid, and I was a threat. "Paul, I need to leave now. I'll be back. Someone will come with aid, and you'll be able to choose staying or going to New Spero."

Paul's tense shoulders seemed to relax, and he stuck a hand out to shake mine again. This time, he pulled me in for a half hug and whispered in my ear, "This better be for real. They need this."

"It is," I whispered back.

After discussing it with the settlers, I answered at least a hundred questions from various people that came together to see me. They all seemed a little happier by the end of it, and hopeful for their futures. A few of them openly cried when I described the Terran sites, and how far we'd been able to go with them. The group swore that those of them choosing to go to New Spero would stick together, because they were family, and it all warmed my heart.

When they finally broke, heading to their homes, Old Bill and Beverly said their goodbyes and headed back out the fence. I was left with Paul.

"Can you give me a tour?" I asked.

"You bet." He started to walk down the LED-lit sidewalk. "We made homes from the storage units. My wife worked for a fabrication company in the real world. She had some experience with turning the units into livable pods. It was practical, and we could do it with limited supplies, though being in New York didn't limit us too much." He pointed at the rows of the units, and it made me think about the base we'd first gone to, with Leslie and Terrance in the back of our truck. They'd used a similar idea, though these units weren't stacked on each other like the ones at the base had been.

"Makes sense. Good idea," I said, counting fifty of the units. "About a hundred living here?"

"Nice guess. One-twenty. Some kids. A few babies." This made Paul stand up straighter, and I shared his amazement at bringing new life into a world like this. It made me ache, thinking about my own baby girl. I missed her and her mother. I wanted all of this to be over, once and for all. It sometimes felt like it never would be, that I'd be on an endless cycle of a new or old enemy coming for me.

"Past the neighborhood, we have a playground." I saw the equipment and wondered if any of it was in the park before, or if they'd brought it all. I hadn't visited this northern section of the park that often when I'd lived here years ago.

We kept walking, and I began to realize how large this compound was. "Crops over here on both sides." Paul spread his arms wide, and I saw corn on the right, and a variety of plants growing on the left. "Potatoes are key. Carrots, lettuce, beans."

The scent of farm animals thickened as we walked, and we arrived at the end of the complex where cows were fenced inside. There were at least forty of them roaming the grass. Pigs were penned beside them, separated by a waist-high fence. Chicken coops lined the right side. Paul smiled at me. "Good for eggs and dinner."

"What happens when the cows eat all the grass here?" I asked.

"We'll move the fence. Just over there" – he pointed to the north – "is prime park grass. It'll take some work, but we have the motivation. Now I'm not sure what will happen. You promise you can help us?"

I nodded. "Yes."

He let out a deep sigh. "This was my reality. Every ounce of me has gone into this."

He'd mentioned his wife. "Where's your wife?" The second I said it, I knew she wasn't there. His posture changed in a heartbeat.

"Gone. She left us the plans from her old job for the storage containers and left in the middle of the night for the last pickup to New Spero. We'd argued for days about it and decided not to go. She took our daughter and left," Paul said.

"Then she's probably still there," I said.

"Yes," Paul said and stood staring into the cow pasture. "I believe she would be."

"*C*aptain? What took you so long?" W asked as I walked toward him. The Jeep had let me out a hundred yards away, and the robot's question made me laugh.

"You saw someone shooting at me. Saw me trip and then let them take me, right near you," I said.

"I'm sorry, Captain. You didn't ask me to be a guard, only a pilot." His monotone voice made it all the funnier. "Why are you laughing?"

I stepped into the square ship, and he followed. "W, let's get out of here. I think we've let them wait long enough. Slate's going to kill me."

"If you say so." W got into the pilot seat and we rose off the grass, away from the settlement in Central Park, and away from my old life.

I woke as we landed in Egypt, thankful for the short rest. Slate was running toward the ship when I stepped to the ground. "What happened to you, boss?"

"I was kidnapped. Again."

"You know that only happens to you when I'm not beside you, right?" he asked. I didn't think he believed me, and I left it like that.

I couldn't deny the truth to his statement. "How's the room coming along?"

"It's done. They're folding it erect as we speak," Denise said as she approached us with Rivo. She looked happy and slid her arm into Slate's. He glanced back at her with puppy-dog eyes.

Rivo stared at me, her jaw clenched. "I'm glad you're back. I was beginning to wonder."

"So was I for a while," I said, and before anyone could probe me on it, I changed the subject. "I want to see the room. Let's test it out."

We neared the newly constructed room. From the exterior, it looked like a large storage container, with a series of even seams across it in squares. We stepped through the opening at the end and were transported into a room inside Udoon, the space station where the drop of the last remaining Theos would take place.

It looked just like the video feeds the Empress had managed to get sent to her, down to a chip in the dull gray metallic wall. I saw the small red dot in the center of the floor and knew that was my marker for the portal wall. I stepped to the far end of the room, where the table was set up, and heard sounds coming from small built-in speakers.

The Empress had someone record the audio from the room on Udoon for twelve hours, and we were going to use the feed for the trap. We couldn't have it go silent, like the portal we'd walked through on the tropical island. That had easily given away the trick. We didn't want them to know they'd been had.

"It looks great," I said. "Now we just need to transport it. How small does it fold up?"

"Small enough to travel in the portals, but we'll need a cart to carry it. You sure this is a good idea?" Slate asked. We'd discussed it with the Empress, and she was behind it. I wasn't sure we had a choice.

"What other options do we have?" I asked.

"We get Karo and blow this Kinca up, along with Lom of Pleva. Solve a few problems at once," Slate said.

"We kill the Kraski leader, and they still come for us. I need to bargain with them. We can't keep wondering if they'll attack. We have a mole on New Spero, possibly a few of them. It won't be safe until we resolve this," I said.

"What if we can't get Karo back?" Denise asked.

I blew out some air I was holding in my cheeks. "Then I've failed him. The Theos helped me when I needed it most, and we're going to help Karo now. Lom wants him for something. If he's behind the hybrids, he's invested in genetic modification. The Theos are able to live for thousands of years. It has to do with gene manipulation. Something about slowing cells down, Karo had said. Lom of Pleva wants that, but we aren't going to give it to him."

Slate stepped from side to side as the robots dismantled our replica room. "We make a deal with the Kraski, fine. But this Lom guy is never going to bargain with you."

"Then we kill him." Rivo said it without blinking.

Denise had a grim look on her face that matched Slate's. I nodded at Rivo's comment. "Good. I'm glad we're on the same page about that," Slate said.

I smiled at them, wishing I didn't have to conceal the real plan from my friends.

TWENTY-FIVE

We arrived at New Spero's portal, and Denise and Slate stepped away from the table.

"Find out what you can about the Kalentrek. Find those bodies. I'll be back in a day," I said.

"Will do, boss. Say hi to Mary for us," Slate said.

W had stayed behind on Earth, and the others were smart enough not to ask me why. I glanced over at my small blue companion. "Are you ready to see Shimmal?" I asked.

"I am. I've heard great things about it. And Sarlun seemed solid," Rivo said. They'd met on Bazarn Five, when Rivo had surprised me by hiding in a bedroom of our suite.

I scrolled through the world icons, finding Shimmal's, and tapped it. With the blink of an eye, we were inside their white portal room. The two guards saw it was me, but their snouts twitched at seeing Rivo.

"It's okay. She's with me," I said, and we walked past them into the hallway. I found a wandering Shimmali woman and asked where I could find Suma. She directed me to a classroom, and I opened the door to see Suma standing at the front of the room, teaching a class to a bunch of pint-sized Shimmali children. They were very young, half as tall as Suma, and she talked to them with an animated disposition, excitedly explaining some law of physics.

After a few minutes, she finally noticed us standing there and held her hand up to the class. They glanced back at us and sat still while Suma crossed the room to say hi.

"Rivo, this is Suma. Suma, Rivo." I introduced the two women. "I'm going to go see Mary and Jules for a while. Do you mind keeping Rivo company?"

Suma smiled and, in English, said, "Not at all. Come, Rivo, you can sit in the front row. I'm just teaching them about pentaquarks."

Rivo gave me an accusing glare before heading with Suma to the front of the class.

"Dean," a voice behind me said, translating into my earpiece.

"Hello, Sarlun." I shook his hand.

"Back so soon? Is it done?" he asked.

"No. We're one step closer, though. We know where the drop's going to be, and we have a plan," I said.

"Good. Lom will not easily be tricked or dealt with. It worries me he's gone dark. No one has seen him for a couple of years now. Be wary," Sarlun said quietly.

"We have no choice. They attacked us at home. They have Karo," I said.

"Dean, remember how I told you to keep quiet about the Theos before all of this started? That there were forces out there willing to destroy worlds for the lifeblood of that ancient civilization?" he asked.

"Yes. I recall that conversation," I answered.

"He's that man. He'll destroy everything for a chance at immortality. Believe me. If you encounter him, tread lightly. He's not like everyone you've faced." Sarlun walked, and I strode beside him, down the sparsely populated halls. When someone neared, he lowered his voice.

"I've been face to face with some baddies, Sarlun. Remember Drendon, the Deltra who wanted to kill me on the Kraski mother ship? Or the entire Bhlat fleet, led by the unforgettable General Blel? How about the Iskios in all their glory, creating the Unwinding, a vortex hell-bent on eating solar systems? I've seen it all." I was talking through clenched teeth.

"No, Dean. Each of those did what they did because they believed in the greater good of their actions. Drendon thought he could be the savior of his downtrodden people. He wanted to give them an out from captivity. Blel was a soldier, trained to destroy opposition. He was doing what he was told to do. The Iskios were an ancient race, one with a goal set into motion countless years ago; an unmovable force.

"Lom of Pleva is a man. A man with a lot of money and power, with a hunger for more. Greed. Greed drives him. Not ideologies or passion for a people. He'll destroy you without thought and smile while watching you die. Don't underestimate him, Dean."

I stood there, watching Sarlun spill out his speech, and I found myself getting worried. He was making good points. At least with the other enemies, I'd felt a connection. There was something I could understand about them. Lom was a ghost to me. I didn't know where he came from, what he looked like, or why he wanted to live forever.

"I'll be cautious. I have to be. I have a family to get home to," I said.

"Good. Go see them. There's a vessel waiting to take you to them." He shook my hand again, and his snout lowered. "If you need anything before you go, let me know."

I told him I would and eagerly jogged down the corridor to the outside. Mary and Jules were close, and I couldn't wait to see them.

The small ship landed near Sarlun's home away from home. The ship was on autopilot, and the door opened, letting in the sweet-smelling fresh air.

"Mary!" I called as soon as my feet hit the ground. I made for the house, which overlooked an ocean below. I didn't even take the time to look at the amazing view; I ran, head down, until I was at the door. Instead of barging in and scaring her, I knocked impatiently and called her name again.

"Dean?" The door swung open, and a worried Mary was stood there. "Is everything okay?"

I hugged her fiercely and kissed her in reply. Eventually, she broke the embrace and smiled at me. "That was one hell of a greeting. What are you doing here? You can't be done."

"Plans have changed. We have a better idea now, but I wanted to run it by you. And I needed to see you guys before I left." I didn't say the "in case I don't make it back" part. It wasn't going to help anyone to hear those words out loud.

"Come in." The door closed behind me, and I marveled at the large open room. We'd spent some time here before, and I recalled the space fondly. It was one of the best times of my life, and the closest thing to bliss I'd ever experienced. Fresh flowers were cut, arranged in a vase on the table.

"Where's Jules? Sleeping?" I asked.

Mary nodded, and she followed me to the back bedroom, where my little girl was dozing softly. I stood watching her for a few minutes as she breathed in and out, her small chest rising and falling. Mary's hands were wrapped around me, resting on my stomach.

"Tell me what's going on," Mary said, but I had other ideas.

I took her hands and led her out of the room. Her hair fell over her eyes, and I brushed it back, leaning in to kiss her. This place held a lot of memories for me: of our first time away together and all that came along with that. Mary seemed to feel them too as we entered the bedroom. I let all my concerns over Lom of Pleva and getting Karo back wash away for a while, and lived in the moment.

"So that's the plan? Are you sure you want to keep that part secret from the others?" Mary asked.

"I am. We have a mole, and until I know who it is, the information exchange ends between you and me," I said, looking out over the balcony view. Jules was beside us, rocking in a solar-powered baby chair as the sun set.

"W is flying the ship as we speak?" she asked.

"The Empress really came through, which means I owe her again." My hands went to the back of my head, fingers interlaced, and I kicked my feet up. "I could get used to this. Being here. The views. You."

Mary nodded, but she was frowning the whole time. "You're sure the Kalentrek is gone, and the Kraski bodies?"

"Yes. That's what I'm being told. This better work," I said.

"Why not just set the trap and blow the ship up after?" Mary asked.

"I've thought about that many times. But I want to be more than that. I want to change things, not just kill without trying to negotiate first."

"Some things aren't negotiable," Mary said, looking at Jules.

"I know. Let me think about it."

Mary took a sip of her sweet Shimmali wine. "And you can get to this Udoon station quickly?"

"There's a portal planet nearby. The Gatekeepers

have a station there, so we have clear access. From there it's a day trip, and according to the Empress' sources, Kinca is meeting Lom there in three days' time. We'll be there waiting." I took a drink from my glass, finishing it off.

"I wish I could be there with you," Mary said.

"No, you don't. I wish I could be here with you and let someone else deal with this, but this is our reality. I'll be back with Karo, and hopefully our old enemy will become our new neutral."

All of the pieces were coming together for this to work.

"Can you stay the night?" she asked.

I looked at my small family and nodded. "I can."

"*W*hat did you find out, Leonard?" I asked. I zipped up the rest of my white jumpsuit, favoring the Gatekeepers garb today.

"We didn't have surveillance out in the middle of nowhere, so there was no evidence of who took it. Patrice figured no one would know where it was, and a camera would only add suspicion. The good news is, the Kalentrek is only tuned to the Kraski, so it can't be reprogrammed to kill anyone else. If we had a psychopath on our hands, they can't adjust it to our 'frequency,' if you will," Leonard said.

"And the bodies? Surely someone saw what happened

to them?" I prodded, hoping for some good news.

Leonard tapped his tablet. "Sorry. They never made it to the medical center on base."

"What about the pilot?" I asked.

"The ship disappeared."

My heart raced. "First, we had a Kraski ship enter our atmosphere using a valid ID code. Then, the Kalentrek used to keep the Kraski away from Earth all those years vanishes, along with the two Kraski bodies from Terran Thirteen. Does that sum it up?" My voice rose, and Leonard took a step back.

"That sums it up," he said quietly. Slate and Denise were on the way, and Rivo stood beside me, keenly listening to our conversation.

"I don't have time for this." I ran my hands over my beard. "We've been betrayed, and I don't know by whom."

"We'll figure it out. Clare's trying to trace the lander's coordinates now to see where the dead Kraski bodies went. She'll have them soon," Leonard said confidently.

"I don't have time. We're leaving now. Leonard, I'm sorry I can't tell you more, but we'll be back. Take care of yourself." The words had a finality to them I didn't like hearing in my own voice. Leonard came over and gave me a hug, which I returned. "I'm proud of you, Leonard."

He forced a smile. "You have no idea how much that means to me."

Slate and Denise entered the portal room, dressed in matching EVAs. "Sorry, Dean," Denise said. "I couldn't get any more information from the team. No one has sighted the ship or noted any suspicious behavior out where the Shield was buried."

"Thanks, Denise. I didn't expect them to have any details. Everyone ready?" I asked.

Slate, Denise, and Rivo all nodded, and Leonard backed out of the room, watching us from beyond the entrance. I found the icon for the Keppe world and tapped it. Step one: finalize the backup plan.

TWENTY-SIX

*L*ord Crul looked amused to see me again. We were back in his private room, just the two of us, all alone.

"And you think this plan will work?" he asked me.

"It has to."

"What aren't you telling me?" he asked, showing how astute a leader he really was.

"I'm only leaving out the details no one else needs to hear. We've been infiltrated, and I can't have anyone knowing the exact strategy. Will you back us?" I asked.

Lord Crul shifted forward in his chair, his eyes staring hard at me. "I've been ready for years. We have ships ready to jump there at a snap of my fingers."

"Jump?" I asked, unsure what he meant. From what I knew, the Kraski colony world was two years away.

"We have wormhole generators and can be there in two days. We're ready."

I didn't fully comprehend the effects of using a generator, but I knew it would take a toll on the soldiers inside. Currently W, the robot pilot, was traversing the universe in a Bhlat ship fitted with one. I was the only person, outside of Mary, who knew the exact location and why he was doing it. I had to keep it that way.

"Then send them. We need to show them we mean business. The Bhlat will be there in three days. Just in time delivery." I laughed nervously. This had to work, or else I was going to owe a lot of powerful races some explanations.

"We get the world afterward?" Lord Crul asked.

"I was thinking we'd leave them with it. I've talked with the leaders at Haven, and they've offered to take a contingency of Motrill and Keppe colonists. Let's start fresh. Share what we have. Humans are there, and another wave is planning to go there to help." I hoped the offer was enough to entice Lord Crul to play along. I needed his fleets.

"Very well. I hate sending a fleet only to sit and play bully," he said.

"Sometimes a show of force is enough. The Bhlat will be there too, and we know how the Kraski feel about them. They should give in," I suggested.

"And what of Lom of Pleva?" he asked.

"Let me deal with that," I said, trying to sound confident.

He nodded, as if he believed me. "Consider it done."

I left the room and was greeted by Rulo. "Dean," she said, "I want to come with you."

We walked down the hall together. The others were waiting for me at the portal. We had a couple more stops before getting to Udoon.

"Why do you want to come?" I asked her. She stood a head taller than me, her arms twice the size of mine, with her skin's armor wrapped around them.

"You clearly need some muscle around you," she joked.

"I have Slate, and Denise. Don't be fooled, she's a tough cookie," I said.

"Human tough and Keppe tough are two different things. I like you guys and wouldn't want to see anything bad happen to you," she said, showing a softer side than normal.

It would be good to have someone trustworthy from the Keppe there with me when I broke the news to the Kraski. "Fine. You can come, on one condition."

"What?" she asked.

"You bring that cool minigun with you."

---

*W*e arrived on the ice world, and the package we'd left there sat in the corner, near the exit. Slate activated the cart's thrusters and used the remote to maneuver the folded room outside.

"So this is where we're going to bring them?" Denise asked, looking skeptical behind her helmet's face mask.

"This is it," I replied.

Rulo was even more imposing in her spacesuit. It was black with gray squares over it; the helmet had a horn on the front, adding to the impressiveness of the display. I didn't want to see her chasing after me on the surface.

"Where do we bring it?" Slate asked.

"Far enough from the portal," I answered as we exited the tunnel and stood on the icy mountain. The last time I'd been here, Mary, Slate, and I had discovered the first clue to find the Theos, which turned out to be a trap set by the Iskios. It was only fitting I was setting my own trap on this planet now, only not the trap the others with me thought it was.

I shot the metal studs from the bottom of my feet to give me stability on the ice, and we started down toward the snow-covered open plains below.

Rivo hovered in her suit and used the built-in thrusters to survey the area before us as we kept moving ever lower. She met up with us an hour later, saying the path was clear. There were no surprises ahead.

Most of our trip was done with little talking. It was snowing heavily, and I felt exhausted as we trudged through heaps of the white powder, toward the middle of a valley a few miles away.

We'd been there for three hours when I stopped us. "This is good."

"Finally. Dean, you sure like to commit to a plan," Slate said, most of the joviality gone from his voice.

The sun started to go down, so we lit lanterns and set them out around us. We let the crates we were hauling lower to the cold ground, and I took over the controls, directing the robots to do their programming. They assembled the folded room that was made outside the Bhlat base in Egypt. Once it was done, we had an exact replica of the room where Lom would meet Kinca of the Kraski, with Karo in tow, on Udoon.

"The Empress better have good information, or

we've just wasted a lot of time," Denise said.

"I trust her," I said, wishing I had more confidence in her sources.

Denise just nodded as we watched the last few pieces of the structure snap into place. When it was done, I entered into it, stepping through before anyone else. It looked just like the video feeds had. I listened for the sounds of the station and could hear them playing through the speakers in the walls and ceiling. If I didn't know better, I wasn't standing in the middle of an ice-covered planet; I was on that space station, hearing music from the bar down the corridor.

"Perfect," I whispered to myself. Denise and Slate flanked me, and my tall friend smiled.

"All we need now is the portal," Slate said.

"I'll set it. Do you guys mind leaving? You're tracking snow inside. We need this place clean." I waved them back outside, and they left without arguing. My heart hammered in my chest as I went through the motions of setting the other side of the portal. I took one side out of my pocket and set it on the floor, but instead of activating it like they thought, I slipped it back in my suit. I counted to five and stood up, then exited the structure. "All set. When we get them to walk into the real room on Udoon, they'll be sent here."

We packed up our gear and started our three-hour slog back in the snow to the portal room. I hoped Slate would be able to forgive my deception when it was all over.

"You guys carry on and procure our transportation. I need to make a quick stop on Bazarn. Rivo, do you mind coming with me?" I said from the portal room on the ice world. Slate knew something was up from my erratic behavior, but I could visibly see him accept it and move on. He trusted me, and it was good to know.

"I'm happy to help," Rivo said.

"Who did Sarlun say to ask for?" Denise inquired.

"A woman named Cee-eight," I replied. "Everything should be ready for us. I'll be there as soon as I can."

Rivo and I stepped away, and I heard Denise ask Slate if I was always this strange. Rulo glanced at me, a hint of worry on her face. Slate agreed that I was weird, and then they were gone, the white light flashing. One moment they were near the icon table, the next Rivo and I were alone.

"What's on Bazarn?" Rivo asked as we stepped to the table.

"Regnig. I need you to get me access to him again." I found the icon for Bazarn, and in seconds, we found ourselves back on Rivo's world. She strode by the guards like they didn't matter, and they let her by, giving me a staredown as we passed.

An hour later, we were back underground, down in the tunnel beneath the surface, where Regnig resided. The Alnod pilot sat still and didn't speak a word as he landed on the perch where the secret library sat hidden from prying eyes. I didn't have a lot of time and jogged to the door, knocking politely at first before banging impatiently after no one answered two minutes later.

Hold on, hold on. I heard the familiar bird man's voice in my head and found myself grinning. Rivo must have heard it too, because she smiled beside me. We'd removed our helmets inside the transport ship; I took a deep breath of the stale inner world air and coughed lightly.

The door slid open and Regnig looked up at me. *I didn't expect you back so soon. I got your message.*

"Can we come in?" I asked the two-foot-tall beaked being.

He waved a wingtip, gesturing us inside. *I take it you found your mate?*

"I did, thank you. She's fine, and I'm now a father." I stepped inside, and Rivo shut the door behind her. Large locking bolts slid shut automatically.

Regnig glanced back at me as he trotted down the hall and into the large open library. Something like a cross between relief and regret covered his expression.

I am glad for you. Now to what do I owe the pleasure of your company? Did you find the other you sought after? Regnig's eyes looked at me with a glossy sheen over them.

"The Theos. Karo. I did." I sat down and Rivo beside me. She openly stared around the room, as if seeking to soak up the image of the beautiful and sacred space to hold close in her memory at a later time.

Karo. How wondrous. They exist? Regnig propped himself up onto the short couch across from us and folded his wings over his small lap.

"They do. Or they did." I set into an explanation of how they'd stored themselves in the portal stones, allowing for travel between worlds. We had a short discussion on the Balance of the universe, and I went over the events leading up to me knocking on his door.

That is a lot of information. Perhaps I shall write a book about you, Dean. Would that be acceptable?

"Sure, if you like. I'll have to survive the next few days, but I'd be happy to talk more when it's all done," I said, not sure anyone would want to read a book about me. I humored him anyways.

Karo. You have to get him back. I would love to speak with him as well. This is necessary for the library.

He had a good point. "Now that's a story that needs to be told," I agreed.

Your message asked me about someone else. What do you know of Fontem the Terellion?

"Nothing. That's why I wanted to see you," I told him.

He was a collector of fine antiquities. Some say he had a fascination with many things, but more than anything, he wanted to find a way back in time to be with his one true love.

I sat back, and Rivo leaned forward, knowing Regnig could weave a great tale if he was prompted.

"He was obsessed with time travel?" I asked, remembering what Crul had said about the young Polvertan, who'd been seeking the same thing. I kept that part to myself for the moment. "Go on, tell us."

Fontem was born on Terell, a backwater world of no real im-

portance. At least, not until he put it on the map. He grew up the son of a tree feller, like his father before him. He had no urge to follow in the family footsteps, and grew tired of the simple life living by a swamp, and cutting down trees to exchange the wood for food. Fontem longed for more adventure, so he left home at a very young age. Tales say he found the nearest city and snuck onto the first ship from space that landed there.

To him, space was the unknown: something he dreamt about but didn't truly believe existed. When he saw his own world from a window, he nearly passed out. His life was changed, and his blood sang in excitement. He'd escaped his path and could seek his own fortune.

The ship's captain found him among the supplies when they were unloading on a small space station, and he tried to capture Fontem, but the young boy snuck away, avoiding a life as a trade slave. He hid on the station until the captain left, but his perfect view of the world had changed.

"Is this a true story, or just something from your books?" Rivo asked Regnig.

You are Garo's daughter, correct?

She nodded.

It's from a book, but often, much truth comes from the words on the paper. Isn't that right, Dean?

"I suppose that's right," I agreed, smiling at Rivo.

"What happened next?" Rivo asked the tiny bird man.

A Motrill trading vessel found the alien youth behind some crates in the common cargo bay of the station and took pity on him.

The Motrill. No wonder Pol knew about this Fontem character.

Regnig continued over my own thoughts. *He was taken*

in, fed, and given a job. He stayed with the crew for a few years, until he was a man. You see, the Terellion were a different species. They were much like you two, bipedal and carbon-based, but a small percentage of them had a flaw in their genetics. They stopped aging when they reached maturity. This created complications for Fontem when he met his mate.

Rivo perked up. "How did he meet her?"

He'd been with the Motrill five years when they happened across another vessel. You see, many of these ships used trade slaves, those taken from worlds by smugglers of low morals. There was no one to police their behavior, and that wasn't the lowest thing they often did.

This particular vessel had such slaves, and one was Terellion. A female. The most beautiful being young Fontem had ever laid eyes on.

I could tell where this was going and wanted to rush Regnig along. I didn't have much time to sit and hear stories. He seemed to sense my mood and raised a small digit at the end of his wing, as if to calm me.

As you may guess, he had the Motrill trade for her life, though it cost them plenty. They traveled with the ship another two years, and she was eternally grateful to Fontem for saving her from the space pirates' clutches. They fell in love, as you would expect two Terellions to do among nothing but other species.

They saved up and made some profitable deals, with the help of the Motrill, and bought a home on Bazarn before it was commercialized.

Rivo's eyes all darted open wide. "Here?"

Here. Fontem started to collect things: some for trade, others for his growing personal collection. He didn't age, though his love did.

His collection of rare artifacts made him very rich, but as his wife got old over the years, he grew bitter. Bitter because they'd been unable to conceive, and bitter that he was so happy but would inevitably lose the love of his life.

Being wealthy changes things, and he had all his contacts search for anything that might help him. Years later, he heard of a time-travel device, but he'd heard of many over the decades. His wife died soon after, and he was lost in grief. When he came to, he searched high and low for this device, spending decades and decades traversing space to find it.

"What happened?" Rivo asked, obviously caught up in the story.

No one knows. His collection disappeared from Bazarn. One day it was in his house, the next the house was vacant, and no one ever laid eyes on Fontem again.

"Wow. Quite the story. Do you think he found a way to travel in time?" she asked, and Regnig shrugged his thin shoulders.

Who's to say?

"That's what I wanted to talk to you about. I've been to his collection…" I started to say, but Regnig shot out of his seat so fast, I thought he was having a heart attack.

What are you saying? Where?

I'd never seen the little man so excited before. "There's a portal leading to a derelict ship that's floating lifeless in space somewhere. On it is a room full of crates. A young Motrill man was there, looking for the same time-travel device you speak of. He didn't find it."

That's because he didn't know what he was looking for.

"And you do?" I asked.

I have a book. The seller claimed it was a code from Fontem's private collection of antiquities. Since no one knew where the collection was hidden, I never thought it would prove to be of any value. It was interesting enough to me, though, because I've confirmed it was written by Fontem's hand.

"Get the book. We'll bring it with us," I said.

"Bring it where?" Rivo asked.

"To the collection. I have the other half of a portal in my pocket that will take us there."

Regnig, the keeper of the universe's largest collection of information, fainted.

TWENTY-SEVEN

I set up the second piece of the portal device in a small room to the side of the library. As I pressed it open, a light emanated from it, expanding as it hit the ceiling and two side walls. It hummed and then went quiet.

This is it? This will take us to Fontem's private collection? Regnig was still pale, but his eyes were wide with excitement.

"It should. At least, I hope it works properly. I haven't tested this one," I said.

"You first," Rivo said with a grin.

"I wouldn't have it any other way," I said and stepped through the invisible wall. My foot set down in the large storage room where we'd met Polvertan. It had been only months since I'd laid eyes inside the space, but it felt like much longer. Many of the crates sat open, pillaged by Rulo and the others as they went through Fontem's prized possessions. There had to be a reason he'd gone to so much work to keep the assembled crates from anyone's hands.

I walked forward as Regnig bumped into my legs, his small beak wide open. Rivo came next, her expression much the same.

It's real. When I said you were a Recaster, I could tell you were important, but you amaze me still, young man. You found the Theos, stopped an ancient race's plan for destroying the universe, and have now brought me to the famed antiquities collection of the one and only Fontem of Terell. Regnig's thoughts were rushed and excited. He hobbled forward, setting his hands on a wooden crate.

These took him a lifetime to collect. Who would desecrate such a thing?

"The Keppe were with me. They were soldiers, looking for loot to bring to their admiral. They're not unlike most races. They think of weapons before anything else," I said, not faulting Rulo, Hectal, and Kimtra for taking what they had.

Regnig slid a small book out of his robe. It looked oversized in his little talons. *Let's begin.*

We spent a few hours going over the book, referencing the catalog numbers in the manifest Pol had been searching through. Once we understood the code for the book, it became much easier. Most of it was interesting, but not what I was after.

I sat back, drinking some water from the small pack we'd brought along, when Rivo called my name.

"We found it. This has to be it. He went to great lengths to hide it among this other useless stuff," Rivo said.

My heart raced, and I crossed the cluttered room, stepping over open crates lying across the floor like live land mines.

This is very dangerous. I've translated his last entry. Regnig ran a talon over the book's parchment, carefully reading Fontem's words. *This is the last entry, for I have found my life's work at an end. It is here. It exists. After all these years of loneliness, I will see her once again. Farewell.*

Regnig didn't have to tell us who "she" was. Fontem spent his life searching for a time-travel machine so he could relive his time with his wife.

"What of the other Fontem? The one from the former timeline?" I asked, unsure I wanted the answer.

That, I don't know.

I looked over the handwriting, noticing the last phrase was rushed, written by an excited hand.

"Where is it?" I asked, scanning the small makeshift desk Rivo had created.

"Here," she said, tapping a wooden box.

"This? It looks so small," I said, holding the box in my hand. I flipped open the nondescript case – meant to keep it looking harmless, I suspected. Inside was an object the size of a wallet. It was clear, and when my finger touched it, the screen came to life. Colors swirled on it, and I set it back down, fearing I would somehow activate it and end up somewhere I didn't want to be.

Careful. This is dangerous indeed. We do not understand the consequences of traveling in time. Do other times exist on separate timelines, or does something changed in the past affect our current reality? This has been a discussion of speculation for countless generations among the best philosophers out there. I've read many tomes on the subject.

I had no answer for him. The only experience I had on the subject was from Eighties movies and books.

"How does it work?"

I needed to know. If things went south, I wanted a backup for my family. I felt Rivo's eyes burning into the side of my face, while I avoided making eye contact with anyone. I thought about the power of such a device. Could I go back before the Event and convince the powers that be to mount a defense against such an invasion? Would I be able to save the countless people that died from that horrible experience?

Or would my efforts mean nothing on our current timeline? Did we have an infinite amount of alternate realities going on right now, changing with each decision? The thoughts were giving me a headache.

Be warned that to play with this could be very disruptive. There was a reason Fontem hid it so well.

"But he did use it. I wonder what happened to him," I said as I looked at the device. I had the urge to close the case, but I was drawn to it. I had to understand how to use it, at least. Even if it never saw the light of day again, I needed it.

———————

I slept for a couple hours back at Regnig's, only because I knew it was safe. I didn't want to leave everyone waiting, but I wasn't going to be of use to the plan if I was sleep-deprived. Rivo took the chance to sleep as well, and Regnig woke us after two hours passed. He had a worried look on his face but didn't say anything further on the time-travel device I had stored in my EVA.

"Here, take this," I said, handing him the second side to the portal.

You want to leave this with me?

"Who better? Sort through Fontem's possessions and see what you can make of them. And if you can find out where the real ship's located, do that." I was more curious than anything to see where he'd hidden it.

Very well. I am pleased to have this opportunity.

"Dean, we better get going. Who knows how long they'll wait for you before heading to Udoon?" Rivo said, stretching her arms and getting off the small couch.

"They'll wait. Slate won't leave without me." I knelt down, setting a hand lightly on Regnig's shoulder. "Thank you for your help. Once again, you've proven invaluable. Would it be okay to visit you soon? Maybe with my wife and baby?"

Regnig's beak opened and closed a few times, his one eye narrowing. *I'd be thrilled for the company.*

It wasn't long before we were once again walking back past the guards in the ornately decorated portal room, ready to leave Bazarn Five.

I found the icon for the world just outside Udoon, and Rivo and I disappeared from Bazarn, only to appear on the distant world milliseconds later.

An alien stood at the doorway to the plain room, casually leaning against the frame like it had nowhere better to be. Its arms were short, only hanging halfway down its long, thin torso. Light green skin stretched tightly over a bony body. Its deep-set eyes stared toward us on the otherwise expressionless face.

"Hi. We're looking for Cee-eight," I said without the translator on.

"I am Cee-eight," it said in my language. The voice was high-pitched, though it could belong to a male or a female, if they had sex differentiation. The universal translator implants seemed to be everywhere, and not for the first time, I considered getting one. "I've been expecting you."

Something about the alien was off. "Where are my friends?" I asked.

"They are awaiting your arrival. The big one with the armored body wanted to leave already, but the smooth pale one you call Slate made them wait," it said, crossing the room to stand close to me. "Dean, I presume?"

"That's me. Nice to meet you, Cee-eight. Thank you for helping us out at short notice," I said, smiling at the creature before me. Rivo looked uncomfortable and cleared her throat. "I'm sorry. Cee-eight, this is Rivo Alnod."

Cee-eight's deep eyes widened. "Not of *the* Alnods?"

"The very same," Rivo said in English.

"You are an interesting group. Three humans, a Keppe warrior, and Garo Alnod's daughter. No wonder the Empress paid so well. I'll be coming with you, by the way," Cee-eight said.

I bristled at the comment. "I was under the impression we were borrowing your ship." I didn't like the idea of other people getting involved with our mission. Too many hands in the cookie jar was never a good thing, especially when you didn't know or trust two of the hands.

"It's *my* ship, and I'm the only one who pilots her. If you have any issues with that, I'll send the credits back to the Empress now." Cee-eight looked pleased.

"You really want to anger her?" I asked, calling the bluff.

"We go way back. We're nearly sisters. Plus, you'll never be able to pull off whatever you're doing on Udoon without a credible known entity like me." Cee-eight was either lying or being honest. I tried to imagine how this strange alien could be tied up with the Empress of the deadly Bhlat, and couldn't. At least I knew Cee-eight was female now.

"Sure. Fine, have it your way. We need to," I said and set a hand on Rivo's shoulder.

"Have it your way, Dean. This way," Cee-eight said, leading us out of the portal room. Like most of them, it was underground, only this one had an elevator at the end of a hall to bring us to the surface.

The space was cramped with the three of us inside, and I was suddenly grateful for having my EVA helmet on, supplying fresh oxygen. Cee-eight wore light fabric over her bony body, and she moved like a branch in the wind, flowing and effortless. Even when she was still in the elevator, she swayed from side to side.

I'd expected a quick ride, but it was minutes later, and we still hadn't stopped. "Where are we going?"

"To my ship," Cee-eight answered.

I didn't question it again. While we rode in silence, I thought about W and hoped he was getting to his destination. The others didn't know about his mission, and a lot was riding on him not encountering any issues along the way. I'd have to sneak away to check on him when we got to Udoon.

Rivo looked about to say something, when the elevator stopped, the doors chiming and sliding open. Now I knew why it had taken so long to arrive. I stepped clear of the elevator and noticed we weren't on the surface. We were in a building thousands of yards above the ground. From here, I could see ships all around the clear-walled open space we stood in, each parked with a blue beam locking them into place. I looked down, through the clear floor, and saw clouds a thousand feet below my boots. My skin crawled as I stepped forward, feeling like there was nothing but a thin piece of glass between me and a freefall.

Rivo didn't seem to be bothered by it at all, and she walked out freely. Cee-eight noticed and smiled at the small blue woman.

"What is this place?" I asked. I scanned the open room to see a line of desks, with aliens of all kinds in line to speak with someone. It looked like a bizarre DMV.

"This is where anyone coming in or out of our planet comes. I have a docking slot here permanently, since I'm always making runs. No one gets in or out without stopping here first." Cee-eight walked past the lines of aliens, some familiar, others as confusing to my senses as anything I'd ever seen. She waved a badge at a purple blob wearing a sash, and it scanned her in, waving a gelatin arm at her. "Thanks, Jossu."

I walked closer to Cee-eight and whispered in her narrow ear hole, "What was that?"

"Jossu? A Cib. They're a good bunch. They emerge from a mother twenty at a time, and sit in a natural rock bowl for the first hundred years of their lives. One by one, they form into their own sentient beings, like Jossu." Cee-eight made this sound like it was normal, and I couldn't help but realize there was still so much I didn't know.

"That doesn't sound too bad," Rivo said with a shrug.

"If you say so," I commented, not sure I wanted to share a rock bowl with nineteen siblings for a hundred years.

We kept moving and arrived at a conveyor belt that rotated the outskirts of the ship dock. Cee-eight scanned her badge, and we started moving. We passed a dozen ships of varying proportions before stopping at a mid-sized freighter ship. It had clasps at the tail end of it, and that told me it was used for hauling objects. For now, they dangled empty.

"This is her. My ship." Cee-eight tapped a code on the clear wall between us and the ship, and an energy field spread out, enveloping it with a soft glow. The wall spread apart at seams I hadn't even noticed, and the floor extended until we got to the ship's lowering ramp. It was an interesting system. Most of the docks I'd seen were indoors, but this one had all of the ships parked outside the facility.

"What took you so long?" Slate was standing inside the ship, a hand on his hip like a scolding mother.

"We had somewhere to be," was all I said. Rulo was inside too, sitting on a chair in the corner of the room. There was no sign of Denise. "Where is she?"

Slate knew who I meant. "Having a nap. We didn't know when you'd be getting back, so we took turns sleeping."

"I hope you were comfortable enough," Cee-eight said to them, and Slate shrugged.

"It was fine. Can we get going, boss? It's going to be close. We need to beat the Kraski ship there. Kinca doesn't seem like the type to be late for a meeting with Lom of Pleva," he said.

"Yes. Cee-eight, how quick can we be at Udoon?" I asked our pilot.

She smiled at me, and with her odd physique, it made me think of a grinning skeleton. "Don't blink."

TWENTY-EIGHT

*I*t turned out I blinked about two thousand times before we arrived, but it was only a few hours. Cee-eight's ship was clunky, with loose wires dangling about. She called them modifications, and I didn't ask any further questions. When she fired up the engines and gunned the thrusters, the lights dimmed, and I could tell she was putting everything into speed, not trip ambiance. I appreciated it.

I sat in the cramped cockpit with her, staring out the viewscreen. The station came into sight, and it looked just like the screenshots the Empress had shown us, only seeing it in person was surreal. The tablet I'd seen on Earth gave it the illusion of a cheap outer-space Las Vegas. Seeing the glowing signs, and arrows directing you to your specific desires, only reiterated the Vegas vibe to me.

There had to be hundreds of ships nearby, each locked into place, much like on Cee-eight's world. I scanned them visually on the computer by zooming in, and looked for a Kraski-style vessel. I didn't see any. We didn't know what type of ship Lom would be arriving in, so it was no use looking for signs of him. I didn't even know what he looked like at this point.

"I'll bring us in. I know where we can get in discreetly, away from any surveillance. There are a lot of... unsavory visitors traveling to Udoon, and many of them would prefer not to be seen or heard. I'm one of those characters." Cee-eight slowed her ship, dancing it lithely around some backed-up space traffic. Rivo stood behind me now, her small frame allowing her to fit in the space behind the chair.

"I wonder if my father's ever been here," Rivo said casually.

"I doubt it, Rivo. You father sticks to classier joints than Udoon." Cee-eight spun the ship around, using her thrusters while descending, lining up perfectly between two larger ships. From most vantage points, her ship wouldn't even be visible beneath the others' bulky exteriors. She knew what she was doing, and I was lucky to have her guiding us.

I hoped we weren't too late. I needed at least an hour to get to the room, and to visit W without anyone noticing. The time-travel device was tiny and light, but it weighed heavily on my mind. I almost wished I hadn't brought it. If it got in the hands of someone like Lom of Pleva, who knew what kind of damage he could do with it?

Cee-eight got up and moved quickly to the back of the ship, Rivo and I following closely behind. The others were waiting for us in the cargo bay of the freighter, their obvious weapons tucked away in large black duffel bags. I grabbed one, and we made our way to the inside of the Udoon station. The room we were in was quiet; a few aliens passed by with obvious destinations, and then we were left alone. The walls weren't clear here, but a plain dark gray, with no viewports or screens to see the blackness of space beyond.

There was a planet called Udoon below, but from all accounts, it was a simple place, full of the Udoon people happy to reap the tax benefits of having a guilty pleasure station above their world. As we walked, I saw a few of the Udoon race, recognizing them from the data packet the Empress had provided me. They walked on four legs, with a head like a small hippopotamus at the front, wearing colorful flowing clothing that stopped just short of dragging on the ground as they walked. Mist blew from collars around their thick necks into their faces, as they were used to a humid environment. I didn't want to go to the planet's surface and experience the instant dampness that must soak your body if you weren't used to it.

Cee-eight stopped one of them, chatting to them in a series of low groans. She came back with a smile. "Let's go. Maintenance will be at your destination shortly. You'll have access while the doors are blocked off from interruption."

The Empress really had thought of everything. I was impressed. "Thanks, Cee." I made sure the portal stick was in my suit pocket, and turned back to the others. "I'll go there with Cee. It'll only take a few minutes. Why don't you guys go somewhere and keep a low profile?"

"There's a lounge close by. Best *tenipro* out there." Cee-eight gave Denise instructions, and Slate walked over to me.

"Boss? You sure going alone is a good idea? What's with you? You don't think one of us is the mole, do you?" Slate looked hurt as he asked.

"No." I hoped that was the truth. Slate had been with me through so much, I couldn't imagine him being the one to stab me in the back, but I had to be careful. "Don't worry about it. A ragtag group like us will draw a lot more attention than a familiar face like Cee-eight talking business with a human."

He nodded like it made sense and leaned in. "We're going to get Karo back. Then we go home. I'm thinking of retiring," he said quietly.

"From what?" It was a serious question.

"From all of this. Denise and I can settle down. Get a house, start a family. Our kids can grow up together, boss." Slate glanced over at Denise, and she looked lovingly back at him.

"That sounds perfect, buddy. I'm with you." I thought about what retirement even meant. Would I be able to step away from the Gatekeepers and all the trouble I constantly found myself in? Did I have a choice as this Recaster, or whatever I was? I was like a magnet for conflict. Would I be happy being mayor of Terran Thirteen, maybe eventually being in charge of all New Spero, like Mayor Patel had suggested? I didn't know the answer.

I shoved the future projecting aside and worried about our current situation. In a few hours, Kinca, the Kraski leader, would be meeting Lom of Pleva with our friend Karo, the last remaining living Theos. That was what I needed to concentrate on.

Cee-eight grabbed my arm and led me away. I grimaced as I looked back to see my gang staring after me before turning to head to some dive bar to wait for me.

We passed dozens of storefronts, lounges, and eating establishments. Some places were blatant in their attempts to get visitors, showing images of various naked creatures, all of which made me want to run away faster. Smells of food lingered in the air, some appealing, while others made me nauseous as we ambled on down the halls.

"Here we are," Cee-eight said, and right on cue, two robots rolled up, wearing yellow vests and holding random tools. They didn't say anything. Instead, they scanned Cee-eight's badge, opened the door, and put a red energy barrier up so no one could get by. Cee-eight stayed outside with them, and I closed the door. With a deep breath, I tried to calm myself. Everything was going to be okay. In a few hours, we could start our trek home.

I pulled out the other side of the portal device and activated it before looking around the now-familiar room. It was exactly the same as the one the Empress' robots and drones had built back in Egypt. The portal glowed until it filled the space from wall to wall, floor to ceiling; then it disappeared. It was invisible to the eye. I stepped through it, closing my eyes and listening for a difference.

The variance of sound was there but hardly noticeable. Once through, I looked around the room, and couldn't see any difference from the one back on Udoon. Everyone thought the portal was going to lead us onto the ice world, where we'd left an identical room, but they were wrong. Instead, it led to the duplicate I'd had the Empress make without anyone else knowing.

I went to the far corner and found the secret latch I'd had the robots add in. With a tug, the panel snapped off, and I found myself in the cargo bay of a Bhlat ship.

"W?" I called, and walked down a corridor toward the compact bridge.

"Hello, Captain. It is nice to see you here." W's voice carried down the hall as I approached. "We are at our destination." He motioned to the viewscreen. We were far from any known sentient beings. The remote corner of the universe, as the Empress had called it. Without her wormhole drives, it would have taken more than my life-time to travel this far, even with the advanced FTL drive.

"Very good. Thank you, W."

He didn't respond to the polite comment. "Is there anything else you need of me?" he asked.

"No. We're going to sneak you out to the space sta-tion with me. We have to be quick. Remember, the others don't know about the ship. They think the portal's going to lead to the ice world."

W stood up, and his electronic eyes stared at me. "I understand, Captain, and will not speak a word of it."

I grabbed my communication device that went direct-ly to the Empress and tapped it on. "Empress, it's Dean Parker."

Her voice carried over the line, and I was amazed at the technology, seamlessly allowing us to speak while so far apart. "Dean, good to hear from you. Did W tell you about the backup surprise?" she asked.

I glanced at the robot, who remained silent. "Not yet. What is it?"

"The ship is armed with explosives. W will give you the trigger. Should you need to escalate things, don't be afraid to use it. There's also a tablet with a live feed of the Kraski colony. Use it to show them your show of force. We're scheduled to jump there in under two hours. The timing should be impeccable."

W reached down and passed me a small pen-shaped object. The trigger. I eyed it, worried I might accidentally set it off. It had a flip top and a button beneath. I slid it carefully into my pocket and sighed.

"Anything else I should know?" I asked her.

"Surveillance on the ice world shows no ships approaching yet. I'll keep you posted on any developments," the Empress said, clearly invested in the outcome. I wondered what it was that had her so involved on a personal level. I decided not to ask.

Could I have been wrong? Was the traitor not as close to me as I'd assumed? "Thanks, Empress. Wish me luck."

"Luck has nothing to do with it, Dean. You will do what you need to do," she said and ended the transmission.

"W, let's go," I said with one last look at the colorful nebulas in the far distance through the viewscreen. The robot bent down and hit a button. The ship shook, and I nearly fell over. "What the hell was that?"

"The engines, Captain. They are now detached. This ship has no weapons, with the exception of the explosives attached to the underbelly, and now it has no way of being flown." W turned and lumbered toward the back of the ship.

I followed him, and we entered the secret room together before I snapped the panel back in place. "Don't say anything once we're through." W didn't comment, and we stepped through the invisible portal, arriving back on Udoon. Everything was set. The space was empty. Apparently, it was a room meant for clandestine meetings. No chairs, no tables; just dark walls and floors. I wondered how many altercations happened here, and how many dirty deals were done right where I stood.

I opened the door, and the maintenance bots removed the red barrier with the touch of a button. I stepped into the hall, and W was close behind. "Cee-eight, get my friend somewhere quiet. Don't let the others see him here."

"Very well," Cee-eight said, giving me directions to the lounge, where the others were waiting. I kept my eyes down, trying to avoid eye contact with any of the different beings that roamed the station. As I neared the lounge, I saw a Kraski trying to hide beneath a hooded robe. Its familiar eyes burned through the shadows as it peered around anxiously. I turned my head as I walked past it and cut into the bar without being noticed.

I instantly recognized Slate's short blond hair from behind and headed for their table. Denise was beside him, hand pressed down on the table. I thought they'd stand out like a sore thumb, but after looking around, there were nothing but motley crews of various aliens hanging out, many in random groups. We might have actually been one of the less conspicuous assemblies in the bar.

Rulo saw me coming and slid over on a bench on the left side of the table. The room was packed and musty, making me sweat from the heat and anticipation.

I leaned in. "It's done."

"Good. Now we just have to wait," Slate said. "But not for long."

"I saw a Kraski in the hall. They're here." My voice wasn't much more than a whisper, but everyone seemed to hear me.

My earpiece buzzed, and Cee-eight's voice came through. "Dean, your target has arrived at the destination. He has the package with him."

I tapped it. "Thank you for the information."

We stood as one, everyone's jaws tight and faces serious. "We get Karo back now and end this Kraski threat," I said. We headed for the room that was waiting for Kinca with my trap.

TWENTY-NINE

*I*t turned out Kinca had entered with Karo – the package – and with two other Kraski. There had been no sign of Lom of Pleva yet, according to Cee-eight. I really hoped I could trust her. My gut was telling me I might be walking into a trap as well. I grabbed the communicator that I had connected to the Empress' own device and programmed it into my earpiece. I didn't want her message getting through to anyone else's ears.

"Do we wait?" Slate asked, and I thought about it.

"Just a few minutes," I said in hushed tones. Solving the Kraski threat and getting Karo back were my main objectives. If I could avoid seeing Lom of Pleva entirely, that would be ideal. I imagined getting this dealt with and sneaking out before he showed up. He would be upset, but then we could deal with him another day. "On second thought, let's go in. Rulo, you guard the door outside. Don't let anyone through. Rivo, you stay out of the way. If anything happens to you, your father will be as angry with me as Lom of Pleva. I can't afford another enemy."

Rivo looked ready to argue but bit her tongue and backed away, heading down the hall.

"Slate and Denise, you're with me." They both

grabbed guns – Slate a pulse rifle and Denise a pistol. We were ready. "No time like the present."

I opened the door to the room, but as I started forward, Slate set a big hand on my shoulder, holding me back. "I'll go first," he said with authority. I let him.

He entered, and Denise and I were right behind him. One step we were on the Udoon station; the next we were in a copycat room, tens of thousands of light years away. My two allies assumed we were on the ice world.

The Kraski leader's eyes went wide, and his guards fumbled for weapons.

"Keep them down, Kinca," I said, recognizing the Kraski with a scar across his face.

"How… where is he?" Kinca asked, looking behind us. I didn't follow his gaze.

"Lom isn't here yet. It's just us." For the first time, I noticed the tall figure in the corner. He wore a black cloak, hiding him in the dark room. "Karo, are you okay?"

His head snapped up as if he'd been sleeping, his eyes dazed and unfocused. Clearly he was drugged.

I spoke slowly but firmly. "This is simple, Kinca. Right now, Keppe, Motrill, and Bhlat forces are surrounding your little piece of heaven you stole from the Motrill. If you don't give us Karo right now, the last of your small foothold in the universe will be destroyed."

"I don't believe you, Parker," Kinca said, his hand ready to grab a weapon from its holster.

"Maybe you'll believe this," I said, pulling the tablet out. I held my breath, hoping the Empress' timing was as good as she claimed it would be. The Keppe were hesitantly following the Bhlat's lead on this mission. Lord Crul must have hated that, and I could only imagine Admiral Yope's stoic face turning dark in anger. He would be leading the Keppe charge at the colony world, using the wormhole tech that was newly fitted to their fleet.

I turned it over, revealing a live feed of their world. A space station orbited around it, a few ships and satellites blinking lights in our view.

"There's nothing there out of the ordinary..." he started to say but stopped as the fleets appeared on the probe's wide camera angle. Dozens of sleek Motrill ships arrived, with the Keppe fleet right behind them. I recognized the markings of *Starbound* and gave a silent prayer for the crew. Magnus and his family were away on an expedition, and I was grateful to keep them out of my crazy plan.

Seconds later, the Bhlat forces materialized through black rifts, twenty huge warships covering the other side of the world from a thousand kilometers away. They'd make quick work of the Kraski world.

"What is this?" Kinca cried out.

"This is me angry, Kinca." I stepped toward him. "First you come to Earth and send hybrids to do your bidding. You made them trick us into befriending them. Loving them, even! They're people too. They aren't disposable creatures!" I was yelling now, thinking about Janine, who I later learned was Mae, and then the second Janine thrust in her place, and how hard that must have been on her. She'd died because of the Kraski, like countless others.

"We had no choice," he said, his voice a low growl.

"There's always a choice," I responded.

"Like how you chose to kill us all," he accused.

"You beamed everyone off Earth and sent them to die. You enslaved the Deltra…"

"We were forced to do that after your new friends, the Bhlat, nearly disposed of every last one of us," he said, running a finger along his scar. So that was where he got it.

"Then we offer you a choice. Give us Karo, release any human hybrids you have, and we'll spare you. Leave Udoon station now and never come back." I lowered my arm and the tablet with it. I glanced over my shoulder to make sure no one had come into the room.

"Then what? Lom of Pleva wants this being," Kinca said, looking behind me nervously.

I had to be quick. Lom would be there any time. "He's just one man."

The scarred Kraski shook his head. "No. He is much more."

My earpiece buzzed, and I tapped it. "Dean, our sensors have picked up activity on the ice world. Ships have arrived and are lowering toward the decoy."

I whispered into the mic, "Whose ships are they?"

"We aren't sure. Something new."

It had to be Lom's people. We'd been betrayed, and the trap was sprung. My eyes scanned back and forth. Was this all a big trick by the Empress to create chaos among the lesser forces out there? Did she have fun pulling puppet strings? My experience with her had taught me she was tough but caring of her people. She didn't treat me with anything but respect, and I doubted she was behind it.

Kinca and I stared at each other for a moment as I tried to figure it out. My gaze scanned from Denise to Slate. Was it one of them? It had to be someone close to us. Rivo? W? Rulo? What would their motivation be? Damn it. I was running out of time.

"Give him to us or perish," I threatened. "I know this is your last home base. You're done if we destroy this world, and you deserve it after your crimes. Give us Karo, you walk away, your people get to live, but remember this moment. Remember the forces I can assemble against you, and never, I mean never, come to New Spero again." My blood was pumping hard, and I was standing inches away from the tall Kraski, looking into his hard eyes.

Kinca stood straight-backed but slouched enough for me to see his decision made. "Let him go," he said, and the guard holding on to the Theos released his grip.

Karo stumbled forward and Slate grabbed his arm, leading him across and through the portal, and I saw him cross back into the real room on Udoon. Of course, the others didn't know they weren't there as well at that moment.

It was time to get out of there, before Lom arrived. "Take care, Kinca. Remember our agreement. Stay to yourself, and don't so much as breathe my name again."

I turned to leave, Denise beside me, when Slate stepped back inside. Denise kicked out, knocking Slate's rifle out of his surprised hands. "Wha…" he started to say, when her fist clocked him in the jaw, a snapping sound filling the room. His hands went up in defense, but Denise just stood there, holding a gun on him.

"Denise, what the hell are you doing?" I asked, reaching for my pulse pistol.

"Don't do it, Dean. Or he's dead," she said.

Slate's eyes were hard, disbelief crossing his face.

"That's right. Or you're all dead. And you don't want that, do you, Dean?" a new voice asked. I'd been so preoccupied with Slate, and Denise's betrayal, I hadn't seen anyone enter the room.

The three Kraski each held guns in their hands now, unsure who to point them at. I backed up, pressing my shoulders against the wall away from everyone, and looked at the newcomer. This could only be one man: Lom of Pleva.

He stood at least seven feet tall. His shoulders were wide, along with the rest of him, bulky in a fit and powerful way. Half of his face was metal, a matte gray material; the other half was scarred and pale. It was then I heard the slight whirring of robotics when he moved. He was half robot, a cyborg.

"Lom," I said, trying to sound tough, but my voice caught in my throat. "We finally meet."

"Yes. Thank you for placing the Theos in my hands, Dean," Lom said in English. He smiled, his half-mouth baring teeth too perfect to be natural.

"Where is he?" I asked, my heart racing in my chest.

"He'll be in my team's hands soon enough," was his

only answer. "Kinca, you've failed me. I've tried to help you for years, but every time, your people fail and fail hard. I gave you weapons. I gave you the technology to beam an entire people off a planet, and you squandered it all. The hybrids… you can't do anything right." Lom stepped into the room, now between Slate and me.

His footsteps were light, soundless in the quiet box. "Lom, we've done all we know how. I think it unfair to say…" Kinca started to say, when Lom brought up an arm, firing two beams from a fingertip of his left hand. The guard to the right of Kinca dropped, then the one to his left.

Kinca stared down at the two bodies and backed himself into the room's far corner. "I've done everything you've ever asked of me. We've paid you everything we had."

"And now that your usefulness has ended for me, our arrangement is over," Lom said casually.

"What does that mean?" the Kraski leader asked.

"It means what you think it means," Lom said. "Dean, would you be so kind as to point that tablet in your hand at Kinca?"

I hesitated but turned the tablet up, seeing the image of the Kraski world much as it had been minutes before. Lom tapped his foot five times, and we witnessed the first explosion go off on the planet. Then a second, a third, and one last fiery eruption. Bright orange energy shot out from the world, and an energy source appeared in the center of the planet's destruction, sucking everything in the area into it.

Ships from the invading fleets struggled against the force; then there was nothing but empty space where the Kraski world had been. Kinca fell to his knees, screaming out.

"You see? I don't like loose ends," Lom said.

Kinca stretched to grab a gun from his fallen guard, but Denise was quicker. She took a second to spin to the Kraski, firing a single pulse at him from her pistol, before swinging back to aim at Slate. Kinca crumpled on the ground, dead in an instant.

This wasn't going to end well. I knew it in my gut and hated myself for getting stuck in the trap. I'd been so foolish. Of course it had been Denise. She had access to things as a policewoman, like cameras, ID codes, and anything else. She was trusted, and she'd integrated with us through Slate. It was just like…

My eyes went wide, and Lom's one good eye squinted at me, his half-mouth smiling again.

The Empress started talking quickly into my ear, but I didn't hear her words. It was all white noise.

Slate looked crestfallen, destroyed. I needed to snap out of it and figure a way to still win the day.

"You see it now, don't you, Dean?" Lom asked, still smiling.

"The hybrids. You didn't give all of the models to the Kraski, did you?" I asked, looking at Denise.

"No, I didn't. They've proven their worth, especially this one." Lom glanced over to Denise, who grinned back at him.

"Denise, is it true?" Slate asked her.

"Shut up, Zeke." She said his real name with contempt. "God, you're so weak. Following this one" – she jabbed a thumb in the air toward me across the room – "around like a lame puppy. It was painful playing this role." Her words were sharp, and Slate looked like she'd just stabbed him in the chest with them.

"What do you want, Lom?" I asked.

During the seconds it took him to answer, I heard the Empress' voice in my ear. "They've touched down at the room on the ice world. If you have to do anything, do it now, before they realize the trap."

I remembered that Denise didn't know where we really were right now. We weren't on the ice world where we'd built the replica of the room on Udoon; we were in a ship far from any civilizations. A ship with no engines and lined with explosives. All I needed to do was get Slate and myself through the portal first, leaving them behind. Then we'd disconnect it and tap the trigger on the pen-like device linked to the bombs.

The realization that the Kraski were gone hit me. There would be a few of them left around, but they had no fleet, no leadership, and from the sounds of it, no credits left to their name. If I could pull this off, we'd be without one of our old enemies and could deal with Lom of Pleva at the same time.

Lom finally spoke. "I want you dead. It's quite simple."

"Then what are you waiting for?" I asked stupidly. I was trying to distract him, to get him pacing the room, moving away from the invisible portal barrier. It worked.

Lom stepped forward. Denise remained still, pointing a gun at Slate, keeping her distance from his long reach in case he tried anything. I huddled close to the barrier, waiting for the moment to act as Lom spoke. "You're a lot of trouble. I've heard all the stories. Very impressive for a weak human. But you're more than that, aren't you, Dean? More than the rest of your pathetic race."

I still held my pistol, waiting for the right moment. Firing at Lom would be a dangerous gamble. He was only half flesh and likely had a shield covering him. I had only one other alternative.

"I'm just an accountant," I said, and his forehead scrunched up, like he didn't understand the word. "Why don't you just let us go our way, and you go yours?"

"You see, I can't do that. But I'll give you an option. I come bearing an opportunity," Lom said.

"What's that?" I asked. My finger twinged on the trigger of the pulse pistol.

"Work for me. You'll be wealthier than you could imagine, live anywhere you want. Dean, you haven't seen the luxuries out there. Your wife would love it. And that little pink baby of yours too."

I clenched my jaw, and he looked amused as he watched me tense in anger. "Relax, Dean. I wouldn't harm them. Not if you agree to my terms. This one will have to die, though. I'm sorry."

Slate was my brother. He was my sidekick and my best friend. I saw Denise step back slightly as her finger tightened on the trigger. I had no choice. I fired once, twice, three times, and she fell to the ground, holes blasted through her body. "Go, Slate, go!" I yelled, and he stared at the dead body in front of him before looking over at me with a sadness I'd never seen on his face before. It was then I noticed he was holding his left arm in agony. She'd hit him. His hesitation was over. He ran through the barrier, and I was right behind him, only something blocked my way through.

"I don't think so, Dean. You're not going anywhere."

THIRTY

I struggled to get past the barrier, but it was to no avail. He had me trapped.

"I've heard you consider yourself quite the intelligent person. Not smart enough to fool me, though, were you? As we speak, a hundred of my soldiers are advancing on this building," Lom said, his voice light and friendly. "Did you really think I wouldn't figure it out? Even without Denise, it would have been simple enough."

I let him talk, hoping Slate had taken the portal down from his end. Lom saw my gaze flicker to where the portal barrier had sat invisible, and he stuck his arm through it. But I knew now we weren't going back to Udoon. Slate had taken the barrier down. Lom of Pleva and I were alone on a ship bound for nowhere, and I had no way out.

That feeling of finality hit me once again. I'd had it a few times. Once when I raced down the roads of South America, with no one but Carey at my side. On the bridge of the Bhlat ship when General Blel fought the Empress for control of their fleet, when I thought Mary was dead. Then only a few months ago, when I headed straight for the Unwinding with a dimensional Shifter in my grip.

This felt much like each of those times, but I didn't have a knot in my stomach or sweat dripping down my back this time.

Calm washed over me as I locked eyes with Lom. He was imposing: part machine, tall and broad, only half a face showing, the other half covered in metal. But I had the upper hand.

Now that I knew he couldn't escape through the portal barrier, I raised my hands up. "You got me. How about we consider this deal you're speaking of?"

Lom measured me with his gaze. "You expect me to trust you?"

"Why not? Have you ever heard of me not being trustworthy? I'm Dean Parker, the guy who cut deals with the Deltra…"

He finished my sentence. "Then killed them."

"You would have too, in my position. And one of the Deltra eventually became a great friend of mine. An inventor named Kareem." His eye widened at this, as if it was news to him. "The Deltra broke the trust first. Hell, I have alliances with your own hybrids. Don't forget the Bhlat. Add in the Keppe now; even the Supreme of the Volim and I are on good speaking terms. Toss in Garo Alnod and his resources, and I have to say I have some good references." I stood up straight and felt the grip of his barrier loosen on me.

"You are persuasive, I'll give you that. Karo. Where is he?" he asked.

I hesitated. "You didn't have men waiting to grab him on Udoon station?"

"I wasn't expecting Kinca to give in so easily. I thought he had a backbone." Lom leaned casually. He started walking for the back of the room. I let him. It was sealed. "How do I get out of here?"

"I'll show you," I said. "What do you need Karo for?" I asked as I walked to the hidden panel that would lead us to the cargo bay of a ship, instead of to the ice world he was expecting.

"The Theos? I've tried for years to find them. Somehow you did it. Karo's blood will sustain me. I'll become immortal, like any man of greatness such as myself should be. And just think of the hybrids we can create. How about some Theos and human genetics mixed together? A race of beings that will live long, without health concerns, and so much more." He paused, and I stopped at the panel, my hands ready to pop it out. "Your daughter could live forever, Dean. Is there a reason you wouldn't want that for Jules?"

"Don't you say her name again," I whispered, not looking back at him. I popped the panel out and motioned for him to pass through.

"You first," he said calmly.

I obliged and entered the cargo bay, running for the far end. He was big and struggled through the opening. I ran, hiding behind a crate, and he growled angrily. "What kind of treachery is this?" he screamed before changing languages and talking to himself. He was likely calling his team on the ice world. He repeated a few phrases, then fired at the crates in front of me, which exploded into small pieces. I dropped low to the ground and crawled ten yards away, behind a larger stack of protection. I was wearing a shield dome, but it wouldn't last more than a few shots. I had to be careful.

"What did you do, Dean? Where are we? Why won't my communicator work?" he asked.

Mine worked because the frequency was programmed into the ship's parameters, but all other signals were dead inside this ship. No one would know where he was. My back pressed hard against the metal wall. I goaded him. "What do you mean? We're on the ice world, like you said."

"No. We. Are. Not!" He pounded his feet across the room, and I heard the top crate crash to the ground beside me.

"We're far away, Lom. Far away, indeed." I pulled a thin object from my pocket and stood up, my right hand on the trigger of my pulse pistol. I knew he'd have a shield on too, so it would come down to whose burned out faster. I suspected it would be mine.

"Where?" Saliva dripped down Lom's chin as he asked the question.

"Look for yourself," I said, and he slowly backed up, heading to the far wall, where a computer screen sat recessed into the wall.

He tapped it a few times, and an image appeared on it. It was the view from the front of the ship, the distant colorful nebula filling half of the screen. Otherwise, there was nothing but faraway stars. "I don't recognize this," he said.

"You wouldn't. You know how the universe is ever

expanding? This is somewhere few have laid eyes on. No one will find you here." I stepped out from behind the crates. There was no point in hiding from the inevitable.

"What's your end game?" he asked.

"Karo's safe. I wanted to work it out with the Kraski, but I guess you did me a favor by killing them all. And my family's safe. We'll go on, and you'll die. Here. Now," I said. I was surprised by how steady my voice was.

Lom smiled then laughed, spittle flying out of his thin lips. "You really do regard yourself highly. To think that you, a puny human, can kill Lom of Pleva. I'm centuries old. I've amassed the most wealth in the universe, and have started and ended over a dozen civilizations. You'll either bend your knee to me now, or you will die.

"Not soon, though. I'll take your beaten body and make you watch as I kill your child, then your wife. You'll view it all from above as I destroy New Spero, and then, as I hunt every damned human out there, you'll be by my side, broken, without a tongue to argue, with no hands to fight. You'll watch your people all die, and then, only then, will I consider letting you join them."

"No. You're wrong." This time, my voice did betray my nerves. There was no leaving Lom here to rot. I couldn't risk it, not after what he'd just said. The others were right. This man was a lunatic. He didn't just speak that threat idly, he meant every word of it. I had no choice. I had to make sure he never made it out of here.

I'd told Slate and the others to never reinstall the portal wall. If I was stuck there with Lom, they were to leave it that way. I'd talk to the Empress through my communicator, letting her know it was over. I tapped the earpiece and spoke to Lom. "You and I will die here together today."

Lom laughed again as he pointed a hand at me. Pulse beams shot out, and I ducked and rolled, my shield dome taking the brunt of the abuse. I fired back at him as I stilled, his shield making only the slightest indication it had been hit. He stalked toward me, and I kept firing until the shield began to weaken. He thought he was invincible, but the truth was, I wanted to wear it down enough that the coming explosion would be enough to kill him.

The Empress spoke into my ear. She wished me luck and called me a warrior. "Tell Mary and Jules I love them," I whispered.

He fired at me. My shield wore down as I sat back against a wall, endlessly going shot for shot with Lom. Finally, I saw his visible eye flicker as he looked down to my left hand. I flipped the detonator cap open and gave him a grim smile.

I pictured Mary and Jules in the short time we'd spent together as a family. I saw them growing older together, me watching from the clouds. Jules with her long curly chestnut hair, and Mary holding her hand on the way to her first day of school. These images flooded my eyes as I pressed down on the button, my body bracing for the explosion.

Nothing happened.

THIRTY-ONE

*L*om's instinct had been to duck and run for the edge of the ship, thinking I had the bomb on my person. I got up, firing toward him as I ran for cover. It hadn't worked. The ship was wired to go off with the press of a detonator, and it had failed. Even though I wanted it to work, I still felt relief at being alive. My mind raced, thinking of ways I could I win the day.

"It looks like your plan to kill yourself alongside me was flawed. I told you I'm invincible," Lom of Pleva said.

I rolled my eyes, knowing he had nothing to do with the malfunction.

He kept talking. "See. It's a sign. Join me, Dean."

An idea hit me like a ton of bricks. There was a way to get rid of Lom and survive. I pulled the small device from my pocket, fumbling with it. Regnig and I had spent some time going over how to work the time-travel device Fontem had spent his life searching for. Now, as I heard Lom walking toward me, all of the research on it slipped through my mind like water through a strainer.

He was close now, and I stood, dropping my pulse pistol. "You win."

"Good. I thought you might say that. Just imagine the

look on Alnod's face when we kill him, you by my side. It will be priceless. You see, he did this to me." Lom ran a hand across the left side of his body, where the robotics whirred, and to the plate covering half of his face. "He thought he could kill me so easily, but not even an explosion that large could end my reign."

"My family will be safe, though, right? That's the deal?" I asked, more to appease and distract him as my thumb tapped the final details into the time device.

"As long as you stay in line, then yes. I'm not a monster, Dean." He said this with a dark half-grin that churned my stomach.

I had to prod him now, to anger him so much he would charge me. It was the only way. Sweat dripped down my torso as I nervously waited to activate the device. "Only, you are. You want nothing but power and credits, and for everyone to fear the name Lom of Pleva. What the hell is a Pleva anyway? A backwater swamp planet? Are you the king and lord of a muddy stink hole, Lom?"

"Watch your tongue." He raised a hand. "Deal's off. You will die like I described. I can't wait to see your face as I peel your baby from your wife's arms."

"You'll never see them. You're useless. Trapped by a human in the middle of nowhere. No communication, no engines, and a shield that's nearly dead. You're impotent, Lom," I said, hoping he'd bite.

It worked. Lom yelled in frustration and stepped closer to me. I waited. The rift would open one yard from me, and he needed to be moving so he couldn't stop.

"Come on, let's do this like men!" I yelled, raising my right fist as if we were boxers in a ring.

He ran now, an animalistic snarl over his face. I closed my eyes for a second and pressed the button. The colorful rift opened in an instant, small as a pinprick at first, then upwards and sideways at the same time.

Lom was able to avoid it, crashing into me. We rolled to the ground in a heap, the air gone from my lungs. I gasped, swinging at him. My hand hit his armor, and crumpled.

"You think to trick me?" Lom was on his feet, kicking me in the ribs. I felt something snap as I rolled away. I stumbled to my feet, Lom stalking after me. He swung an arm, his long reach catching me in the shoulder. I spun but kept my footing. Lom was standing right in front of the fold in time.

It hung there, a blotchy circle, reds, greens, and blues cascading around like a whirlwind. He didn't even seem to remember it was behind him.

A blade shot from his left hand, and his face was a mask of horror. "Let's start with the tongue." The sharp edge came at me, cutting into my cheek. Blood poured out, and I took the chance. He was off-balance from his thrust. I kicked low, hitting his right knee. It twisted, going to the ground. I kneed him in the head, on the flesh side.

His blade caught me in the leg. A searing pain coursed through me, causing me to bend over.

"You'll never beat me," Lom shouted, but he was wrong. As soon as he was looming before me, I pushed forward, planting both hands on his torso, shoving him back with all my remaining strength. He stumbled back, entering the colorful vortex. His yells cut off as soon as his head disappeared into the time fold.

I staggered around it, seeing I was alone in the room. I tapped it closed and fell to the ground, my back pressed against a stack of crates. It worked. Lom of Pleva was gone, sent into another time.

I pressed a palm to my cheek, which stung fiercely, as did my wounded leg. Each breath came with a sharp pain, and I knew my rib was broken.

I looked down at the device and double-checked the stats. My stomach knotted up tightly when I saw what I'd done. I'd meant to send him into the future, far away, so I wouldn't have to think of his name ever again. The device wasn't built on Earth years, so the math was suspect, but I'd intended to program it for two thousand of our years.

But in my rush and half-concentration, it was set for around twenty Earth years.

I sat there, staring at it, wondering if he'd arrive in our own timeline twenty years from now, or if he was on a parallel one. My head pounded as I got to my feet, the blood loss becoming worrisome now.

"Empress. Communicate with Slate. Tell him to open the portal again. It's done. I'm coming home."

---

*W*e sat inside Cee-eight's ship, ready to start the trip

back home. Rulo remained quiet, her pride shaken after Lom of Pleva had blasted a shield around her and walked by her at the doorway. I told her it wasn't her fault he got through. There was no way to prevent it, but it didn't seem to help. Rivo was the only one of us with some energy. She was thrilled at the outcome and couldn't wait to tell her father that his nemesis was gone.

Karo was there, eyes bright and wide as he stared out the viewscreen. I think he assumed his time was over, and he hadn't spoken much since we'd gotten him on board. Lom's hired goons had broken when Cee-eight bribed them as they engaged her ship, holding Karo. She told them Lom was dead, and they hadn't put up much of a fight.

Then there was Slate. He was in the small quarters, lying on a bunk that was too short for his tall frame. I made my way inside the room and closed the door.

"Slate, I'm sorry," I told my friend. He didn't move, and his back was to me while he faced the wall. My face was bandaged; all of my injuries had been fixed, but I might have scars. They'd remind me how close it had been.

"It's not your fault. How could I be so stupid, Dean?" Slate asked, and I noticed how he called me by my name, and not "boss." It sounded good, like we were equals. He claimed he didn't mean anything by the term "boss," but it always made me think he felt like my subordinate, instead of my co-conspirator or friend.

"What do you mean?" I asked.

"She was a hybrid. Looking back, it's so obvious. Of

course she was the mole. Damn it, Dean. The first woman I fall in love with, and she's using me." Slate now turned and swung his legs off the bed, his feet hitting the ground softly.

"I understand that only too well," I offered. "It seems we both had the same thing happen."

He thought about it and gave me a weak smile. "You're right." His gaze averted from mine. "We even killed each other's."

Slate was clearly still ashamed for killing Mae back on the Bhlat station, but I'd long ago forgiven him. "Forgive me, Zeke," I said, using his real name. I went and sat beside him on the bed, and put my arm around his wide shoulders. "Forgive me for having to kill her like that in front of you."

"She was about to shoot me, so I can only say thank you. We're even now, I suppose," Slate said.

"Can things go back to normal between us?" I asked him.

He nodded. "They already are." He said the words, but I could see the pain racking his body and mind. It would be a while before he'd heal from this one. He held his arm close to his body, and I saw the fresh pink skin. Cee-eight's medical kit had cleaned up his injury well, but a damaged arm was something we both shared.

Slate leaned back, his right arm propping him up. "Dean, I'm sorry I didn't come help you."

"You weren't supposed to."

"Do you know how hard that was? I thought you were going to die," he said.

"I know. But I didn't. I have too much to live for."

"You do."

"And so do you. You'll get over this, Slate. You'll be stronger for it. Believe me," I assured him.

"Thanks. Do you mind if I have a few minutes alone?" he asked, and I got up, shaking my head.

"Take as much time as you need." I shut the door and heard him fall back down on the bed in a heap.

EPILOGUE

One Year Later

"What do you think?" I asked, taking the blindfold off Mary's eyes.

She stood at the precipice of the rooftop, glass safely keeping her from falling down, though she still took a step back. "It's amazing."

"That's it? Amazing? I mean, this is pretty spectacular. How about life-changing, or revolutionary? I'd even take absolutely fantastic." I waved my hand as if I were a model on a game show.

"It's great, Dean. Perfect." Mary stepped over and slid her hand into mine as we looked over our newest colony. It felt strange to think of it as a colony, but that was really what it was. Earth reborn. Dozens of high-rises stood nearing the clouds. It was modeled after the Terran sites on New Spero, only this one had a lot more houses and acreages surrounding it. We gave those to the people working the crops and tending the animals needed to survive in Middle America. From this spot, you could see for miles and miles, all the way to the canola crops near our eventual destination.

Mary had been so busy with the new site on Haven

that she hadn't seen this one with her own eyes. "I have a surprise for you," I said.

"More surprises?" she asked with a smile.

"Come on, get in," I said, picking Jules up off the ground. I passed her favorite little doll to her, and she shook it and hugged it tight as we made our way to the lander.

"Where are we going?" Mary asked, taking Jules from me as I shut the door to the small ship and lifted off. "And since when did you learn to fly these things?"

"I figured it was better if I learned to get around myself. I can't always have a Magnus or a Mary around." The reference to my friend got me thinking about them. We'd spoken a few times, and they were enjoying their mission on the Keppe's exploratory vessel. So much so, they were considering staying on permanently.

Mary rubbed my shoulder. "Well, you can have a Mary around you most times."

"I can handle that," I said. A few drones hovered around the new buildings, but the city was mostly ready for living. I was happy to be leaving it in the capable hands of Paul, the same man I'd met running Central Park's settlement.

I lowered us as we passed the edge of the city, and I moved to the south, toward the familiar landscape. Mary's mouth formed a knowing smile. "What's this?" she asked.

"Do you recognize it?" I asked.

"Only from your descriptions." Mary had never seen my parents' acreage, but we'd spent countless hours regaling one another with tales of our childhoods. "What are we doing here?"

The house was fixed up, looking like a classic farmhouse from the Forties on the outside – only with no rotting wood, a new paint job, and new shingles. "This is our new home, if you're happy with that."

"But we already have a home," she said.

"The way I figure, we need a place to stay on New Spero, on Earth, and on Haven, if we're in charge of the colonies. I hope you don't mind, but I thought this was the perfect place to raise Jules while we're here." The lander touched down in the field between the huge garden and the house. It was July, and the sun was high in the sky, the garden in full bloom.

"How did you…?" Mary was looking to the plants, tears in her eyes. "It's beautiful, Dean." She grabbed Jules and set her down on the thick green grass. Jules started to run around, her shoulder-length hair bobbing in the wind, and our house door opened. Maggie raced across the yard and to Jules, licking our daughter's face like she hadn't seen her in a year. It had only been three days.

"Papa," Jules said, raising her arms to me.

"I got you." I picked her up, and we walked toward the house. It held so many great memories, and I hoped Jules would have the same experience and love as I'd had growing up here.

Slate stood at the doorway, and Mary's smile grew when she saw him. It was his turn to grow a beard. I'd shaved mine off when the ordeal with Lom was over. I needed a new start. Now Slate had a bushy beard, mostly blond, speckled with brown and red hairs. His hair was longer, and he was almost unrecognizable.

"Mary, great to see you." The two of them hugged, and Jules stretched her arms out for Uncle Slate, who happily took the little girl. "And it's good to see you too, Princess Jules."

"Dean, the house… it looks so inviting." Mary walked through the doorway, and I followed. We were greeted by all of our friends.

Rivo and Garo were there, talking with Clare and Nick. Sarlun and Suma were in the kitchen with Regnig and Admiral Yope. Rulo stood at his side, smiling. Cee-eight had taken us up on the invite, and she was sitting on our couch beside the Empress of the Bhlat, whispering into her ear. James and my sister were there, and she waved at me as I entered. The room smelled of roast chicken, and a Bhlat delicacy that reminded me of fish. I didn't ask what kind of animal it came from.

The only people missing were the ones we'd lost along the way, and Magnus and Natalia, who were far away, with little Dean and Patty at their side.

Mary greeted them all, and later, when she asked why the big event, I told her the truth. I wanted to celebrate. We'd all been through so much over the years, and it was time to enjoy each other's company and treat these years like they were special, because they were. The threats were over for the time being, and everything had some-how fallen into place.

I thought about Kareem telling me to change the uni-verse, and I wondered if he would be proud. If I'd done enough to make it safe for us. Time would tell, but for now, I wanted to enjoy it.

There was a knock on the door, and Paul stood there, wearing a tie. It almost looked out of place on him, but I liked it. He was embracing his new role as leader of Earth 2.0. "Glad you could make it. Hi, Sammy. And hello, Brittany," I said to his wife and daughter. They'd been reconnected shortly after I got word to New Spero that Earth was still inhabited.

Terrance and Leslie arrived with Karo, who was staying on Haven. He enjoyed the peace out there and had integrated himself into their community with ease.

The house was full of laughter, beverages, and good food, and when everyone left for the night, I got Jules to bed, and told Mary I'd be right up. She kissed my cheek, and her cool hand lingered on my neck for a moment.

I went downstairs and stepped outside. The air was still hot, the sun just down. A coyote howled in the distance, and it was oddly comforting to hear. I walked around the house to the cellar that led beneath our home. It had a padlock on the door, and I used a key from my pocket to turn it. That one was just for show. There was also an invisible shield, which would let only my biometrics through. I stepped down, pulling a chain to turn an incandescent light on. The steps were made from carved-out earth, and soon I was at the bottom of the small cellar.

I went to the wall, opening a secret compartment. Inside was half of one of Fontem's portal devices. I activated it, knowing where the other half was mounted. I stepped through it, and onto the ship where Lom had been sent to the future. Only the Empress knew of the ship, and only W knew the coordinates, so it was as safe a place as any. I popped the hidden panel out of the copy of the room from Udoon, and entered the cargo room.

I slid a small device from my pocket. It was the small Kalentrek weapon that I'd found on the space station so long ago. It was the one I'd loaded Bhlat DNA into, killing everyone on a Bhlat outpost. I set it in a locked case, hidden under three other crates full of useless tools. Beside it was the time-travel device.

I held it in my hand and marveled at how small it was. No one could get their hands on this. Here it was safe. Twenty years. We had twenty years until Lom of Pleva potentially dropped from his sentence through time, and into our lives again. I silently hoped we were done with him. The Kraski were gone, and for once, I felt safe while I slept at night.

I closed the case, making sure the dangerous weapons were secure, and went back through the portal, into my cellar, to the outside. A few minutes later, Maggie was following me upstairs. I checked on Jules, who was sleeping soundly, like only a sixteen-month-old could. I kissed her forehead before going to our new room, and climbed into bed, wrapping an arm around Mary.

"Everything okay?" she asked quietly.

"Couldn't be better." I closed my eyes and couldn't help but feel like the luckiest man on any world.

The End

ABOUT THE AUTHOR

Nathan Hystad is an author from Sherwood Park, Alberta, Canada. When he isn't writing novels, he's running a small publishing company, Woodbridge Press.

Keep up to date with his new releases by signing up for his newsletter at www.nathanhystad.com

Sign up at www.scifiexplorations.com as well for amazing deals and new releases from today's best indie science fiction authors.

32753586R00182

Made in the USA
Middletown, DE
07 January 2019